Pure Blood

The Pure Blood Chronicles

Book 1

Cris L. P. Olsen

WestBow
PRESS

Per the Author, this work of fiction is considered PG-13, and is not intended to be read by persons under the age of 13.

First Edition

This is a work of fiction. Names, characters, places and incidents either are the product of the author's imagination or are used fictitiously.

This novel and the story incorporated herein by reference includes trademarks, service marks and trade names not owned by Author. All trademarks, service marks and trade names included in or incorporated by reference into this novel are the property of their respective owners.

Of Love and Evil by Anne Rice, used with permission from Anne Rice. Alfred A. Knopf, New York, Toronto, 2010, a division of Random House

Scripture quotations marked NIV are taken from the HOLY BIBLE, NEW INTERNATIONAL VERSION®. Copyright © 1973, 1978, 1984 Biblica. Used by permission of Zondervan. All rights reserved. The "NIV" and "New International Version" trademarks are registered in the United States Patent and Trademark Office by Biblica. Use of either trademark requires the permission of Biblica.

Scripture quotations marked NLT are taken from the Holy Bible, New Living Translation, copyright 1996, 2004. Used by permission of Tyndale House Publishers, Inc., Wheaton, Illinois 60189. All rights reserved.

Scripture and references in this work are often paraphrased by the Author. Scripture is taken from the King James Version, New International Version and New Living Translations of the Bible.

WestBow Press books may be ordered through booksellers or by contacting:

WestBow Press
A Division of Thomas Nelson
1663 Liberty Drive
Bloomington, IN 47403
www.westbowpress.com
1-(866) 928-1240

Because of the dynamic nature of the Internet, any web addresses or links contained in this book may have changed since publication and may no longer be valid. The views expressed in this work are solely those of the author and do not necessarily reflect the views of the publisher, and the publisher hereby disclaims any responsibility for them.

ISBN: 978-1-4497-6465-4 (hc)
ISBN: 978-1-4497-6464-7 (sc)
ISBN: 978-1-4497-6463-0 (e)

Library of Congress Control Number: 2012915549

Printed in the United States of America

WestBow Press rev. date: 09/10/2012

For my beloved husband, and cherished son.
I adore you both more than words can say.

Acknowledgements

Cover Model
Dylan B.

Photographer *(Cover and Author Photo)*
Lydia Rose
Assistant: Sarah Rose

Photographer *(Cover)*
Andy McElroy
www.PerishPhotography.com

Hair, Makeup and Body Art *(Cover Photo)*
Emilie Proctor
www.makingfacesbyemilie.com
Info@makingfacesbyemilie.com

Tattoo Stencil Artist
Eleanor Rogers
www.SwaggerThat.com

Creative Design *(Cover)*
Todd LaSota
www.Toddjamesmedia.com

Research Assistant
Chandra Prather

Critique and Editing Assistance
Kelly S. Lynne
Franchesca Romero
Jessica Randall

Thαηк ψου

Thank you, Almighty God, for giving me the incredible dream that turned into this amazing story. Thank you for guiding me through this awesome, tedious, scary and rewarding process!

To my wonderful and loving husband, John; you are the most patient and humble man I've ever known. I'm proud to be married to you and our son is lucky to have you as his father. My beautiful son, thank you for being so patient with Mommy and giving me uninterrupted time to write! Thanks, Mom and Dad, for giving me a firm foundation and raising me in the ways of the Lord. Although I strayed for long enough to drive you crazy, I eventually returned to my foundation of faith. Thank you to my sister, Chandra, for spending countless hours with me talking about this book. Your research assistance and ideas helped shape the story. Thanks to my marketing manager and friend, Fran. Without you, I would still be lost. Kelly, your critique turned Pure Blood into something real; thank you! Lydia, what can I say, your photos are divine. Thank you for taking your precious time to spend with me on this project! Dylan, you're beautiful inside and out! I couldn't have created a more perfect person to represent this story. Thank you for enduring hours of tattoo torture to become *Pure Blood*'s Jonah! Ellie, working with you was a pleasure and your art turned out better than I could have possibly imagined! Emilie, with a steady hand and lots of patience, you created the most beautiful art on Dylan's back – you rock! Todd, from your heart, you accepted the challenge of creating the cover – your mad skills are amazing, thank you!

I also want to thank all of the people who made it possible for me to develop this story. Without your never-ending devotion and friendship, *Pure Blood* never would have happened! Thank you to my friends, Denice, Jessica, Sylvana, Rebecca, Jami, Theresa, Pastor Scott, Bryna and Pastor Clark for reading copy after copy of the manuscript and giving me awesome feedback each and every time.

Thank you, WestBow Press, for getting this book into the hands of the readers.

And finally, thank you, fans of *Pure Blood*! Thank you for reading this story for what it really is – a beautiful love story and a chance at redemption. I pray that you find the Truth woven within this story and that you accept the invitation that's been offered to you, so that we will meet each other in heaven at the end of our days.

With Love,

Cris

Chαpτξr 1

My eyes shot open as I awoke to the sound of footsteps climbing the creaky hallway stairs to my bedroom. A rush of blood raced through my body. I sat up and furiously yanked my hair to the side, swiping it out of my face just enough to be able to peek through the long, tangled strands. My own ragged breathing echoed within the bare walls of my room, muffled by the rapid pounding of blood that rang in my ears. I scanned the room intently. Empty walls stared back at me, illuminated by the full moon outside as it blazed white light through the half-open shutters that covered my window. Bright moonbeams cast sharp lines across my crumpled covers.

Cold from somewhere unseen trickled into the warm, stuffy room, raising goose bumps on my bare arms. In that moment, I regretted my pajama choice of a pink tank top and lavender plaid boxers. In any other instance I would have welcomed the draft, reveling in the coolness cutting through the torrid, late-summer heat that was trapped in this box of a bedroom. But this was an unnatural cold; cold from a source that didn't belong in this world. More than anything, I wanted to grab the covers and wrap them around me tightly, but I sat frozen, unable to move.

I stared at the door, waiting for it to be opened by someone or something that did not belong in my home, but I knew that a door wouldn't stop what I suspected to be on the other side.

Puffs of condensation escaped my mouth into the frigid air with each hot breath, as the cold wound its way into the room. It wrapped itself around me with almost visible, icy tentacles. With it came the ominous, ancient scent of the otherworld; a scent that is only detected just before contact.

The doorknob squeaked as it turned ever so slightly. Something was coming for me.

A low, feline growl rumbled from deep within Nicodemus's throat, as he stood on the end of my bed with an arched back. Fiery hairs of his orange fur bristled up along the ridge of his spine, silhouetted against the moonlight. His growl grew, until a loud hiss sizzled out of his mouth into the icy air. Wide-eyed, his gaze fixated on the closed bedroom door.

The doorknob stopped turning and quickly spiraled back into position at Nicodemus's warning. My body shuddered at the sound.

A scuffle began on the other side of the door, followed by a loud thud that shook the wall. A deafening screech hissed through the air. Then it was silent.

My face and fingers turned numb as blood drained from my limbs to feed my pounding heart. Spotty dizziness filled my vision just before everything went black.

When I awoke again, the spot where I lay had become moist with sweat, as the heat of the September night had completely dissolved the chill of the event. My pulse quickened when I realized that I was hanging halfway off of the bed. You don't get a choice where you land when you faint.

I sat up and stared at the door for longer than felt comfortable, waiting for further evidence that what I experienced was real, when the flick of a white-tipped tail caught my attention. I peeled my eyes away from the door, blinking furiously to ease the hot dryness that had filmed over them to find Nicodemus fast asleep, twitching his tail as he dreamed. My pulse and breathing began to slow, only after I saw that he was at ease. He was my gauge. If he was calm, then there was nothing to worry about. But still I sat, waiting.

I watched as the early morning sun slowly began to illuminate the dreary room, changing the color of the walls from a shadowy gray, to pale yellow. My fuzzy pink alarm clock blared, telling me that the day was beginning. I had been sitting in the same position for so long that it took of all my effort to wrench my body out of its stiff state and reach over to tap the snooze button. With the haunting cold long gone, the hot sun began to heat the room.

My dreams had been getting the better of me lately, surely exacerbated by watching too many *Ghost Hunters* episodes recently, spurring my overactive imagination to come alive. I only watched to ease my own insecurities. If these encounters happened to other people, maybe I wasn't the only one who was haunted by them.

Sometimes it was hard to determine if these brushes with the other side were real or just my imagination. That didn't make them any less frightening though, for I knew all too well that there had been those few apparitions in the past that had made full contact.

When I was seven, my therapist labeled me as being "spiritually sensitive." It took me years to figure out what that meant, exactly. I stumbled across clarity late one night, after a particularly pungent-smelling gossamer figure spoke directly to me, threatening me with ancient words that I didn't understand. It desperately tried to get through to me, inching closer and closer until I could smell its decrepit breath. It pulled at my hair, pleading with me to respond. Then, succumbing to defeat, it vanished, leaving a thin, shiny film on my bedroom floor.

The otherworld and I were connected in some way; a way I had no control over. Whatever the connection was, it haunted me over and over again. I had always wondered why. Why *me*? Were these ghosts watching me? Were they sent by something bigger to terrorize me?

Maybe my soul was more open. I sensed these beings that roam the Earth; beings that are always there, even when not seen by others. They were drawn to me for some reason, and that scared me the most. Being a supernatural magnet . . . being sought after, was my biggest fear. I knew of no reason for it and had no defense against it. I was an easy target.

In my early childhood, my parents reluctantly believed the stories of my encounters. They sympathized with me when I was young, which always left a lingering doubt in the back of my mind. I always wondered if they ever had any of the same experiences. If they did, they never told me. I quickly learned not to talk about my episodes. Although they claimed to believe me, my stories scared my mother and angered my father.

I never understood their erratic reactions. Sometimes my mother comforted me. Other times my father went into a wild frenzy, locking all the doors and windows.

Like that would help.

I had my first encounter when I was a toddler, so the existence of the supernatural had always been a reality for me. Denying, or even doubting the existence of the metaphysical wasn't an option. I knew for a fact there was another world out there . . . somewhere.

The episodes stopped over the past few years, which gave me hope that I had outgrown my sensitivity. I could only be so lucky. To my dismay, they had recently returned, no doubt spurred on by the recent change in my life circumstances.

I was newly alone. I had no one looking out for me. I had no one to confide in. No one.

Imaginations can do funny things when you don't have a chance to divulge your inner thoughts and feelings on a daily basis. Imaginations can run away with you when you don't have anyone to share your life with.

The alarm clock blared again, this time reminding me that I had to get up. Class would start in an hour. I reached over, carefully switched it off, then grabbed the mess of covers and pulled them toward me slowly, so as not to disturb Nicodemus's slumber. When he was within arm's reach, I scooped him up and stroked his mangy fur until I heard a loud purr resonate from deep inside his throat. He cracked open his yellow eyes just enough to find my hand, then pawed at it, imploring me to continue scratching his belly. I bent forward and nuzzled my nose into his face.

Nicodemus had become a good watch-cat since I found him tortured, starving and left to die in a dumpster a few months ago. As soon as he regained his strength, he became a loyal protector, never leaving my side whenever I was home.

"Ni-co-demus, what was that all about last night, huh? You heard it too, didn't you? You scared it away, you big lion, you! Good boy!"

He rubbed against me, happily purring while he gave the tip of my nose a soft lick. I hugged him snugly.

He let out a sharp *meow* and batted at my chin before running to hide in the closet to lick his wound. I accidentally touched a tender spot on his still-recovering body.

"Oh, Nico, I'm so sorry, baby!" I whined, as I followed him. On my hands and knees I could see him back in the corner, whimpering.

I knew what would make him feel better.

I ran out of the room and down the stairs to the kitchen, flung open the cabinet and pushed my way through empty cereal boxes to find a bag of his favorite treats.

"Only two left. I better make them count," I whispered.

Bounding back up the stairs, I fell to my knees at the opening of the closet door and began to coax him.

"Nico, baby, come here Nico," I pleaded as I scratched at the floor to entice him.

His temper was easily swayed by the fishy-smelling treats that I reserved for times just like these. I put the first one on the floor in a neutral spot, halfway between the two of us. He skulked toward it, then gobbled it up eagerly. I put the second one on my knee and waited for him to crawl into my lap to retrieve it . . . worked every time.

A few snuggles later, he was content and on his way to find a sunny spot to lay in, which was good because I was now in fear of being late to my first class of the day.

My stomach growled for breakfast. I raced down the stairs and found myself standing in the kitchen, staring into an empty refrigerator and bare cupboards.

A wave of nausea washed over me; a common occurrence recently, when reality came crashing into daily life. I had only made a few trips to the grocery store since my parents died.

I had unwillingly been thrust into adulthood only seven months ago when their plane went down in the Pacific Ocean on their way back from a Hawaiian vacation; a trip to celebrate their twenty-fifth wedding anniversary. Since I had turned eighteen only weeks before it happened, I was now "of age." No one was required to care for me, which left me rattling around in my childhood home alone. I had no uncles or aunts, no grandparents, no siblings. I was alone; abandoned by the circumstances of a small family.

The full understanding of all that I now possessed still hadn't completely sunk in. I was the sole owner of a house, three cars, and holder of a trust account that had been recently engorged with my parents' life insurance money. I should have been ecstatic. Most teenagers would be if they had an almost endless amount of shopping money. But to me the money was tainted, wrong, bloody. My parents had to die for me to get it. I didn't want it.

My stomach growled again as hunger overtook the nausea. The walk to campus usually took about twenty minutes, but today I had to speed it up. Most meals came in the form of fast food these days. I needed to grab some breakfast before class.

Barreling back up the stairs, I threw off my pj's and headed straight for the closet. I opted for my running shoes, knowing they'd be hot, but they would get me there faster than my flip-flops. I paired them with shorts and a nondescript fitted T-shirt, channeling a plain, athletic style. There was no need to be fancy. Anything I wore would need a good washing by the end of the hot day.

I stood in front of my mirrored closet doors and glared at my reflection. I'd spent most of the summer grieving inside this dreary, empty house and my pale skin showed it. The turquoise flecks in my blue eyes popped against my pasty white complexion. Usually by September I had a golden tan and sun-bleached auburn streaks through my chestnut hair, but not this year. I sighed apathetically and threw my hair up into a messy pony tail.

The morning sky was clear and the air completely absent of any moisture at all, leaving no barrier of protection in the atmosphere from the hot sun as it blazed down onto the earth in dry rays. Short on time, I began a swift walk. By the time I reached the Price Center in the middle of the UCSD campus, trails of sweat streamed down my face.

I dashed into the food court, taking in a deep breath of cool air as I slowed my pace and swiped a napkin from an empty table to wipe off my face and neck. The heat wave had knocked out half of the air conditioning units around campus, and as I walked through the crowd of students, I secretly thanked the building maintenance staff for keeping the air conditioning running in this particular building – one I visited often.

As I stepped up to the counter at Jamba Juice, the guy at the register greeted me with a pre-emptive strike. "Let me guess . . . non-dairy Maui Wowie with a soy protein boost?" he asked eagerly.

"Yes, thank you," I muttered.

He clicked the side of his cheek and shot a finger gun at me. Although he was pleasant-looking with spiky black hair, brown eyes and brown skin, his overcompensation for lack of confidence did nothing to attract me.

He had memorized my "usual" the first time I made my daily trip to the order counter, and he gave me a discount – again. I suppose I should have felt grateful for the continued savings, but this wasn't the sort of punch-card discount that you would expect. This was an, "I've asked you out three times and I'll keep giving you discounts until you go out with me," sort of discount. He eyed me unabashedly while he blended my smoothie.

I made a point of not learning his name the first time he came on to me. There's less accountability when you don't know someone's name. I would never accept his invitation, but until he got the point I would have to endure his advances, all the while getting an extra thirty percent off of my daily breakfast.

I tossed him exact change before grabbing the smoothie out of his hand, carefully avoiding an accidental brush of skin . . . no need to give him further encouragement. I nodded and backed away, quickly disappearing into the crowd.

Glancing at my watch, I was pleased that I had time to casually climb the steady grade toward the Humanities building. The pathway was forgiving as it was lined with eucalyptus trees on either side, providing shade from the sweltering sun. The heat of the morning cancelled out the usual shiver I got by sucking down my morning smoothie too quickly.

Amid the bustle of chattering students packing the walkways, a presence disturbed me. I felt as if I was being followed.

I sighed heavily. "The smoothie guy is very persistent this morning," I grumbled to myself.

Ready to tell him once and for all, that I wasn't interested, I abruptly turned a full one-hundred and eighty degrees to face him, head-on. But the pathway behind me was eerily vacant – as if a bubble of empty space had been following me. The students seemed to notice nothing as they unknowingly veered around the invisible emptiness.

An arctic breeze cut through the hot, dry air, sending chills over my entire body.

No smoothie barista, just that phantom, cold like last night.

The frigid breeze blew past me again and I caught a whiff of the ancient stench of rotting corpses and desperation. I turned on my heel and ran as fast as I could toward the Humanities building, straight into class.

Chαρτξr 2

"Miss Immaculada?" the professor called out. Eyes shifted around the lecture hall but no one spoke up.

He looked down at his roster and called again, "Ananiah Immaculada."

The girl sitting next to me elbowed me in the ribs. "Professor Dhampir is calling on you, Anna," she whispered.

Popping my head up, I aimed my focus down to the front of the room. "Oh, uh, s-sorry Professor Dhampir."

I peeked around and paused for a second, trying to remember where I was. I strained my memory, hoping it would give me a clue as to what the professor had just asked.

After a long pause, I sighed in defeat. "I apologize, what was the question?"

Professor Dhampir pursed his lips for a moment as his eyes bore into me. "I know it's hot in here, but if you're going to daydream or fall asleep, please go do it in someone else's class!"

My face turned hot as the blood rushed to my cheeks. The stifling temperature in the room only aggravated the flush I felt in my face.

As he stared at me, he let the uncomfortable moment linger to make an obvious point to the rest of the class of my inattention. His gaze pierced through me, glimpsing vast nothingness. I hadn't been daydreaming as he had accused. My mind had been completely blank.

As he turned his focus back to the class, I whispered a quiet "thanks" to Beth, the girl next to me. Beth had introduced herself the first day of school and found a seat next to me every class since then. She had spoken to me several times, attempting to draw me into conversation, each of which I had brushed off. After the year I'd had, I wasn't ready to befriend someone new yet.

A hot breeze trickled in through the cracked windows doing nothing to make up for the broken air conditioning, leaving the room sticky and suffocating. Beth was fanning herself with a piece of lined paper she'd folded into a makeshift fan, as were many of the other students. She directed the flurry from the page my way for a few beats, blowing tendrils of hair that had escaped from my ponytail against my skin so that they stuck to the sweat that polished my forehead.

Professor Dhampir's deep voice started up again, booming out to the entire class. "I was asking if anyone knows about the myths and folklore history of the Giants. I was asking if anyone has heard of the Titans . . . the Twelve Olympians . . . the Greek gods . . . Goliath?"

The class was dead silent. Of course we had heard of these figures, but no one wanted to speak up.

"I know this is Mythology 101 and you're all new to this, but come on, people! This is the University of California, San Diego," he roared with dignity. "You should have already been studying your syllabus, not to mention that there have been books written about these characters in history that are required high school reading!"

The class sat still as stone. The fanning stopped as Professor Dhampir's voice grew louder. "There have been movies made about these mythological figures. Surely you've seen some of the movies!"

Beth leaned toward me, covering her mouth with her homemade paper fan as she spoke in a whisper. "The guys are too intimidated by him and the girls are too busy drooling over him to answer."

I could see her point. Just his sheer size made him look intimidating. He was every girl's dream and every guy's nightmare. His short, black hair was an updated Caesar style cut, which would normally look bad on anyone except Russell Crowe in *Gladiator*, but somehow Professor Dhampir pulled it off with finesse. He looked like he should be modeling for a Greek god cologne or an underwear ad. The Polo shirt he wore stretched tight around his thick biceps and across his chest. His confidence and obvious narcissism would make one think that he was wearing the tight shirt on purpose to show off his bulging pecks, but his chest was so big he was likely wearing the largest size he could find. His olive skin was flawless and the five o'clock shadow he carried on his face was just enough to darken the crease in his cleft chin and make him look the slightest bit rugged.

It was his eyes, though, that seemed the most daunting. They were the darkest brown I'd ever seen . . . so dark that they looked completely black, like a great white shark zoning in on it's prey. Every time he looked up at the students, their heads bobbed away quickly to avert his gaze.

This was the second week of the fall quarter. You'd think some of the students would have thawed by now and been more comfortable speaking up.

Beth leaned toward me and muttered in a hushed whisper. "He must be what, six-foot-seven, at least? And look at those hands, they're huge!"

I'd sat next to Beth for only a few classes, yet she seemed completely comfortable blurting out whatever was on her mind and usually directed her thoughts toward me.

Her attention focused back on the Professor, and I peered over at her while I really examined her for the first time. Faint freckles over her nose and cheeks speckled her delicate face. Her dishwater blonde hair hung straight, just past her shoulders and the gold streaks in it brought out the flecks of gold in her hazel eyes. It was obvious she spent a lot of time outside as she had perpetual sun-kissed, golden skin. Every time I saw her, she donned shorts, a tank top and flip-flops; typical ultra-casual San Diego style.

Though I repeatedly shot down her invitations for conversation, her noticeable effort to befriend me was appreciated. She exuded a casual and friendly demeanor and I'd never seen her with a frown on her face.

A retort to her comment entered my mind and I decided to finally acknowledge her friendliness with a reply. I leaned toward her, snorted a quiet giggle and whispered. "He must have an issue with his size. He's giving us a research assignment on mythological *Giants*. He must be totally infatuated with himself and wants everyone to discover just how awesome he thinks he is."

I regretted the words as soon as they exited my mouth and sat back in my chair with a silent humph. *Nice going, Anna.* A feeble attempt at a conversation with her and I'd said something mean and gossipy. What was wrong with me?

On the outside, I suppose I looked like a normal teenage girl . . . long, auburn hair, blue eyes, curvy figure. It was the inside that was a mess.

Instantly memories of the past year flooded my mind. These were the exact memories I'd been trying to blank out when Professor Dhampir called on me.

In the past seven months my parents had died, I graduated from high school, then my boyfriend was killed in a car accident. Everyone important in my life was gone. Death seemed to follow me wherever I went. Sitting in the middle of class, surrounded by a hundred students, I suddenly felt alone.

Why was I even here? Why didn't I take a year off from starting college like everyone said I should? Oh, right. I *wanted* to be here. Staying at home was just too depressing.

A sigh voided the air from my lungs as thoughts of my dead boyfriend invaded my mind without my permission. Professor Dhampir's voice faded and a daydream appeared before me, transporting me back to high school.

Seth was the star basketball player. He was six-foot-four and all the girls flirted with him. He loved to shake his shaggy, blond hair after the game and spray sweat all over them. They loved it. I hated it, but he was my boyfriend, so I just nodded and smiled.

Looking back, I'm not really sure why I went out with him in the first place. We met in the sixth grade. We were always in the same class and despite the alphabetical gap between our last names he always seemed to end up sitting next to me. We were casual friends and regular study buddies in class, but I was never a part of his crowd.

Everything changed as soon as I turned sixteen, though. Within a week of my birthday, he began asking me out. He became persistent as time went on, wearing me down before I finally conceded. It took two months before I said yes.

On our first date he gushed compliments, noticing every facet of my attire, how I fixed my hair, even my shoes. I had never really found any redeeming qualities in him, but his charm was hard to resist. He was typically macho, tall, cute and attentive so I let him continue to date me, despite the fact that my feelings for him were only lukewarm. But the best thing about him was his popularity.

I had never been particularly concerned about being part of the "in" crowd, but living my elementary school years as the earliest bloomer in class gave me a complex about fitting in that I had never outgrown.

Puberty hit me at about eight years old. The years following my early blossoming were uncomfortable as I started to grow into a woman while the other girls were still . . . girls. By sixth grade I had all the "goods" which granted me unwanted extra attention from the boys. I quickly learned to keep my wardrobe "PG" and "sweet" to counter the voluptuous shape of my more mature body.

I spent years refining my style to help downplay my early development. I discovered Mary Jane shoes and had my mother buy them for me in every shape and color. My favorites were charcoal gray and glittery with a flower on the buckle. They made me feel sweet. I grew out my hair and kept it long to my waist. Headbands usually kept it out of my face and it was easy to accessorize them with flowers or sparkles. For years I felt like the oldest girl in school because of my body, so the Mary Janes and headbands made me feel younger, feminine, girlish. Although early blooming was a part of growing up, I did very little actual growing. I had always been the smallest girl in school and was teased about being "vertically challenged" even though I was four foot nine by high school graduation; just tall enough to be taken seriously, or so I thought.

When I stood next to Seth I looked like a child, but I became one of the elite as soon as we were known as a couple – popularity by association. Popularity wasn't what I was aiming for, but as I suspected, the teasing stopped as soon as the student body saw me on his arm and the word spread that Seth, the most coveted boy in school, had a new girlfriend.

I had always wondered why Seth was attracted to me. He always seemed to be drawn like a magnet to the practically naked cheerleaders – the tall blondes that made him the target of their cheers. He gravitated toward the ones with the worst reputations. At least those were the type of girls he always toyed with after the games. But he chose me as his girlfriend. I decided to go with it until something better came along.

When my parents died, Seth was the only one who stuck by me when I stopped talking to everyone. His macho side turned soft as he took gentle care of me those first few months. He came from a wealthy family, so he had the means to help ease my grieving and assist in the recovery process in the most basic of ways. He had someone stock my pantry and refrigerator every week. He had someone cut the grass and water the plants. He even had someone fill my car with gas.

My father never liked Seth, so the advancement of our relationship had been suppressed with strict house rules. Having no reason to stay away now, his presence was constant in my home. His parents were continually away on business, which left his own home empty more often than not. His need for company was almost as desperate as my own. At first, he properly bid me good night, returning to his mansion every evening. But over time, his stays grew longer until he found his way into my bed each night. His repeated attempts to consummate our relationship became urgent. He made it clear that I owed him a debt for the generosity and care he gave me. Separating me from my virtue was the payment he sought.

At first my refusals were gentle, but as his attempts grew more forceful, I resorted to pleading with him to find patience with me. I wasn't ready to let go of my virginity. The more he begged, the more I realized that I didn't want *him* to be the one to take it . . . ever.

Five months into this new solitary life, Seth disappeared. Days passed without a single word. One overpowering feeling arose above all the others . . . relief . . . relief that I might no longer have to fight him off; relief that I wouldn't have to give into his advances, fearing each night that I would succumb to a premature and forced deflowering. I had fought to retain my virtue – and won.

I hated to admit it, but my father was right. Keeping Seth under close watch was the only thing that had kept him under control and out of my bed.

After three days of Seth's absence from my life, curiosity won over my reasoning to just let it go and I began searching for him. I drove by his parents' house first – all dark. No surprise there.

Thinking the worst, I headed to the nearest hospital. I didn't have any sort of biological connection to him, so I wouldn't be on the list of people to be contacted in case of emergency. Besides, I hadn't decided if I wanted to actually talk to him even if I did find him. I still had my anonymity.

I entered the main doors and made my way to the emergency room waiting area.

Two nurses passed by, talking about a patient. "The police said that the car accident should have killed him instantly. He's been in a coma for three days, but he's healing *so fast!* The doctors are astounded," one of them said.

"I've asked for a double shift," the other boasted. "They expect him to wake up any time. I want to be here when he does." The tall, slender nurse wrapped her long, blonde hair into a bun as she walked by. "He's hot," she whispered as they disappeared through a door marked "ICU."

Seth had been gone for three days. They *must* be talking about him!

The female nurses had formed an attraction to him as he lay in his hospital bed unaware. His good looks colored the way people thought of him, before they even knew him. My stomach churned. If they only knew who he was on the inside, they might not lust after him in such a way.

I snuck in behind the next doctor to emerge from the ICU and kept my head down as I walked into the ward. I only passed by two rooms when I saw him. I stared at him from behind the glass door. The name badge on his door read "John Doe." No one had come to claim him.

It was hard for me to see him lying in a hospital bed, defenseless. He had always been so strong and . . . vital.

"Do you know who he is, Miss?" a nurse asked.

"No. I-I'm looking for my brother," I lied. "This isn't him."

My answer startled me. It seemed as though my subconscious had just decided his fate. I saw all I needed. I hoped that when he awoke he wouldn't have any memory of me. It would be a clean break.

The story of the mysterious John Doe hit the news two days later, when hospital security had to chase away a midnight visitor from his room. He died only hours later. The police were calling it a murder. They were actively looking for the person who had sabotaged his life support. For the police, Seth's death was still a mystery that had yet to be solved. For me, it meant I was alone – again.

Although I was relieved that I wouldn't have to fight him off ever again, without him, my life was desolate. I struggled over and over between deciding which was worse . . . having Seth in my life, knowing that my virginity would have quickly been a thing of the past, or being completely alone in the world.

My regular psychotherapist, Ms. Seraph and I had become close over the course of my life, but I hadn't seen her since my parents died. She called persistently, trying to get me to come in, but being on my own for the first time, I had no one to force me to go.

Being the kind and benevolent woman that she was, she sought me out again when she heard about the mysterious John Doe. Somehow, she knew it was Seth. We started regular sessions again, this time at locations other than her office, which brought back too many memories of the family that I didn't have now. We met at the park, the beach, the mall. Her presence soothed me and was much more welcome than I had anticipated. She said I was processing everything well. But nothing seemed to keep the loneliness away.

I was relieved when classes started. College was still new and the novelty hadn't worn off yet, which kept my mind easily absorbed in the new environment. The task of homework filled my head with enough to drown out the thoughts I tried so desperately to rid myself of. The numbness of my parents' death began to fade. The guilt I felt about Seth's unfortunate departure from this world eased. I began yearning for distraction.

Beth had to nudge me to let me know class was over. "Want to go to Espresso Roma for a latte?" she asked boisterously as she stood up and slung her bag over her shoulder.

It was time I let someone in. It was time I attempted to reconnect with the world again. Sweet Beth seemed like a good person to start with. I took a deep breath. "Sure, just give me a sec," I followed with a smile and a nod.

Her face lit up. "On me!" she squeaked in a high, cheery voice. "You look like you could use some caffeine"

Was she always this bubbly? She seemed the type, but I was spacing out half of the time, not paying attention, which was something I would have to change quickly if I wanted to pass Professor Dhampir's class. I was already off on the wrong foot with my non-answer to his Giant's question.

I took my time gathering up my books as I shoved them into my bag. Putting a minute or two between Beth and me would avoid small talk on the walk between the Humanities building and the on-campus café. After all that had happened in my life recently, my socializing skills were rusty at best.

I hurried along as I lagged behind her, mustering up the determination to begin a new season in my life – a new school, new friends, a new me.

I quickened my step to keep her in view, feeling safe knowing that someone was expecting me shortly. Keeping her within my sight gave me a feeling of security. Someone was accountable for my whereabouts, which helped ease the feeling I had lately of a presence following me.

She darted ahead and into the café. Through the floor-to-ceiling windows, I could see that she was already in line. I jogged to the café just in time to place my order as Beth got to the front of the line. "Iced, decaf, soy, hazelnut latte, please."

Beth turned to me with a look of shock on her face. "Really? What's the point of ordering if you're going to suck down something with no caffeine and fake milk?"

I felt judged. My dietary restrictions played a huge part in my life. They stopped me from enjoying so many good things. "Caffeine and I don't agree and I'm lactose intolerant, so as much as I love coffee, this is about the only thing I can order."

"Bummer," she spouted.

She ordered an iced frapuccino with lots of caramel, whipped cream and caffeine . . . rocket fuel. She'd be bouncing off the walls in about T minus thirty seconds. I was glad we didn't have our next class together. There's no way I could handle a triple dose of her bubbly cheer.

"Thanks for the coffee," I said, sincerely as we found our way to the outdoor tables of the Price Center.

"Pffft, any time!" she said, as she waved her hand in the air like it was nothing.

As we sat under the cover of a blue umbrella at the last shaded table, my thoughts drifted back to the embarrassing moment in Professor Dhampir's class. Every pair of eyes in class judged me as I fumbled about for an answer to a question I hadn't even heard. I was so consumed in my unwanted daydream that I hadn't even noticed if he assigned the research project he had been talking about for the past few classes.

Embarrassed, I forced a smile and turned to Beth, trying to put on my best apologetic face. "Are we supposed to be studying something for next week?"

"Wow," she said, wiping her mouth daintily with the back of her hand. "You were really out of it in there. Yeah, we're supposed to start our research on the Giants. You know, who they were, where they came from, what their story was. I think I'll focus on the Titans. I like the idea of writing about half-naked demi-gods who fought battles wearing breastplates!"

I snickered. "You just like saying the word 'breastplates' don't you?"

I'd caught her sucking in a huge mouthful of her iced frapuccino. Her eyes squeezed together tightly as she tried to force the huge gulp down quickly.

"Brain freeze?"

She nodded and giggled.

I was about to stand up and say goodbye when she burst out with, "I have chemistry after this, but then I'm going to the library to start my research on the Giants. Want to come?"

I took a deep breath and pulled my lips in between my teeth, trying not to show my hesitation.

Reenter life, Anna. "I have calculus now, then that's it for the day. Why don't we meet back here in two hours?" Beth's sugar rush should have worn off by then. I might be able to handle an extended period of time with her if she was crashing off a sugar high.

A sly smirk crossed Beth's lips and one eyebrow slowly snuck up. "I want to see if they have any books with good art. I like the Greek guys in their skirts!"

When I thought of mythological Giants, I envisioned something dark and mysterious. Beth wanted to gawk at their hairy legs! I giggled at the thought.

I had a feeling Beth and I were going to become great friends. She was yin and I was yang. We balanced each other out.

Chαpτξr 3

Blowing over the city was a sweltering Santa Ana wind that had moved in from the desert. September was usually the hottest month in San Diego and this year was no exception.

Beth had stalled under the protection of a shade tree on her way to meet me. She was closer to the library. It was my move. I shoved on my sunglasses and braved the blistering sun as I made my way to her. The fiery rays penetrated the skin on my arms until I reached the dense shaded area she had claimed.

Her chatter began instantly. "We have to do this totally complicated lab next week in chemistry class. I'm so lost!" she announced, as she babbled on about beakers and Bunsen burners. "You don't have chemistry this term, do you?"

I let out a short grunt. "Science and I don't mix. Chemistry is a class I'll be avoiding at all costs. Does the professor have a TA? Maybe you could get help that way? Or you could get a tutor?"

She giggled. "Yeah, there's a TA, but I'd rather not let on that I'm struggling already. I've got a tutor at home who can help me. I'll just ask him."

A tutor at home? One of her roommates must be a chemistry major or something. I was curious about her comment, but I was afraid to open a new can of worms for her to babble on about. This afternoon was about Giants, anyway, not chemistry.

I headed toward the library, zig-zagging from shade tree to shade tree, hoping to get as little sun exposure in between as possible. Beth followed. The final stretch was through a concrete atrium, flanked on either side with blue glass windows that reflected the sun directly onto the students dashing through the heat. As the coolness of the air-conditioned building beckoned me forward, I focused on the sliding doors ahead, forging a path in a straight line to get there as quickly as possible. Just before crossing into the hard line of shade from the building, Beth stopped, tilted her head back and just looked up.

Her mouth fell open as she spoke. "Isn't it amazing how this building is actually standing? It's shaped like a diamond standing on its tip. You'd think it would just topple over, right?"

She was totally right. It looked like fingers were holding a shiny blue diamond in their hands. It was huge – eight stories tall and one of the biggest buildings on campus.

Beth bounced toward the door. "Okay, let's do this!"

Not yet familiar with the library, I gestured my arm forward for her to enter first, hoping she would know where to go. As we wandered through the door, a waft of cool air greeted us. The stark difference from the hot, dry air outside sent my body into a shiver.

Cool and warm pockets breezed past us as we wound through the maze of shelves. The musty smell of the books reminded me of visiting the local library with my mom when I was a little girl. We would go once a month and check out books that we would read together at bedtime.

As I closed my eyes and took in the familiar scent of the worn pages, an image of my mother and I snuggled under the covers, reading silly books, filled my head. Mom had the loveliest auburn hair that I would play with as she read. I could practically feel the silky texture of her wavy locks in my fingers. The sound of her soothing voice was almost tangible as I pictured images of Thing One and Thing Two stirring up chaos for poor little Sally and her brother. She read in a quick-rhyming cadence, as if she knew the words by heart. She probably did. The tongue twisters never failed to trip her up, though. By the end of reading time, our giggles would overcome us to the point of tears.

A small chuckle escaped my throat.

"Ow!" Beth screeched.

In the midst of another daydream, I had smashed right into her.

"Oh my gosh, I'm so sorry!" I said, as I fluttered my hands down at her feet, trying to make it look as though I was doing something to replace the skin I'd just stripped off of the back of her heel.

Beth shook her head and bent down to rub at her foot. "Daydreaming again, Anna?"

She jerked up, smiled and pulled out a chair for me. "Voila! We have computer lab liftoff!" she announced.

Students' heads popped up, as glaring eyes swept over us. A chorus of "shhh" echoed within the room.

Beth plopped into the seat in front of her and I carefully navigated into the chair at her side. Setting my bag on the floor, I caught sight of Beth's poor ankle. It was bleeding so badly that it was dripping down the back of her heel and pooling in her flip-flop.

"Oh, Beth, I'm so sorry . . . your ankle. The front desk probably has a first-aid kit. I'll go get a bandage or some gauze or something," I apologized in my most sincere whisper.

She shrugged. "Nah, I'm fine. No worries." She concentrated so hard on her computer screen that I could see it was an obvious ploy so I wouldn't feel bad for skinning her alive. Her consideration in trying to make me feel comfortable was sweet.

"Yeah, right, Beth. When you stand up to walk out of here, you're going to spray blood all over the place. Look at your shoe."

She looked down at her injury for the first time. "Ew! I didn't know it was bleeding so much. Blech!"

"Okay Little Miss Stubborn, I'll be back in a minute with some surgical wrap and a drop cloth so you don't stain the library floor while you bleed to death."

She shot me a crooked smile and gave me a nod. "Fine," she said, with a sweet, sarcastic sigh.

I wandered this way and that, looking for any semblance of medical help until I finally came upon a guy pushing a book cart. His back was to me, but I could see he was reading the spine of a book he had in his hand, about to re-shelve it – a library clerk.

"Excuse me, can you tell me where I might find a first-aid kit, please?"

Not even looking up from his task, he pointed to a box hanging on the wall right next to me with a fat red cross on it. I felt like a dork.

I guess it's help yourself. Just open up the little clasp on the metal box and grab a bandage . . . yank, grunt, "REALLY!" I wrestled with the stupid thing for at least five minutes. Finally, I yanked it open, sending first-aid supplies flying halfway across the room.

A few feminine giggles, followed by a low, resounding "niiice" rang out from behind me. I didn't have the courage to look back. I picked up rolls of gauze and disinfecting swabs by the handful and shoved them into my shirt, using it as a sling, and carried them back over to the box. As I carefully placed them one by one back into the kit, I noticed each one I touched had a red line of fresh blood on it.

What? I sliced my finger? My humiliation had overwhelmed me to the point that I hadn't even noticed the pain. "This sort of stuff always happens to me!" I growled quietly. I quickly wrapped my finger in gauze, shoved the last ankle wrap thingy back into the box, and swiped some gauze pads and antibiotic ointment before starting my trek to find the bathroom to grab a mile of paper towels to clean up Beth's poor blood-soaked shoe.

Standing in the middle of the massive building, I turned in slow circles, not seeing a restroom sign anywhere. With no other library staff near me, I'd have to ask the guy pushing the book cart where the bathrooms were, now.

"Well, I already made myself look like a total idiot, why not go for the gold?" I whispered to myself in a sarcastic tone.

Hoping he was still nearby, I shuffled in the direction he had gone and found him four rows down from the first-aid box. I felt a twinge of relief that he may have missed the show I'd just put on that had won me a round of snickers.

"Ahem," I cleared my throat softly as I prepared to embarrass myself again.

He turned toward me, his attention still focused on the call letters of a book he was holding. His head slowly rose until his gaze fell on me.

I unwillingly gasped as my heart leapt into a gallop. He had the most crystal-clear, emerald eyes I had ever seen. A lock of wavy espresso hair fell across his forehead. His muscular forearm flexed as he raised his hand to run his fingers through his hair and pushed the curl back into place. He wasn't a boy, but he wasn't a man either. He was simply . . . gorgeous.

I approached him sheepishly, taking timid steps forward. "I'm sorry, excuse me again, where might I find the restroom?" I winced as I asked.

His voice was alluring and smooth as he spoke. "The ladies room is at the bottom of the stairs," he replied, with a cool smile.

He glanced down at the stash of supplies I had wrapped in my shirt. "Are you all right? It looks like you raided half of the supplies out of that first-aid kit."

I felt my cheeks blush, my pulse quicken. The way his mouth moved when he spoke was captivating.

"Uh-h," I stuttered as I began. I was a moron. "M-my friend's heel needs some attention. She's waiting for these." I opened the temporary shirt-sling showing him the hoard of supplies that would most likely last Beth and I all week. As I looked down, I peeked at my finger that I had been hiding beneath the edge of my shirt to check on my wound – it felt wet. The gauze I had wrapped around my sliced finger had soaked through, outing me of my self-inflicted injury of stupidity.

I heard a distinct sniff and looked up to find him noticeably sampling the air, as his eyes searched me for the source of the odor he detected. His eyes widened as he caught sight of my bandaged finger, then his gaze shot up to meet mine. A crease formed between his eyebrows as he pulled them together, before blinking furiously; an attempt to shake off his reaction to seeing the bloody gauze that encased my finger, no doubt.

Some people aren't good around blood. I'm one of them.

A deep breath filled his chest, then the edge of his mouth tipped up into a crooked smile that revealed a deep dimple in his cheek. "It looks like you need some attention, too," he said, as he reached for my hand. He caressed it as he bent down to take a closer look.

As our skin met, a bolt of electricity shot through my body. My hand impulsively jerked out of his.

"Sorry," I apologized. "The Santa Ana must be creating a lot of static electricity in the air today." I tried to hide the magnitude of what I had just felt. That was no static shock. It felt like I put my finger in a light socket.

A look of complete adoration swept across his face as his eyes met mine. "I'm Jonah," he announced, coolly. "Is there anything that I can assist you with this afternoon, other than getting you to the emergency room for stitches?" he joked, as he reached out for my hand again. His face twisted into a half-smile.

My breath quickened.

I pulled my hand back, just out of his reach. "Oh, no thank you. I'm fine."

"Quite the contrary," he said. He reached into the shirt-sling, retrieved a gauze pad and tore it open. Persistently, his hand found mine again and embraced it as he unwound the soaked bandage, exposing my wound.

I inhaled a series of jagged breaths as the electricity from his touch coursed through my body again. His green eyes amorously brushed over me as he touched the open wound with his thumb several times while he wrapped the clean bandage around my finger. I wondered if he could feel my racing pulse.

"There," he cooed. "You should be okay for a while, but you should have that looked at."

I pulled my hand abruptly out of his, turned and hastily headed toward the stairs. "Thanks," I called back over my shoulder, peeking back to take a last glimpse of him. He stood with his arm outstretched, as if summoning me back.

I flew down the stairs finding the restroom at the bottom, just as Jonah had said, and entered into an empty ladies room. Leaning over the sink, I stared at myself in the mirror. "What was that?" I asked my reflection.

I closed my eyes and imagined the beautiful boy I had just met. His strong jaw gave him an air of confidence and he carried himself in the most debonair way, like a gentleman from the old days. And those eyes . . . I could get lost in those eyes for days. Despite the electric jolt, his touch was incredibly tender as he bandaged my cut.

Someone entered the restroom and headed straight for a stall, closing it with a click that echoed loudly off of the tiled walls. My eyes snapped open and I stared at myself in the mirror again. The girl that stared back at me looked tired, as if the world had trampled her like a wilted flower. I stood up straight and took a deep breath. "Forget about him. Concentrate on school right now, Anna," I whispered to myself and stuck out my tongue at the counterpart staring back at me.

I unwrapped my finger and inspected it. Jonah's bandaging technique should be patented; the bleeding had stopped already. I tossed the bloody gauze in the trash and opted for a small flesh-colored bandage, hoping a less obvious dressing would help it go unnoticed. I would hate to be forced to relive this dumb self-inflicted injury incident again by giving Beth a play-by-play.

I walked out of the bathroom, not realizing I had forgotten the paper towels until I was standing empty handed at the bottom of the stairs. After darting back in to grab some, I emerged from the bathroom a second time and surveyed my surroundings. I had no idea where I was in this massive building. I was now on a different floor than Beth and didn't have a clue how to get back to her without passing by Jonah and the first-aid kit giggling squad again. There had to be another way back to the computer lab. I wandered through rows and rows of books, finally stumbling upon a volunteer behind the reference counter. She gave me rambling directions which I followed as best as I could and eventually found my way back.

"Oh my gosh, Anna, where have you been? I was ready to send out a search party!"

"Huh." A sharp, sarcastic grunt flew out of my throat, loud enough for those around us to hear, targeting me for their glares again. "Be glad you didn't come with me," I whispered. "You would have been subject to complete humiliation and totally flustered by a hot library clerk."

"Here." I shoved the handful of first-aid supplies at her, immediately grabbing back a disinfecting swab. I ripped it open and sat on the floor to begin doctoring up her heel. The tinny metal smell of the blood made me feel queasy, but I was determined to fix what I had broken without passing out in public.

Beth's nails tapped on the keys of the keyboard while she babbled on about Titans, gladiators, skirts and swords. "Ouch!" she squealed. I had just pressed the disinfecting swab to her skin.

"I'm so sorry Beth, really. But I'm almost done. Can you hang in there?"

She flinched, then nodded and went back to ogling pictures of Greek gods on her screen.

By the time I was done, there was a pile of bloody paper towels, bandage wrappers and antibiotic ointment packets surrounding me on the floor. Who would have thought that such a small cut could make such a big mess?

I wrapped up the bloody evidence of Beth's torture in a clean paper towel and crammed the ball of medical waste into a nearby trash can.

"Done," I said, as I wobbled into my seat.

Chαρτξr 4

Beth was up to her elbows in art of the gods, her eyes glued to the screen as she scrolled through photo after photo with a smile plastered on her face. She seemed set on focusing her research on the Titans.

I'd have to choose a different angle for my paper. First, I'd have to familiarize myself with who and what these things were. I began with the most fundamental research – encyclopedias. The basic encyclopedia didn't hold the information I needed, though, so I searched until I discovered encyclopedias on ancient deities and cultural mythology.

"I'll be in the Reference section if you need me," I whispered to her.

The Reference section being next to the computer lab, it only took a minute to locate the volumes I needed. I pulled down four gigantic books and carried them to a nearby reading lounge, nearly dropping them on the way. The books took over the two-seater couch as they landed on the cushion with a loud thud.

The giant creatures weren't buried in the text as I had expected. The depictions of them and the supporting evidence of their existence jumped off the page. The words blazed a trail in my mind as I read.

Greece – Titans: Giants. A race of powerful deities who fought a war in Heaven against Zeus and were overthrown by the Olympians. The Titans lost and were imprisoned in a cavern near the underworld known as the Tartarus.

How do you search for mythological Giants and avoid the Greeks? If I was going to base my paper on something other than the Greek mythology, I'd have to dig a lot deeper than this.

> Ireland – Fomorians: A Celtic race of semi-divine, demonic Giants that were said to be gods of darkness, who inhabited Ireland after the Flood.

> Scandinavia – Jötunn: A race of hostile spirit Giants with superhuman strength. Early theology portrayed the Jötunn as gluttonous flesh-eating, blood-thirsty man eaters.

Hmmm, Scandinavia. Were these early predecessors to the Vikings? The Vikings were supposed to be huge in stature as well.

> Egypt – Og, the King of Bashan, ruled over the "land of the Giants." Later Goliath and his four brothers (Giants) as well as the Anakites (Giants) inhabited Egypt (now known as the Gaza Strip).

Giant jackpot!

Definitions were only a beginning. Now I needed the in-depth story on these ogres. I returned the encyclopedias to their respective shelves and made my way back to the computer lab. BS1800's was the section I needed to find, now.

"I'll be on the fifth floor for a while," I whispered to Beth.

"Right-e-o," she said, as she gave me wink.

I rose from the table and chose to climb the four flights of stairs instead of using the elevator. It was the only exercise I would get today without breaking into a drenching sweat from the heat outside.

I wound through the stacks, following the call letters on the end of each row. There it was, stack number twenty-eight. My fingers traced the gold lettering on the spines of the well-read books as I sauntered down the narrow aisle. BS1430-BS1860. Dozens of books about ancient folklore lay before me. How to choose? I grabbed as many as I could hold and brought them into a private study room with glass walls on two sides. As I peered out the windows, students buzzed about below in the honeycomb, maze of campus. It only took a few seconds for the height of the building to spawn a flash of vertigo. I backed up slowly and stayed to the interior corner of the room for the remainder of my study session.

The crinkly sound and feel of the aged pages added a layer of mystique to the words as I read. I imagined myself in an ancient Egyptian tomb, reading the markings of an extinct civilization.

Giant after Giant, a growing connection between these beings and the supernatural threw me. Legends, myths, folklore; the meaning behind these words tumbled around in my mind. My understanding of them meant that the characters in these stories were made up. Until now, I had never really thought of the metaphysical aspect of folklore.

People with fantastical imaginations have been admired for centuries for their ability to conjure up images and stories from their minds. This creativity, I was learning, had a source. A celestial source that was open to a thousand different interpretations.

It had always been my understanding, though, that ancient stories were written from truth, chronicled as they happened. Fiction hadn't even been conceived as a written form until the last few centuries. This led me to believe that at least part of these myths . . . this folklore, came from real happenings.

I wandered back to the computer lab with pages and pages of notes in hand and sat quietly in the empty chair next to Beth. She startled me when she squealed with excitement, as she poked me repeatedly in the arm. Gawking and giggling at drawn depictions of some of the great characters from Greek mythology without any clothes on, her fingers waved over the screen frantically, pointing out their bulging arms and legs. What was this, junior high? Her giddy attention to the mature pictorial content seemed childish, but I appreciated the innocence it brought out in her. She was having fun. Anyway, who was I to judge what granted a good giggle? I had just put on a first-aid kit flinging show that got lots of laughs.

As I thumbed through my notes, something struck me. All of these Giants were divine in origin somehow. Divine meant they had a supernatural or heavenly beginning. Could that really be?

Most mythological stories were fraught with tales of war and deception, fighting to the death for power. How could all of that be sourced from such a divine place as heaven? The Titans were gods and so were the Olympians. They battled over control of Mount Olympus; ruling from Mount Olympus meant control of the world.

Maybe the subject of "Giants" was a metaphor. Maybe Professor Dhampir wasn't talking about physical size, but power. Power must surely be a part of it, but I was sure physical size was the basis for his assignment. The class was Mythology 101 and the professor had an *obvious* preoccupation with size.

"Re-pha-im," a low voice whispered around me. An icy chill ran down the back of my neck. I turned my head nonchalantly from side to side as my eyes darted around, searching for the source of the voice. I skimmed a glance over to Beth, who was happily typing away with a smirk on her face.

"Just your imagination, Anna," I whispered to myself through clenched teeth. This wasn't the time or place for this to happen. My interloping imagination was beginning to take over; first the stairs last night, then the cold following me to class and now this? I turned back to the screen and tried my best to focus on my task as I began outlining my paper, but I couldn't shake the voice that had just whispered around me.

The encounters that had given me messages in the past were usually persistent until I followed up on them. I slowly typed r-e-p-h-a-i-m into the search field on the screen and hit "go."

Israel – Rephaim: An ancient race of Giants from the Iron Age. In the biblical narrative, the Israelites are instructed to exterminate the inhabitants of the promised land of Canaan where the Anakim dwelt. The Anakim were people of great height and were the descendants of the Rephaim. (*See also "Nephilim" and the "sons of God" in Genesis 6:1-3 and Numbers 13:32.*)

A shadow darkened my line of sight. My eyes shifted to the floor. Two huge feet stood next to my chair as a deep voice purred over my head.

"Hmmm . . . interesting find, Miss Immaculada. Immaculada is an unusual name, as is Ananiah. Did you know your name means 'pure one, protected by God?' Do you believe in God, Ananiah? Do you think you are protected by a higher power?"

The hair on my arms stood on end. I looked up to find Professor Dhampir hovering over me, staring at me with his black eyes, waiting for me to answer.

"I, uh," I stammered. No words would come.

He loomed over me, slowly moving closer and closer until he placed an ice-cold hand on my shoulder.

"Do you feel safe, Miss Immaculada?" he whispered. His icy breath cooled my warm forehead as he spoke. My eyes were locked in his. As hard as I tried, I was unable to break my stare. When I finally blinked, he vanished.

I whipped around in my chair. "What the . . ." I stood up and spun in circles, catching wary glances from the students around me. "Why are you just sitting there? Didn't you see him?" I whispered hastily to Beth as I slowly slumped back into my chair.

"See who?" she replied with a tired sigh. Hadn't she seen what Professor Dhampir had just done?

My mind had wandered off into daydreams quite a few times today, but this was different. Could I have imagined . . . no! This one was *so* real!

I sat, perplexed, staring blankly at my computer screen as it glared the definition of "Rephaim" at me.

My goose bumps hadn't yet faded when Beth decided she'd had enough studying. "I'm done for the day, how about you?" she said, as she stretched her arms over her head. Her head was tipped back in mental exhaustion. "We've been here for two hours! I'm hungry, let's go for burgers!"

As soon as she mentioned food, I realized that I was starving. I have issues with getting delirious when my blood sugar dips too low. If Beth didn't see it, did it really happen?

An uncontrollable shiver ran down my entire body. Either I was finally going crazy, or I needed food . . . badly. The thought of pushing through a crowded restaurant for burgers wasn't appealing in the slightest, but neither was going home to an empty fridge.

What I really wanted to do was go home and plop down on the couch, but that wouldn't fix my growling stomach.

"Sure, but this one's on me," I sighed, straining a smile and adding some fake pep into my response.

"Aww!" she whined. "Then I get to drive! How about Islands?"

Islands would definitely fix my hunger. As for what just happened with an evidently invisible Professor Dhampir, I guess I would have to come to terms that I imagined him. Blowing off my hallucinations for the sake of appearing sane was something I had lots of practice at, only none of them had ever touched me like *that* before. A few had pushed me from behind, one grabbed my hair, but this was different. There was no mistaking Professor Dhampir's frigid hand on my shoulder.

Worried I would have to go back on my medication, a pang of loneliness stabbed at me. There would be no one to monitor me. The last time I was on my meds my parents were still alive. They always took care of me when my hallucinations got really bad. They always made sure I was visiting Ms. Seraph regularly, too. I hadn't seen her in over a month now.

"Ready?" Beth bounced out of her chair and nudged me with her hip. With an empty stomach and food on the way, it only took us a few seconds to pack up and head out the door.

By the time we emerged from the library, the sun had just dipped below the trees and a balmy summer breeze cooled the evening. September blooming lavender filled the air, casting a noticeable calm over the students milling about in the quad. It only took a few deep breaths for it to cast its spell over me as well. My nerves settled.

"Did you get very far with your research?" I asked Beth as we hurried along.

"I got hung up looking at pictures," she giggled. "I have a lot more work to do. How about you?"

I definitely had an angle for my paper, but how could I share my findings with her and not sound insane? "I found some Giants, but I'm not sure what to make of them. I have more research to do, too."

A loud growl came from Beth's stomach. "Okay, I'm starving," she said. "Race ya!"

Her race pace was a slow jog. I kept up with her easily, thanks to this morning's shoe choice. We walked in circles as I followed her around the parking structure.

"Now, where did I park? You'd think my green car would stand out, but I always forget where I parked!" She pressed the alarm button on her key chain, waiting to hear a familiar "chirp chirp," but it didn't come.

I spotted a shiny green VW bug. "Is that it?" I asked, pointing across the aisle.

"No, it's a Prius."

We walked around for at least ten minutes looking for it. My blood sugar was dropping fast and I started getting silly about the fact that she'd lost an entire car. We ran through the aisles giggling and appearing completely foolish looking for the thing. I hid behind some monstrous gas-guzzling SUV and waited for her to walk past.

I jumped out, "gotcha!" I yelled.

She screamed and began running. Two seconds later she stopped in her tracks. "Oh, my, gosh," she said, smacking the heel of her palm on her forehead. "I'm such a dork. I parked it on the street today!"

I rolled my eyes. "Seriously! Blonde much?" I couldn't help the sarcasm, but she giggled, taking it in stride and led the way out of the garage.

There it was. We had walked right past it on the way from the library to the parking structure. A shiny green Prius.

She tried the alarm button on her keychain again. "This stupid thing! This is the second time the battery has died since I got the car. It must be defective!" She struggled as she unlocked the car with the actual key. "Okay. Get in," she ordered in an exasperated tone.

Chαpτξr 5

A straight shot down La Jolla Boulevard, followed by a few short blocks south and we were there. My growling stomach was glad the short drive made up for the drawn-out search for the car.

I yanked open the heavy door to the restaurant and gestured for her to enter.

The hostess seated us at a table that looked like an old-fashioned balsa wood surfboard with red and black stripes down the middle. Videos of surfers on longboards hanging ten and wiping out, were on the flat screens hanging high above us.

I pulled out a menu, intent on ordering and filling my stomach as soon as possible, but Beth seemed distracted. Her eyes darted around the restaurant, searching intently for something when a smile beamed across her face. I turned and glanced behind me. A cute waiter walked toward our table from the tiki hut bar. He was wearing the traditional Islands uniform of a Hawaiian print shirt and khaki shorts, but the uniform didn't look like a uniform on him, it looked like something he might wear every day. His hair was bleached blond and straight on the top with light brown curls underneath. As he approached, his brown eyes sparkled in the overhead lights. He was extremely tan and well-developed biceps bulged out from below his short sleeves. Around here, a raging tan coupled with big guns were the tell-tale signs of a surfer.

"What can I get you lovely ladies to drink today?" he asked in a well-spoken and intelligent tone.

The grin on Beth's face was obvious. She liked him. "Ananiah, this is Zechariah, Zech this is Anna. Zech is the TA in Professor Dhampir's World History class."

He reached out his hand toward me for a handshake. Obliging, I swung my arm around and grasped his palm firmly, giving it a few sharp shakes and a nod to convey a business-like attitude.

His grip was firm as he introduced himself. "Pleased to meet you, Anna. I hear you and Beth are classmates in Professor Dhampir's Myth 101 class?"

I nodded and retracted my hand quickly. Beth had been talking to Zech about me.

"That's a great class; you'll really like it. Let me know if you need any help. It's just my area of expertise!"

Zech took our drink order and disappeared into the kitchen.

"He's cute," I teased her.

She gushed. "Yeah, he's super smart, too! He started college as a seventeen-year-old sophomore! He's working on his Masters in Judaic Studies and he's only twenty-one! His class is going on an archaeological excavation in Israel's Negev desert later this year! Kind of like Indiana Jones, you know?

This, I could relate to. Indiana Jones was one of my favorite fictional characters. I could totally understand the draw to such a seemingly obscure area of study, now. "That's really cool! And Zech gets to go on the dig later this year?"

Beth was glowing as she spoke of him. "Yeah, he's really excited about it. That would be a fun trip to tag along on, wouldn't it? Oh, Anna, he's so sweet and super smart," she said, with a dreamy look on her face. "I'm actually shocked he doesn't have a girlfriend!" She sighed.

I had never seen anyone swoon before. Witnessing it for the first time, I saw how unguarded Beth was, like Zech could swoop in and absolutely destroy her with one malicious word. Most people put walls up to protect themselves from such vulnerability.

My own self-preservation kicked in for her, but I had to keep it light. I didn't want to burst her bubble.

"And how do you know he doesn't have a girlfriend?" I teased her, lightly.

"A girl has her ways of finding out things when it comes to a cute boy. Plus, I overheard another girl totally hitting on him the other day, and she asked him if he had a girlfriend. He said no, then gave her a very polite brush-off," she said, as her chin rose with confidence.

She looked at me and snickered. "He actually gave me a few pointers on how to succeed in Professor Dhampir's class last week."

"Really? How?"

"Huh," she grunted sarcastically. "Don't get on his bad side."

"I already failed that lesson," I snorted, as I remembered Professor Dhampir's eyes blazing into me when I couldn't answer his question.

I flashed a look over her head. "Shh, here he comes."

He walked up to the table, set my drink in front of me and nodded politely. As he set Beth's drink down she grabbed for it. Their fingers brushed, turning Beth's face a bright shade of garnet. Zech smiled, and watched her intently as the blush raced down her neck.

I saw an opportune time to leave them alone so they could get some good flirting in. "Uh, I'd like the teriyaki burger please, medium-well, wheat bun, no cheese." I smiled up at Zech, then I leaned across the table and shielded my face with my hand. "I'm running to the little girl's room, be back in a minute," I whispered.

I escaped from the table and quickly ducked down the hall. Hidden behind a wall, I did a one-eighty and peeked around the corner at them. They were adorable. Zech traced circles on the table with his finger and Beth batted her eyelashes shyly. The blush on her cheeks brightened every time he smiled.

She picked up her glass and took a sip of her iced tea. When she set it down she kept her hand resting on the table close to him. Zech was quick to pick up on her cue as he rested his fingers on the top of her hand.

Seconds later, he pulled a phone out of his pocket and keyed in some numbers. Then, nodding politely, he turned and walked back toward the kitchen. As soon as he was out of Beth's sight, a colossal grin swept across his face. Only a half-wall separated the dining room from the kitchen. He pulled out his phone again, stared at the number and smiled before shoving it into his pocket.

I felt the need to make my trip to the bathroom official, so I dashed in and washed my hands before venturing back to the table. When I returned, she was caressing the spot on her hand where Zech had touched her.

"Is he watching?" she asked.

I tilted my head up and looked toward the kitchen area. "No."

She couldn't hold in her excitement. "He asked me out!" she said, as she held back a squeal. Her toes tapped the ground in an animated frenzy under the table.

While we waited for our food, Beth couldn't contain her exuberance as she prattled on about Zech and how cute and smart he was. "Can you believe he asked me out? Of all the pretty girls he must meet every day, he picked me!"

I looked at Beth affectionately. She was so unguarded. It made me see her in a different light. She was pretty, but not exotic, almost cute. You only had to know her for about half a second to recognize the inner radiance that came from deep inside. It was obvious she wore her emotions on her sleeve, which was very reassuring. I never wondered where I stood with her. She was transparent and honest. Those were good qualities in a friend, especially when someone like me was trying to start fresh and didn't want to deal with chaos and secrecy.

"Beth, you're adorable and sweet. Any guy would be lucky to go out with you."

I was feeling good about finally getting something positive and nice out of my mouth, when only seconds later my good mood burst.

A tall, skinny waitress with a sour expression stalked up to our table. She was wearing far too much makeup and her black hair was teased into a pouf on top of her head before being pulled back into a ponytail; a look that seemed to require far too much energy for a girl of her obviously pessimistic nature to have created. A silver scale-textured snake ring slithered into the piercing in the side of her nose and her tan uniform shorts hugged her legs so tightly, they made red lines on her thighs.

"My name is Mara. I'll be your server for the remainder of your visit. Zech just went on break." She glared at Beth, flipped her hair and walked away.

Beth's mouth fell open. "Did she just . . . ?"

"Totally," I replied. Either Mara is the worst waitress ever, or she witnessed the exchange between Beth and Zech and was jealous. Now she was taking it out on us. Why else would she be so snitty?

I began to feel woozy from lack of nourishment. To my relief, Beth blew off the Mara thing and started jabbering on about her favorite TV show, completely occupying herself with the one-way conversation. I'd never seen the show before, but it was something about two vampire brothers being in love with the same girl and a diary or something like that.

After what seemed like forever, Mara finally showed up, slapped our food on the table and pranced off.

"Think she spit in it?" Beth asked worriedly.

"She may be a brat, but the kitchen is pretty open. She would have to be Houdini to hide something like that. I would guess we're safe."

Spit or no spit, I practically shoved my face into the burger. It was delicious, but completely unsatisfying, seeing as I scarfed it down in three minutes flat. I picked at my fries while Beth daintily nibbled on her monstrous burger.

The rest of the meal lacked enthusiasm. Beth was bummed out because Zech had disappeared and I was perturbed because not only had the waitress been snotty to sweet little Beth, but now she was M.I.A. with the check. Beth was the closest thing I had to a real friend in over a year. She didn't deserve to be treated like this and she was too sweet to say anything bad about "Mara snippy pants." I felt the need to defend her, but making a scene would be sinking to Mara's level and I wasn't about to go there.

Beth finished her meal, sighed and made a concerted effort to snap out of her funk. "Hey, I have *Clash of the Titans* at home. Sam Worthington is *hot* in that movie, and guess whaaaaat," she sang out. "He wears a breastplate and a skirt, hee hee! Wanna come back to my house and do some 'research'?"

I'd had enough socializing for one day. "Thanks for the invitation, but I'm beat and I should really get home and feed my cat. I think I'm gonna do a little studying and go to bed early," I said, with an apologetic wince.

Beth slumped her shoulders in disappointment. "Are you sure?"

I pressed my lips together and nodded.

She let out an exaggerated sigh. "Okay. I'll take you back to campus so you can get your car," she said.

"Actually, I walked today. I only live a few minutes from here."

We sat in the car in front of my empty house with full bellies, both of us agitated from the experience at the restaurant. I pivoted toward her in my seat and was surprised when a genuine smile crossed my face. "Thanks for the study date. I don't have many friends and you've been really nice to me. I appreciate it."

She beamed and lunged at me from her seat, giving me a huge bear hug. "We're going to be best friends, Anna," she said, as she gave me little baby pats on the back.

She snatched a piece of paper out of her bag and wrote her cell number on it. "Here," she said, as she shoved it into my hand. "You can call me anytime, day or night. I'm always up for a study date or shopping or whatever!"

"I will," I lied. I wasn't the shopping type. I tucked the paper in my pocket and stepped out of the car. The door closed softly with only a small nudge. She pulled away from the curb, making a U-turn before yelling out her driver's side window as she passed by. "Call me if you get bored this weekend!"

Chapter 6

As I poured over my textbooks, an orange, mangy ball of fur jumped on the kitchen counter, begging for Saturday morning breakfast. In the absence of another human body around, little Nicodemus had become good at keeping me company. He had a bad habit, however, of plopping down right in front of me, no matter what I was doing. He quickly found a spot he liked on my open calculus book and sprawled out, meowing at me for attention.

"Hello, Nicodemus," I said, softly as I gave him a luxurious belly rubbing. "You're looking a tad bit plumper today, aren't you, old boy?"

The night I heard his agonizing cry from inside the dumpster, I found him all but skin and bones. Most of his fur was gone, looking as if it had been pulled out in clumps on purpose, leaving patches of dried blood and open wounds that were in the beginning stages of infection.

It didn't take me long to climb inside that huge stinky box and rescue him, once I realized that the pitiful cry was coming from a live animal. I rushed him straight to a twenty-four hour emergency vet.

The miserable skinny tabby hung on by a thread, behaving himself through test after test, and was a particularly good boy while being hooked up to the IV. I waited for days in the lobby, clinging to hope that the poor thing would survive. I felt connected to him somehow. The way he looked up at me when I pulled him out of the dumpster was a plea for life. He didn't even fight me.

The staff repeatedly urged me to go home and wait for a phone call, but I just couldn't. We already had a bond. I knew he wanted me close. My days waiting for him to pull though gave me a lot of time to think, and since school hadn't started yet, I usually just sat there, worrying.

The vet told me that he would have certainly died within days, but saving him gave him a second chance. I remembered a story of a man named Nicodemus sort of coining the phrase "born again." I decided if he made it, I would name him Nicodemus in hopes that he would start a new life with me.

Nicodemus had indeed been given a new chance at life and it warmed my heart every time I noticed him filling out. As I rubbed him, I inspected his body, taking note of the patches of fur that were still missing. Some of them were just now starting to grow back while some of them would be scars forever, void of any of Nico's beautiful orange fur.

Though I had been studying for over an hour, the sun was just coming up. Nicodemus meowed for breakfast again, so I shuffled sleepily to the pantry and pulled out one of the only edible items in the house . . . Nico's cat food. He devoured it as soon as I poured it into the bowl. At least one of us would get fed this morning.

I decided to concentrate on calculus instead of my hunger and sat down to run numbers again. Nicodemus sauntered over and nibbled at the end of my pencil as I wrote. He playfully grabbed it away from me and batted it around until it rolled up against a folded piece of paper I'd carelessly tossed on the counter the night before. Beth's phone number.

I scraped together the last bits of food from the fridge and ate a poor man's lunch, then studied until my brain was mush. Toilet brush in hand, I headed upstairs to scrub already sparkling clean bathrooms before rattling around the house, accomplishing various chores as I tried to ignore the folded paper on the counter. I passed it at least a dozen times, then finally picked it up and dialed the number. I held the phone in my hand and just stared at it. Instead of pressing "send," I added the number to my phone book.

Beth was my friend; a brand new friend who didn't know about my past or watch me go through it; a fresh start friend.

Connecting with people was never difficult for me, but I hadn't made an effort to reach out in a long time. The thought of calling her made me anxious. What would I say? Even though I felt completely comfortable with her, I didn't know her well enough to know what she would want to do on a Saturday night.

Sundays were usually quiet on campus. There were those who frequented the usual social spots, but the library was a place of cool serenity today.

The first-aid mess took so long last week that I barely got in a sketchy hour of research. I hadn't even scratched the surface. My notebook was filled with notes that didn't seem to make sense to me – leads that I was going to follow-up on today.

As I stepped through the sliding entry doors of the library, anxiety coursed through me at the thought of possibly seeing Jonah again. I still hadn't been able to figure out what happened the day I cut my finger. Jonah's touch was like an incredible electric force – hot and powerful. I hadn't stopped thinking about him since that day. How would I ever be able to enter this building again without imagining those piercing green eyes?

My thoughts confused me. Did I *want* to see him, or avoid him at all costs? My knees suddenly became unsteady.

I covertly dashed from stack to stack, concealing myself behind each row. Relieved when there were no familiar faces in the computer lab, I settled in, and poked the button on the sleeping CPU. The monitor hummed to life, signaling the beginning of my Giants journey today.

I cracked my knuckles in anticipation, readying myself for the search. Okay, what did Professor Dhampir say? Giants, Titans, Goliath? I searched "Goliath."

Childhood Sunday school lessons came rushing into my mind. I remembered this story. Goliath was a Philistine soldier who stood over nine feet tall. He came out each day for forty days, mocking and challenging the Israelite army to fight. They were terrified of him.

As I read about this very story, other biblical references flanked the side of the screen. A certain word kept popping up that I'd never seen before. I ignored it for a while, thinking the searches were pulling up results that had nothing to do with the subject of Giants. But I kept seeing it. I felt my nose wrinkle up as I whispered to myself. "What is a Nephilim?"

As I searched for a definition of this strange word, the reference to a certain Bible verse appeared over and over again. Things never seemed real unless I found them amongst the pages of a book. A book was something I could hold. The pages were tangible and real as I rubbed them between my fingers. I marched over to the Reference section and easily found multiple copies of the Bible, each larger than the next. I pulled the smallest one off of the top shelf and rested it comfortably in my lap as I sat on the floor and turned only a few pages before I found it . . .

> When men began to increase in number on the Earth and daughters were born to them, the Sons of God saw that the daughters of men were beautiful and they married any of them they chose. The Nephilim were on the Earth in those days; and also afterward; when the Sons of God went to the daughters of men and had children by them. *(NIV)*
>
> —Genesis 6:1, 2, 4

What the heck? Who were the "Sons of God?" And why were they having children with the daughters of men? I went back and searched multiple sources for a definition of these "Sons of God" but only found reference to an ancient script.

> Sons of God – also referred to as Watchers or Angels – When men started to multiply on the Earth, God sent Watchers to protect many of the humans He had created. In Genesis six, "Sons of God" refers to Fallen Angels who lived on Earth and

> married human women. Their consummation bore
> Giants of extra human strength called Nephilim.
> —Book of Enoch / Book of the Watchers

No way could this stuff be real, I thought. Then it dawned on me; the second I pulled a Bible off of the shelf, everything became real. I was brought up to believe that the stories in the Bible were chronicles of real happenings, a book containing tales of the past.

> The Lord saw how great man's wickedness on
> the Earth had become and that every inclination
> of the thoughts of his heart were only evil all the
> time. The Lord was grieved that He had made man
> on Earth and His heart was filled with pain. So the
> Lord said "I will wipe mankind, whom I have created,
> from the face of the Earth – men and animals, and
> creatures that move along the ground, and birds
> of the air, for I am grieved that I have made them."
> But Noah found favor in the eyes of the Lord. Noah
> was a righteous man, pure among the people of his
> time and he walked with God. *(NIV)*
> —Genesis 6:5-9

Noah? Seriously? Meaning God sent the "Great Flood" to wipe out the Nephilim . . . the Giants? I don't remember ever learning *that* in Sunday school!

Was this really the common thread I had been searching for? I couldn't wrap my head around that. There was *no way* all of the Giants in so many cultures stemmed from the Old Testament Great Flood . . . was there?

> The Nephilim consumed the possessions of
> man and when all had vanished, and they could
> obtain nothing more from them, the Giants turned
> against man and devoured many of them, eating
> their flesh and drinking their blood.
> —1 Enoch 7:3-5

Blood drinkers – like vampires? Vampire legends stemmed from various cultures all over the world. These were the exact sorts of stories that are retold and changed throughout the ages, ending up skewed and far from the truth.

From my research last week, I also remembered that the giant Jötunn race from Scandinavia were blood drinkers as well. I scribbled a note connecting the commonalities between the two myths.

Okay, so, if God sent the Flood to wipe out the Nephilim, what happened to the Angels who came down from heaven and fathered the Nephilim in the first place? Did they fly back up to heaven? If God was that angry, would He have welcomed them back? They were, after all, the ones that started the whole mess.

I searched for that answer for a long time. My heart sank as I read the fate of the Angels who fell.

> For God did not spare the Angels who sinned, but cast them into hell and locked them up in chains in utter darkness in gloomy dungeons, where they are being held until the day of Judgment. *(KJV, NIV, NLT)*
>
> —2 Peter 2:4

These short Bible verses seemed so small, so random. I anxiously searched the card catalog, wondering if I'd find any books about the Nephilim. Was this a subject others wrote about? The answer was an overwhelming "yes." Six were here in this very library.

I pulled as many of the books I could find and headed back to a table to spread them out. As the information from each book entwined itself together, an extraordinary story of love, gluttony, desire and evil filled the pages in my notebook as I furiously wrote the highlights of these tales in my notebook.

The Nephilim turned on the human race, devouring and corrupting God's creations. God literally rained His wrath down on the Angels, their offspring and the wicked mortals who walked the earth with them, for creating this horrific predicament. He turned the Nephilim from beautiful creatures into hideous monsters and they fought each other to the death. He flooded the earth to finish them off, sentenced their spirits to roam the earth hungry and thirsty, stripped the Watchers' wings so they couldn't return to heaven and then locked up the worst of them in a dark prison until Judgment. Finally, He limited humans' lifespan to one hundred and twenty years as punishment.

I always wondered why people in the Old Testament lived to be centuries old. Maybe we would still live that long, if not for what the Fallen Angels did in the time of Noah. Humans barely make it to one-hundred these days.

Angels; I had always thought God made them out of love, their purpose to protect, guide and inform. But they must have been created with free will just like humans. And that was the age-old dilemma, wasn't it? How can you guide or protect anyone if they choose not to listen, not to participate, not to obey?

Obeying was one thing my parents were very strict about. There were no doubts about what we would be doing on Sunday mornings. Church was from nine to eleven and we attended with no exceptions. The structure they set up in my little life didn't waver; until suddenly we stopped going altogether. I was twelve. They told me to never return. It wasn't safe.

In those few years of attending without fail, I had retained a lot more than I could've imagined. I never thought that my lessons in Sunday school would ever be useful for anything, but in the past few days, flashes of those childhood Bible stories raced through my mind. When these stories are taught to a child, they're portrayed as light and whimsical. Now, knowing the real story, my perception had changed. The epic battle of good versus evil is *very* real.

Of all the Bible lessons I remembered, one in particular stuck with me. It wasn't often we were taught Revelation, but I recalled a lesson about the stars and how a third of them were swept from heaven when Satan fell.

God created Lucifer as the most beautiful of all the Angels. He was God's right-hand man, but that wasn't enough for him. He wasn't content being second best. He was hungry for more; hungry for power. He chose to turn away from his Creator in an attempt to become more powerful than God himself. He "fell" and took one-third of the Angels with him.

Angels *must* have free will, or how could that have happened, right?

I scanned the pages of the many books open in front of me, looking for more clues as to what came next. My findings unsettled me.

I spent the rest of the day digging deeper, hardly believing what I found. Some believed Goliath was a Nephilim. Some people believed the Titans were ancient Nephilim.

God told his archangel to incite hostility among
the divine ones, so the giants killed each other.
—1 Enoch 10: 9-10

Hence the legendary Battle of the Titans.

Every Giant I researched came back to the Nephilim origin somehow. The more I read, the more obvious it became that this was true. With knowledge of the Nephilim, one only needed to read between the lines and connect the dots to confirm it.

It was as I suspected. This wasn't mythology, it was history. I wasn't just researching Giants, but ancient historical facts.

After all I had read, one thing haunted me about the original Genesis 6 verse. It said, "the Nephilim were on the Earth in those days; *and also afterward.*"

I'd come across quite a few references to the idea that there were Nephilim on Earth after the Flood, but I'd set them aside until I read something that seemed to pull it all together:

> We saw the Nephilim there, the descendants
> of Anak. Next to them we felt like grasshoppers,
> and we looked the same to them. *(NIV, NLT)*
>   —Numbers 13:33

This verse made no sense to me until I remembered the story of Moses . . .

> *When Moses led the Israelites away from Pharaoh's rule, he parted the Red Sea and they escaped from Egypt. When they reached the other side, they spent forty years in the desert traveling until coming to a city called Canaan. Moses sent spies to Canaan to check it out. When the spies came back, they told Moses how they had encountered giant beings and how they felt as small as grasshoppers next to them.*

Moses came centuries after Noah. That meant that there were hundreds of years for more Angels to fall and procreate again to form a new race of Nephilim – the Anakites.

This was definitely the poignant topic that everyone seemed to have a theory about – if there were Nephilim on Earth after the Flood. What I couldn't understand was how these scholars and historians had to theorize about it. Didn't they read the Bible? It seemed to be pretty clear to me that there were – and maybe even still *are* – Nephilim on Earth.

> Just as it was in the days of Noah, so shall it
> be also in the days of the son of man. *(KJV, NIV)*
>   —Luke 17:26

I think I just discovered the thesis for my paper.

Chαptξr 7

The Nephilim giants, who are born from the
spirits and flesh, shall be called evil spirits upon
the earth, and the earth shall be their dwelling.
And the spirits of the giants will afflict, oppress,
destroy, attack, do battle, and work destruction
on the earth, and cause offences. They take no
food, but nevertheless they hunger, they take no
drink but they thirst. And these spirits shall rise
up against the children of men and against the
women, because they have come from them.

—1 Enoch 15: 8-12

The Nephilim were physically exterminated.
Though their half-mortal bodies could be slain,
their half-angel souls could not, nor could they
be held in chains. They remain on the earth, their
disembodied souls wandering through the world at
will as a race of demons. Though they are chaotic
and destructive, they will not be punished for their
deeds until the Final Judgment, in which the great
age will be brought to an end.

—Anonymous

As the words sank in, the thought crossed my mind that
these Nephilim spirits roaming the earth have a modern day
equivalent – demons . . . ghosts.

These could be the very ghosts that the *Ghost Hunters*
follow. These could be the very demons that stalk me. I had
always wondered why they're here on Earth when they should be
somewhere else – another dimension, another world. Now it all

makes sense. They're trapped here until Judgment; not allowed to ascend into heaven as Angels, because they're not Angels and not allowed to die as humans, because they're not humans. They're half-breeds.

No doubt the devil, with his cunning and deceptive ways, lures them to do his bidding. They are hungry. They are thirsty. They are evil. They have been around for thousands of years. Surely they have learned how to be deceptive in the most insidious ways. Surely they have mastered the craft of evil to please the only one who will listen. Satan.

> And no wonder, for Satan himself masquerades
> as an angel of light. It is not surprising, then, if his
> servants masquerade as servants of righteousness.
> Their end will be what their actions deserve. *(NIV)*
> —2 Corinthians 11:14-15

Cold stirred around me, raising the hair on my arms. I didn't wait around to find out why. I logged out, grabbed my bag and headed out the door.

The warm evening air hit me, calming my fears of another encounter. If the air was warm, I was safe.

As I walked, frustration added a new layer of heat to my already flushed cheeks. After all I had experienced, I was still unable to determine if many of the occurrences I'd had in my life were real or just my imagination. Some I knew *for sure* were real. But some were so elusive, it was hard to tell. For all I knew, there was no dark presence back in the library. The air conditioner could have just turned on. I kicked the ground in disgust.

Even though the sun had set, walking the two-hundred feet from the library to the Price Center created a thin sheen of sweat that covered me from head to toe. Now that the dry desert air of the Santa Ana was gone, a muggy ocean breeze blew in from the west, leaving the atmosphere heavy and sticky.

I entered the food court, inhaling the mixture of various cuisines, prompting my stomach to rumble. A bowl of dry cereal for breakfast and an apple for lunch hadn't given me much energy. This would be my main meal of the day.

My mother had always taken care of shopping and meals at home. After that it was Seth's staff that stocked my pantry. It had only been a few months that I had been on my own, now. Getting into new habits, like visiting the grocery store, was difficult. I was still just surviving.

I gobbled down a quick dinner before leaving the lighted security of the quad to begin my twenty-minute walk home. Twilight peeked through the tall trees, silhouetting them against an indigo sky as dusk chased the shadows away. The trees had forged their roots into the ground, only to meet dense clay a few feet below the surface. The roots, searching for their survival, snaked their way under the concrete squares of the sidewalk, uplifting them into a jagged series of obstacles. Although the groundskeepers had filled the gaps in with sloping asphalt, I was still not yet familiar with the rollercoaster of pathway.

As I navigated the maze of hills and valleys, I was comforted by the sound of my shoes shuffling on the pavement. The pungent smell of eucalyptus arose from the leaves crunching under my feet. With each step, home drew closer.

My mind was in the middle of creating a world of Angels and Giants when a pocket of cold air hit me. Although everything around me was the same, it was as if I had entered another dimension. I was still standing on the sidewalk of campus, but the smell of the eucalyptus trees had vanished, replaced by the now-familiar ancient, musty scent of the otherworld. The sound of the warm summer breeze rustling in the trees had ceased and a deafening silence filled my ears. I stood frozen, listening carefully for anything I should be running from.

Soon, I recognized the pattern of footsteps. Not looking back, I crossed the street to see if the sound would follow me. The rhythm of the steps quickened. A lump lodged itself between my vocal cords. If I needed to scream, would I be able to? I began to run, my heavy backpack thump, thump, thumping as it banged against my back. I wasn't moving much faster than when I was walking, thanks to the added weight of the books I had checked out from the library. The frigid cold surrounded me. My panting created dense puffs of condensation in front of me, further impairing my limited vision from the lack of light.

Footsteps closed in behind me. Looking back for the first time, I saw a tall hooded figure. It seemed as though the otherworld and this figure following me were working together to trap me.

Crap, crap, crap!

I mentally charted an unexpected path in an attempt to outwit my stalker that would end up in a well-lit parking lot. I turned quickly to execute my move, suddenly aware that there was another figure running directly toward me. Was this an ambush? I tried to stop. The momentum of the heavy backpack jostling around behind me created an unsteady inertia, sending me stumbling as I tripped over one of the asphalt root ramps. I fell directly into the figure's arms.

A shock of adrenaline filled me as the boy's arms wrapped around my waist, catching me inches from the ground.

He was wearing jogging shoes, shorts and a T-shirt, masquerading as though out for an evening run. Or was that what he was really doing? Maybe this wasn't an ambush. Maybe this guy had just saved me from uncertain doom.

"There's someone following me." The words came out in a rush as I jabbed my thumb over my shoulder behind me.

I struggled to stand up, clumsily wiggling out of the jogger's grip. The heavy backpack fell off of one shoulder, toppling me over as I caught it in the crook of my arm. I managed to stay on my feet.

I turned back and scanned the empty street. My imagination, again? It couldn't be! I was positive of what I felt, what I saw! There were no shuffles behind the jogger and me. The street held no sounds except our labored breathing.

Being in the proximity of the jogger, I felt completely safe and warm. The cold had vanished.

"I was certain I saw someone following me; someone tall, wearing a hoodie."

"I saw someone, too, but they seem to be gone now," a deep, comforting voice replied.

I stumbled as I struggled with my heavy backpack.

"Are you okay, Miss?" he asked between heavy breaths.

The unmistakable song of his alluring voice meant only one thing. I turned from the empty street and looked up at the beautiful face peering down at me. I was greeted by emerald green eyes.

Jonah!

"Miss?" He dipped his head down to catch my gaze.

In my shock, I hadn't answered. I just stood there, open-mouthed, gazing into his clear eyes.

His hand rose and rested on my bare shoulder as he tried to get my attention.

I gasped as his electric power coursed through me. I staggered back. His arm dropped to his side, breaking the contact between us. The electric surge stopped immediately and a cold sadness flushed through me.

"How's your finger?" he asked.

Oh, great, he recognized me. Ugh! My affinity for awkwardness seemed to bloom in his presence. First I pelted him with stupid questions, now I was outrunning some sort of phantom stalker. He must think I'm deranged.

"I'm fine!" I defended as I struggled to get the backpack on my empty shoulder.

He took a step closer. I froze. My emotions were mixed between desire and fear for him to touch me again. My body could only shut down until my mind decided which reaction to succumb to. Neither, it decided. I just stood there like an idiot.

He reached over and carefully pulled the backpack strap into place. His body was close to mine as his hand lingered on the strap. The dusk gave only enough light to barely make out a bead of sweat as it trickled down his temple. I inhaled deeply. In the middle of a run, most people smelled of sweat. He smelled like a clean ocean breeze after a hard summer rain that finished with a sweetness that was familiar, yet I could not place it.

His eyes focused on my neck before darting up to my face. "May I accompany you to your destination?"

I stood, not moving, not answering. My fantasies about him between when we met and now did no justice to his beautiful face.

Thoughts of him had plagued me since our first meeting. How could a few minutes of interlude explode into such a magnetic feeling toward another human being?

As much as I longed to spend more time with Jonah, the last thing I wanted to do was open myself up to more chances to act like a fool in front of him. I should cut my losses now and run.

"Don't let me interrupt your run. I'll be fine. Thanks for catching me. I would have definitely gotten some nasty road rash there if you weren't around! They should really fix this sidewalk! Have a nice night," I said, as I stepped around him to continue my trek home.

"If you don't mind, I would very much like to walk with you. You know, strength in numbers . . . if there *is* a strange guy roaming the campus, I would hate for either of us to get mugged this evening."

He made it easy for me to nod in agreement. He wasn't focusing on my situation. He was concerned for himself as well, like *I* would be protecting *him* somehow. I chuckled under my breath.

We walked in uncomfortable silence until we reached a grocery store parking lot.

I pulled out my phone and quickly texted Beth.

Hey, would you mind picking me up at Whole Foods? I think there was someone following me and I don't want to walk the rest of the way home.

I pressed send. Thank goodness I had put her number in my contact list the other day.

"I need to do a little shopping. I just texted my friend to come and pick me up. I should be fine from here, how about you?"

He looked at me and smiled sweetly. "Are you sure? I don't mind shopping with you and accompanying you the rest of the way home." His eyebrows pulled together as his face turned serious. "I feel a bit responsible for your safety, now."

My phone buzzed. It was a reply from Beth.

Of course, I'll be right there.

I looked up at Jonah. Even in the harsh floodlights of the grocery store parking lot, he was beautiful. "I'll be okay, really." I flashed my phone at him. "See, my friend will be here in just a few minutes. Thanks for walking me to safety. You have proven that chivalry isn't dead."

"It was my pleasure, Miss . . ."

He was fishing for my name. I wanted to tell him so badly, but then he would have a name to attach to the clumsy girl who kept literally running into him. I promised myself right then, that I would tell him if we ever met again. It would be fate if I tried to trample him a third time.

"Thanks," I whispered. I turned and forced my legs to walk, one step, two, then three, into the store, alone. An invisible force beckoned me back as if there was a gravity pulling me toward him. I fought with everything in me not to race back to his side. He disappeared seconds after I entered the well-lit safety of the market.

I sat on an empty bench outside of the glass doors. Shoppers passed by, at first with empty carts, then emerged with full bags.

"Anna!" Beth yelled out of the car window from across the parking lot. I could see her bouncing up and down in her seat with impatience as a white-haired lady pulled slowly out of a parking spot, blocking her path to me. Beth squeezed her green Prius by the old lady's Lincoln with only an inch to spare and yelled out the window, as she frantically drove up to where I was sitting. "Anna! Are you hurt? Are you okay? Get in!" She leaned over to open the door from the inside.

I sat in the seat and hugged my backpack tight to my chest, as if it would act like a shield from the flood of questions she fired at me. What should I tell her, exactly? What had really happened? My entire life was like this . . . always wondering what was real and what was not.

"What the heck happened?" she squealed.

"There was someone following me. Then I ran into this jogger and the guy following me must have been scared off or something because he just disappeared. It was really weird." I couldn't explain the cold, or the smell, or the deafening silence. Any more details would bring more questions. Questions I didn't have answers to. "I'm sorry I bothered you. Thanks for showing up. It's really sweet of you to be so worried about me."

"Bothered me! Are you kidding? Your text scared me to death! I'd never let anything happen to you, Anna! You're like, my only friend here! Are you still scared someone's following you? Do you want to come back to my house?" Beth asked with a hopeful look in her eye.

"I'm sorry that you had to drive all the way here, but I'd really just like to go home, if that's okay."

"Anna, you really shouldn't be alone. Are you sure you want to go home?"

Being alone never felt so isolating, but home offered a familiarity that I craved at the moment. Plus, Nicodemus would be there and I could always count on his snuggles.

"Definitely. I'll be fine."

"Okay," she answered, reluctantly. She put the car in drive. "Directions, please."

Chαptξr 8

Each morning, the sun rose a few minutes later as autumn approached, although the temperature didn't show any signs that the season was changing. Shadows moved across new parts of the bare wall it hadn't touched in a year. The hot, dry sun, reflecting off of the changing fall leaves of the tree outside, created an eerie red hue that filled my dreary, gray bedroom.

The walk to school wasn't quite as sticky this morning. Another dry Santa Ana had moved in, sucking the moisture out of the air. In place of the mugginess, a static electric field permeated everything.

Beth and I found our usual seats in myth class and barely had time to get out a "hi" before Professor Dhampir entered the room.

I felt incredibly guilty about the twilight rescue last night. Beth jetted to my assistance, only to take me straight home afterward. She had peppered me with so many questions that my replies were cut off before I had a chance to answer. We were at my front door before her assault stopped. I was relieved not to have to explain in detail. I flung open the door before she even had a chance to bring the car to a complete stop, dashed out and yelled back a quick "thanks!" My escape was awkward and cowardice.

We both kept busy taking lecture notes like studious pupils when my guilty conscience took over.

> Beth, I'm so sorry about last night . . . bailing like that after you came to my rescue. I'm so embarrassed. I'm a horrible friend. BTW, did you have a good weekend?

Cris L. P. Olsen

Passing notes wasn't usually my style, but it was the only form of communication I could use and still keep my guilty face concealed by the wall of hair I had created by bowing my head over my textbook. I couldn't face her while I put my tail between my legs and begged for forgiveness.

She anxiously read the note and furiously scribbled words back to me.

> Anna, you don't have to apologize, really. I was happy you thought of me when you needed help! I'll always here for you, babe. No worries!
>
> I had an awesome weekend! Zech took me on a date! He has a friend that works at the San Diego Zoo and he got us a private tour to see a bunch of the habitats behind the scenes. I got to touch an elephant and feed a giraffe! It was the best date I've ever been on!

She was so sweet about the whole thing. Maybe I was the one blowing everything out of proportion. She must not have felt it was as huge an imposition as I did. With all of my insecurities, Beth seemed like the perfect friend to have: gracious, forgiving and kind. Thankfulness to a higher power filled my heart at the thought of this budding friendship that lay before me.

My attention shifted back to the note and the heart she had drawn around Zech's name. A pang of jealousy flowed through me. My happiness for her stellar date was tainted with selfishness. Our friendship was just beginning, just like her relationship with Zech. I secretly hoped he wouldn't distract her so much that our friendship couldn't even get off the ground.

The muscles in my forehead began to ache. I was scowling. *Blech, Anna, how callous*, I scolded myself in my head. I should be totally happy for her. She's so sweet and she's never been anything but nice to me.

I had to mentally sluff off the icky jealousy and selfishness that wrapped its sticky fingers around my mind before it grew and showed outwardly. She deserved the best date ever. I was happy for her! I nodded a small sharp nod to myself, hoping no one noticed.

A deafening clap tore through the class as Professor Dhampir smacked his enormous hand on his desk, as he described the battle of the Titans. The entire class jumped at the sound and all began taking notes feverously.

Beth clenched her fist and pulled it toward her sharply. "Yes!" she whispered at her excitement of the subject matter. The Titans were the topic of her Giants paper. Her fingers flew across the keys of her laptop, typing virtually every word he uttered.

The lecture was intense today. I felt exhausted by the time class was over. Beth swiftly packed her bag, making good use of time as she simultaneously apologized to me.

"Sorry I can't grab coffee today, but I have that lab in chemistry class next and I'm really nervous about it. I'm going to get there early and try to get a few pointers from the TA before class starts. I'll see you Friday, okay?"

I nodded as I watched her dash off. My shoulders slumped. Spending time with her was going to have to wait until the weekend. A feeling of melancholy ached in my chest.

I made a point to wait until the last possible minute to get up Friday morning. I threw on some clothes and stared into the mirror at my clear, blue eyes and my pale skin as I brushed my teeth. I looked the same, but I felt different . . . I was excited. The thought of spending time with my new friend brought a smile to my face. I gave Nicodemus a scratch on the head, filled his bowl with food and raced out the door.

Myth class hadn't started yet, but everyone was already there. No one wanted to call attention to themselves by sneaking in late and catching Professor Dhampir's intense glare. Thank goodness, Beth was already there and had saved me a seat. The class was packed.

I focused on the floor as I climbed over a girl with four-inch wedge sandals before stepping on the foot of a boy with extremely large feet. I was in the middle of finagling my way across the row when Professor Dhampir walked in. An instant hush swept over the room. Just like everyone else, I froze. Stuck standing in between two very annoyed students, I caught Professor Dhampir's eye immediately as he turned to address the class. His glare shot daggers at me. I was the only one not ready for his lecture. With a flick of his wrist, he motioned for me to continue. The entire class turned to watch me trip my way to the seat next to Beth. My face turned hot with embarrassment. I quickly pulled out my book and sat as still as possible.

His lecture began. As soon as the tension in the room eased, I scribbled a note to Beth.

He must be PMS-ing today!

She giggled and his eyes shot up at us. He boomed out a question directly to us. "Have any of you come across any supernatural aspects to your Giants research?"

What kind of question was that? It all seemed supernatural! This must be a trick question.

His black-eyed gaze sliced into us. I heard Beth swallow hard. She straightened her back and spoke aloud.

"I've been researching the Titans. They're called gods. Of course there's a supernatural aspect; that's not something we see here on Earth."

He chuckled to himself as a sly smile grew across his face. He turned so his back was facing the class and scrawled methodically on the board, "gods on Earth" was all he wrote.

Despite my interest in the subject matter, I could barely focus on the words he spoke. I studied his body as he paced at the bottom of the stadium seating lecture hall. He moved around the floor with calculated grace. His deep voice rattled the windows and his mouth curled up at the edges when he mentioned the gods. What was it about him that was so commanding? He was totally hot in a Gerard Butler sort of way, but bigger, more chiseled and not nearly as approachable.

The students fidgeted in their seats as the lecture ran over the allotted hour and a half, stealthily slipping their books and notes into their bags as to not draw attention to themselves.

Professor Dhampir became noticeably agitated as he could sense everyone's Friday angst. With a wave of his hand as a dismissal, the class stood up in unison to escape.

Beth and I turned to make our way across the row when we heard a deep "ahem" from the front of the class. Our heads automatically turned to the direction of the disturbance. There stood Professor Dhampir with his arm outstretched, pointing directly at me. His enormous hand turned over slowly as his finger curled, summoning me to the front of the class.

Beth shot me a wary look. She squared her shoulders and linked her arm through mine as an act of unity. We waited for the row to clear, then made our way down the stairs to him.

We reached the front of the class and stood at the side of his desk. He was even bigger up close. His sly smile was back as he opened his mouth to speak.

"Ananiah Immaculada, I presume?"

I nodded slowly as his voice vibrated around in my head.

"And who is your little friend?"

The words wouldn't come. Visions of the last time I imagined him speaking my name haunted me. I couldn't decide if Professor Dhampir was creepy or the most masculine and handsome man I had ever seen. Beth squeezed my arm.

I gulped in a breath of air. "Yes, I'm Anna and this is Beth."

He eyed me up and down carefully, which made me feel extremely uncomfortable. Beth seemed to be enjoying the close proximity to him. She covertly shuffled closer to his direction.

One of his eyebrows lifted. "How are you coming on your Giants research, Anna?"

He slowly walked around his desk and sat on a tall stool, casually putting one foot up on a rung as if posing for us.

"I, uh." My mind bounced back and forth. Is Professor Dhampir creepy or sexy? Creepy or sexy? My mouth wouldn't move.

Beth poked me in the ribs just as I found my voice. "I think I've stumbled on a common thread with most of the Giants I've been reading about."

"Hmm," his voice purred, "and what sort of common thread is that?"

Unable to answer, I struggled with what it was about him that rubbed me the wrong way, when it dawned on me. He wasn't creepy *or* sexy. He was dangerous; the worst kind of dangerous there was! In a position of respect and authority, he could make anything happen at the snap of a finger. That had to be why he seemed so intimidating and intriguing at the same time. I wanted to escape, but Beth, linked to my arm, kept shifting her weight as she inched closer to him.

One can't intimidate you unless you let them. I wouldn't let him. A surge of inner strength arose in me and I spoke clearly. "The Giants are all connected biblically in some way and I think I know how."

The Professor squinted. His daunting stare caused me to involuntarily take a step back. I had to tug on Beth to move with me. One corner of his mouth curled up.

"That's interesting. Not many of my students have come up with that theory, let alone a freshman. So tell me, how are the Giants of old linked, exactly?"

His lips pursed, he stared at me expectantly. My eyes searched the ground as I spoke softly. "I'd like to further research my theory before telling anyone about it if you don't mind, Professor Dhampir."

His eyes narrowed.

I had pushed back; not given into his demand.

"Miss Immaculada, being your professor, I am privy to these things before they are concluded. I may be able to help refine your ideas if you divulge your theory."

He was trying to bully me. I held steadfast.

A buzzing coming from his pocket interrupted his stare. He breezed off of the stool and toward the side door of the front of the lecture hall. He plunged his hand into his pocket and brought a cell phone to his ear. In a flash he was gone, out the door without another word to us.

I gave Beth's arm a tug.

As soon as he was out of the room, Beth seemed to snap out of a trance. "Whew, saved by the bell! Let's get out of here!" she whispered.

With me on her heels, Beth sprinted up the stairs to the back of the lecture hall just as Professor Dhampir was reentering through the side door. We had barely passed through the doorway, when I peeked over my shoulder to see Professor Dhampir searching the room for us.

"Girls!" he boomed out, but we kept running.

Chαρτξr 9

We ran across campus as fast as we could, helping each other as our heavy bags fell off our shoulders. At first it felt as if we were running for our lives, then a different feeling crept in. We were having fun.

We hit a grassy patch in the quad and one of Beth's flip-flops flew off. I kicked it and it flew up and hit her in the butt.

She let out a peal of screaming laughter and spun in circles as she searched the ground for it. Still trying to run, she hopped along, making three attempts at getting it hooked back on her toe, before she realized it had broken. She gave up entirely and threw it across the grass.

We ran straight to the Café, rolling with laughter at the sound of her one-shoe clip with no following clop. As we reached the door, I flung it open and we ducked inside as if to hide.

My face flushed with heat and adrenaline. Our laughter had turned into silent convulsions as we tried to mask our mania from those around us. Passing students stared and shook their heads as we attempted to calm ourselves.

We found an empty table inside the air conditioned food court and slid in, sighing in exhaustion. Beth leaned against the glass window and rested her head back as she stared at the ceiling and I leaned forward and put my head on the table, averting my eyes from her. If I couldn't see her, it would be easier to stop giggling.

"Smoothie?" she asked in a singing tone.

I agreed by bobbing my head up and down, tapping it on the table with each nod. With my forehead still pressed against the table, I grabbed my wallet out of my pocket and blindly held it up to her.

"On me," she spouted.

There would be no use in arguing with her. I dropped my wallet in my lap and gave her a thumbs up. "Oh, no dairy, please," I requested as my breath moistened the tabletop.

"Right," she said, as she flitted from the table to order the smoothies. As her footsteps faded, I rotated my head to look out the window, pressing my cheek against the cool wood. Warmth from the hot September day outside radiated through the glass. It was typical for the summer heat to linger into early autumn here, but there wouldn't be many of these warm days left before fall started to nip in the air.

My worries of Professor Dhampir vanished and the happiness I felt at the current moment made me smile. Beth was my best friend. Life had found its way back into my soul. I reveled in the feeling with my cheek on the cool table when I heard Beth's snap-thud of her one flip-flop stride snapping toward me.

I raised my head just as she shoved a smoothie in my hand. With a straw between her teeth, she gestured toward the door with her chin.

The cool air of the food court wafted out of the doors as we stepped out into the sun. We found a spot outside on the grass, beneath a shade tree, and plopped down. Both of us let out a sigh. Beth lay back on to her elbows to relax, the warm breeze blowing strands of her straight blonde hair across her face. I crisscrossed my legs and straightened my back to stretch and breathe in the summer air. We sat in silence, sipping our smoothies, taking in one of the last days of an Indian summer.

This was the first time we had just sat and Beth hadn't babbled on about something. It gave me time to think. It gave me courage to want to confide in her. I wanted our friendship to go to the next level. Friends can't really be true friends until they know all about each other. I wanted to tell her the tragedies that I'd been through in the last year. She was sweet and optimistic, and she had definitely made an effort to be my friend. I was ready.

I nudged her leg. "Thanks for the smoothie."

She shook her head and smiled widely, revealing a strawberry seed stuck in her teeth. "No problem."

I giggled and tapped on my teeth, signaling to her to check her own. Her tongue searched out the seed. After a loud sucking sound she smacked my knee. "You know how many people wouldn't let someone know they have something stuck in their teeth? Thanks!"

She was adorable and sweet, and right then I knew I could trust her.

The confidence of the emerging new me swelled as I considered what I was about to do. I opened my mouth to begin my confession, but paused.

"Are you okay?" she asked, sensing my hesitation.

I pressed my lips together between my teeth and after a deep breath, I nodded. I squeezed my eyebrows together and bit my lip as I began. "I want to tell you something, but I'm not sure if I'm ready to tell it. I haven't really talked to anyone about it since it happened."

She gave me a look of understanding. "Whatever it is, you don't have to talk if you're not ready."

She didn't even know what I wanted to say, but already she was kind about it. I took a deep breath. I wasn't sure how to begin, but once I started, it all came gushing out. For over an hour I told my story. A feeling of abandonment rolled through me as I explained how I withdrew from my friends after my parents died. My head burned with anger and my cheeks flushed with embarrassment as I told her how Seth pushed me for sex and how I had fought him off. Then an empty feeling filled my stomach as I explained how he died and how I was all alone. I told her everything that had happened in the past seven months, well, everything except the cold encounters I'd started experiencing again. People understand the physical, they can relate to flesh and blood. As much as I wanted to tell Beth everything that was plaguing me, the coldness that was stalking me was something I never told anyone except my parents and Ms. Seraph. No one needed to know I had some sort of strange connection with the other side.

I could see that it took all of Beth's restraint to just listen without commenting until I finished. I desperately hoped she had some sort of life experience that would help her sympathize with my situation.

"Anna, I'm so sorry for your losses," she said sincerely, then paused for a long time as she worked something out in her head. "So, you're living by yourself, now? That must be lonely. Is there anything I can do to help?"

Her thoughtfulness comforted me, but I knew that no one could help heal the pain I experienced every day. No one had the ability to magically heal my soul. I took each day as it came.

"You already have. It felt good to get it all out. I've never told anyone the full story before. You've actually really helped by just listening, thanks."

Beth gave me a wink and a smile.

I shook my empty smoothie cup and surveyed the surroundings. The afternoon had changed. The sun was no longer high in the sky, but at a sharp angle that cast long shadows across the quad.

"I have a perfect idea!" she blurted. "I didn't get a chance to watch *Clash of the Titans* last weekend! Let's go do some research!"

She attempted to distract me, to pull me out of the past and into the present. And I welcomed it. She grabbed my hand and pulled me up so quickly that I didn't have time to stabilize myself on the one foot that hadn't fallen asleep. I wobbled there for a moment.

Beth instinctively reached her hand out. "Here, lean on me."

I flopped my foot around like a dead fish, wincing as pins and needles stabbed at my skin. She had listened compassionately to me ramble on for over an hour. I knew then, that I could lean on her for support that went deeper than a tingly foot. I gave my leg a few more shakes and grabbed my books.

"You don't mind coming to my place, do you?" she inquired with a smile. "I can bring you back after the movie."

"Of course not." My answer was brief. I didn't want to sound overeager.

"Great!" she beamed. "I'll just call my mom and tell her to set another place at the table for dinner!"

She picked up my empty smoothie cup and dashed off to the trash can, cell phone in hand. She still lived with her parents? I had just gotten comfortable having a new friend, but going to her house and meeting her family, too? I was *not* ready for that!

She grabbed my hand again and pulled me along behind her. The sun in our faces blinded us as we searched for her car. I was glad when she led me straight to it and we didn't have to play the "find Beth's little green car" game again.

Her keychain alarm button still not working, she fumbled about, trying to get the key in the door.

I tapped on the hood with my fingernail to get her attention.

Her head popped up and she craned her neck around the front of the car to see me.

"Um, Beth?" I asked her in a quiet voice. "Would you mind keeping what I just told you to yourself? I don't know if I'm ready to have it all out on the table in front of a whole family yet."

"Of course!" she replied in a sweet, reassuring voice as she returned her attention to the key. "I don't gossip about people's private lives. We all have our issues . . . our secrets. I've really been looking forward to making some new friends since classes began. You're the only one who seems real around here. Everyone has a past. I like to focus on the future," she ended with a flash of a smile.

Her tone was so confident and optimistic it gave me a sensation I hadn't experienced in a long time. I couldn't quite put my finger on it. I think it was hope. Just being around Beth made me feel special, like I was the best friend she'd ever had.

"How do you do it?" I asked as we slid into the hot car.

"Do what?" she echoed as she turned the key and blasted the A/C on high.

"Be so happy and cheerful all the time?"

She beamed a smile. "I guess that's just the way God made me! I've always been like this." She put the car in reverse. Within seconds we were on our way.

Chapτξr 10

I had no idea where Beth lived, but we headed west which could only mean she lived near the beach. As she drove closer to the coast, the setting sun lit up the sky, blazing orange and yellow. She navigated through a maze of confusing residential streets, then pulled over and came to a stop on a road where a thick hedge was the only thing separating us from a tumble down a cliff to the sandy beach below.

Thin bands of clouds caught glints off of the deep navy blue water, turning them lavender and pink. I had lived in San Diego my entire life and hardly ever made it to the beach. I had a world of beauty right at my fingertips and rarely took advantage of it.

Beth sighed. "It's beautiful isn't it? I haven't seen such a colorful sunset in weeks!"

Weeks? She must come here a lot. It was nice that she thought to drive me here, too. After the story she heard about my life this afternoon, maybe she thought the beautiful scenery would be soothing for me.

"Sometimes taking the scenic route is worth the extra time," I said. She shot me a knowing smile and pulled away from the curb. There wasn't anywhere to go except to turn around or head into a gated residence. To my surprise, Beth clicked a button clipped to the driver's side visor and an ornate gate opened slowly. The Prius rolled through the massive iron entry and began to climb a steep flagstone driveway that curved toward the ocean. The view took my breath away. A small, deserted beach lay far below, save for one lone surfer in the water.

As we crested the hill, a modern Tuscan villa appeared before us. I only got a quick glance of the house before Beth pulled into a four car garage and turned off the engine.

The soothing feeling I had from taking in the ocean view vanished and panic shot through me. The entire way to Beth's house I was thinking that my couch and TV at home seemed like a much better idea than meeting her family and having to struggle with small talk over dinner. Worse yet, being a first time visitor meant the conversation would be directed at me. The questions of "so, where are you from" and "what do your parents do" would inevitably come. Then the judgment and nods of pity would begin.

Ugh! I can't do this.

Beth grabbed her bag but I paused, resting mine in my lap. My stomach flip-flopped.

"I'm not so sure about this. You're my first new friend in a really long time. I don't know if I'm ready to meet a whole family."

I felt so vulnerable. It occurred to me that I didn't actually know much about her except that she had way too much bubbly cheer for one person's body to contain and she lived with her parents in a huge house on a cliff overlooking the Pacific Ocean.

She gently put her hand on my arm and looked me sweetly in the eye. "Don't worry about it, really. My family's great. They won't give you the Spanish Inquisition or anything like that. They've been through a lot. They look to the future and don't dwell on the past. Well, except for my brother, but he's really nice. You'll see."

Not just parents, but a brother too? This dinner is going to be torture!

She bounced out of the car and motioned with her hand for me to come along.

I gave myself a quick pep talk. *Okay. I'm here. I need to make new friends and rejoin the real world. It's been nothing but blah for long enough. I can do this.* I tried to convince myself.

I took a deep breath, held it until I felt dizzy, then let it out in a gust of air.

As I got out of the car, I noticed three other cars in the garage, two of which were hybrids and one that was old and shiny. It looked like a restored vintage automobile.

I closed the car door and took a few quick steps to catch up with Beth. As we rounded the corner to the front of the house, a warm, moist breeze caressed my face. I closed my eyes and breathed in deeply, trying to center myself. The scent of salt and seaweed from the ocean heavily laced the air.

I opened my eyes and took a small step forward into the warm sun and looked down. Separating the house from the cliff below was a flagstone patio surrounded by a glass wall, just taller than waist high, and to the North, a staircase led from the sand right up to the patio. There must have been at least a hundred steps.

"C'mon, Anna! My mom can't wait to meet you!"

Beth told her mom about me? I prayed she was telling the truth when she said she didn't talk about people behind their backs, even if it was to her own mother.

I caught up with her, just as she stepped up to the front door. Beth reached for the knob, but it turned on its own and opened to reveal a beautiful woman standing inside. Beth's mom was waiting at the door to greet us.

"Hello, girls. I heard the garage open, but then didn't hear you come in," she said, with eager anticipation.

The resemblance between her and Beth was remarkable. Their hair was the exact same color, but Beth's mother had hers pulled back into a bun at the nape of her neck. She had warm, brown eyes with small kind lines around them that appeared when she smiled.

Her slim physique was apparent under her gray pantsuit and white ruffled blouse, and basic black heels poked out from under her pant cuffs. Her clothes seemed generic instead of designer, as I would expect someone of her means to be wearing. Her outfit looked common and unassuming.

"Hi mom." Beth gave her mom a hug and they kissed each other on the cheeks.

"This is Ananiah Immaculada, but she likes to be called Anna. We have Mythology 101 together."

By the way she introduced me, she must not have told her mom anything about me yet.

Beth's mom looked at me affectionately, gave me a smile and held out her hand. I gently gripped it and started to shake. She put her other hand on top of mine. "It's a pleasure to meet you, Anna." Her soothing voice helped relax the tension in my shoulders.

Beth snorted. "I'm sorry, I didn't actually introduce you. This is my mom, Rebekah Gwenaël."

"Nice to meet you Mrs. Gwenaël," I said.

"We welcome our children's friends here like family, Anna. It's very polite of you to call me Mrs. Gwenaël, but please do not feel shy about calling me Rebekah."

"Um, I'll try." My parents had taught me to always address friends' parents formally and with respect. I would have to consciously work at not calling her Mrs. Gwenaël.

As she spoke, I peered through floor-to-ceiling windows that lined the wall facing the ocean, as a guy carrying a surfboard walked from the beach stairs across the yard. The board blocked his face, but he seemed familiar to me somehow.

He wore a tank top that exposed his muscular arms and large square shoulders. His board shorts revealed well-defined calves. As he turned, I glimpsed a tattoo across his shoulders that peeked out of the armholes of his tank top on either side.

My gaze no longer focused on Mrs. Gwenaël, but darted behind her. She noticed my distraction and turned around to catch sight of him, just as he disappeared around the corner of the house.

"Oh," she commented, "that's Beth's brother. He must have just come in from surfing. He will join us for dinner. You can meet him then."

Why was my heart pounding? I *really* wasn't ready for this!

"I'm sure you and Beth have things to do, so I won't keep you. I need to change my clothes and start making dinner, so I will leave the two of you to it. If you're hungry, please make yourself at home and grab anything you'd like from the kitchen."

As nice as Mrs. Gwenaël seemed, I couldn't stand the thought of having to explain my solitary life to her . . . and Beth's father . . . and Beth's *brother.*

Beth put her hand on my shoulder. "You okay, Anna?"

"I'm fine," I said, as I cracked a sliver of a smile. "Actually, I'm a little hungry. A smoothie isn't much of a lunch. Can we get a snack?"

Beth's eyes lit up. "Oh, yeah! Food! Yum! The kitchen is over here," she said, as she bounced along in front of me.

I followed her in silence, walking slowly through the front room that faced the ocean. The outside of the house looked Tuscan, but the inside felt much more casual. Two chocolate-brown leather couches faced each other and rested on a huge shaggy white rug, framed by sage green linen chairs on either side. In the middle of a large round coffee table, sat a silver bowl filled with all sorts of shells, sand dollars and starfish. I wondered if Beth and her brother had found those down on the beach and started a collection.

Beth's brother – something about him seemed familiar, yet elusive, as I thought about the boy with the surfboard. Emerald green eyes flashed through my mind and I instantly knew why I recognized him. It was Jonah.

My palms turned clammy and a tingle rose to the surface of my skin. Should I tell her I knew her brother already? I felt embarrassed to admit that just the mere sight of him made my heart pound. He was so beautiful. Surely, over the years, she had endured her friends drooling over him. I didn't want to be one of them; I was here for her.

As we walked deeper into the house, the sun streamed in through the arched floor-to-ceiling French doors. Hot rays glinted off of the white marble floor so brightly that I had to shield my eyes as we walked past. Every door stood open, carrying the salty scent of the ocean into the house as the sea air wafted in.

I followed Beth into the kitchen. A gourmet chef could only dream of such a beautiful room. Black marble counter tops cut through a sea of antiqued white cabinets. Every top-of-the-line stainless steel appliance you could imagine polished off every crevice. I gawked at the room as Beth started opening the cabinets, searching for a snack. Thirsty, I walked over to the refrigerator. "May I?"

"Of course! Whenever you're here, please make yourself at home! Don't ever hesitate to grab anything from the fridge or rummage around the cabinets for snacks!"

Beth made it sound like I was going to be here often.

I pulled a Vitaminwater out of the fridge for each of us. Beth handed me a one hundred calorie pack of graham crackers. A large bowl of fruit rested in the middle of the island. A pear sounded delicious right now, but I knew I could only eat organic. Anything else would give me a dreadful stomach ache or hives. Living with food allergies and intolerances was frustrating. I had to watch everything I ate.

I peered into the bowl and noticed the "organic" stickers on them. I was in luck! I grabbed one and followed Beth.

"C'mon, I'll show you the rest of the house!"

We walked through a casual living room, where a huge flatscreen hung on the wall, surrounded by bookcases filled with what could amount to a zillion books, then past a library . . . more books. Tons of them!

I turned and Beth had disappeared. I surveyed my surroundings wondering where she could have possibly gone to, when she popped her head around a corner.

I scrunched up my nose and shot her a curious look.

"I know, weird, right? I didn't know this was here until I literally ran into it the first time," she said, giggling. She vanished behind a hidden wall. This time I followed closely as we ascended up a secret back staircase.

Jonah was in this house somewhere. The thought sent a rush of blood pounding through my body. Maybe I shouldn't think about him like that. He's my friend's brother and that's an "off-limits" thing when girls are friends. Then I remembered every moment I had thought about him, fanaticized about him, dreamed about him. I *wanted* to think about him. I hadn't been able to think about anything else since we first met.

I followed Beth to her room. A thousand shades of white and cream covered practically every surface. Bold textures in a fluffy bedspread contrasted the smoothness of a sleek white leather chair in the corner. A rustic, pine four poster bed rested against the far wall and a matching pine desk sat under a huge picture window that framed the side of the cliff. Bookcases on the wall were filled with baskets of shells, sand dollars and starfish. Beth must spend a lot of time on the beach.

She walked over to French doors, opened them and stepped out onto a balcony. Her hair blew in a gentle ocean breeze. Invisible swirls of air came into the room, gently moving sheer, white curtains as they passed by the door. Finally reaching me, they wrapped caressing tendrils of sea air around my skin.

My thoughts turned inward. I was making progress. I made a new friend, told her about my past and was now at her house, about to have dinner with her family.

Maybe I can do this!

I inhaled the heavy sea air deeply. My confidence was growing; confidence to meet new people; confidence to trust a friend with my fragile soul; confidence to live my life again.

Chαpτξr 11

"Hey, why don't we take a walk on the beach before dinner? We can watch the movie after, then Jonah can watch with us. He loves *Clash of the Titans*," Beth said, as she strode back into the room.

"Jonah?"

"Oh, that's my brother."

My heart pounded at the thought of sitting in the same room with him for two hours in close proximity, maybe even on the same couch. I forced slow breaths.

Beth and I walked quickly down the secret stairs and headed out the door toward the beach. I tried to keep my mind on anything but the impending formal introduction to Jonah. Would he out me? Would he explain our first meeting at the library and our second meeting when he saved me from falling face first into the pavement? I remembered the promise I made to myself. If I ran into him a third time I would finally introduce myself. My stomach churned with anticipation.

I counted the steps as we descended down the huge staircase from their backyard to the sand. Seventy-three steps in all.

The wet sand cooled and massaged my feet as we began our exploration of the beach.

"So, have you lived here all your life?" Beth blurted.

Serenity gone . . . here it comes . . . twenty questions. "Yeah. Not far from here, actually, but I never made it to the beach much. It's always too crowded and hard to find a parking spot. I never even knew this beach was here."

"It's totally protected by the cliffs on either side. See over there and over there?" Beth pointed to a cliff about fifty yards away. About equal distance behind us was another cliff, almost a mirror image of the one in front of us.

"You can only get to this beach by the staircases from the houses or if you swim around the cliffs, which is really hard because the waves crash up like crazy against the rocks."

I counted the sets of stairs I saw. "So this is a private beach for just the four houses here?"

"Well, all California beaches are supposed to have public access, but there really isn't any way for that to happen here, so, yeah. Isn't that awesome? I love it here. The surfing is good if you paddle out far enough and the current washes all sorts of stuff ashore. I've found tons of sea creatures and shells and stuff. Look, there's a sand dollar!"

Following the direction of her outstretched finger, I saw a purple circle in the sand.

After rinsing it off in the lapping waves, she handed it to me. "Here, your first treasure from our beach!"

"Thanks. It's beautiful!"

"We can clean it and preserve it. The fuzzy stuff will fall off and it will turn white."

"That's cool."

"Yeah. Jonah knows a lot about the sea. He taught me how to clean and preserve all of the things we've found on the beach since we've moved here."

"You just moved here?"

"About three months ago. After Jonah and I graduated, we moved here so we could go to UCSD."

I guess that answered my question as to why Beth didn't have any other friends.

"So, you and your brother are twins?"

Beth giggled. "Why would you think that?"

"If you both just graduated, you're the same age, right?"

A look of understanding washed across her face. "Ooooh. No, Jonah just graduated from college and I just graduated from high school. He's four years older than me."

"I didn't think he looked like he was eighteen," I murmured.

Beth smirked. "You know him?"

Crap! She heard me. Why did this seem so awkward? Why couldn't I tell her I knew him the second I saw him carrying the surf board?

"I saw him walk up from the beach." That was true, right?

"Oh, right."

We shuffled along, squishing the sticky, wet sand between our toes, collecting as many sea creatures as we could find. I knew any second Beth was going to ask me another question. I searched my mind for a neutral topic before she could throw Question Number Two at me.

"So, your parents must be pretty environmentally friendly. You all have hybrid cars."

I didn't say it like a question so I didn't really expect an answer, but I'm learning that Beth never shies away from conversation.

"Yeah, we try to do what we can to help."

"Help what?"

"Help anything . . . anyone. My mom's a social worker and my dad's a *pro bono* lawyer. We recycle and have hybrid cars . . . well, we all have hybrid cars *except* for Jonah. He's really attached to his Morgan. My mom's been trying to get him to go green for years, but he won't give it up."

Beth's parents' occupations puzzled me. "A *pro bono* lawyer is a lawyer who works for free, right?"

Beth nodded. "He is now, but he used to be a big hot-shot attorney in New York before . . ." Her voice trailed off. She wasn't telling me something.

"Did you know that *pro bono* is Latin for 'public good'?" she blurted. "He's very proud to be able to help those who need his services who would otherwise be unable to pay for them," she said, as she tilted her chin up with pride.

"So, if your mom is a social worker and your dad is a *pro bono* lawyer, how do you have a huge beach house and new cars and everything?"

I instantly regretted asking the question . . . talk about prying! Putting my foot in my mouth was common for me. I'd been working on it for years, but it still reared its ugly head when

I was nervous. I didn't want her to ask me questions, and here I was asking about her family's income. *Bad form, Anna!*

Despite my brazen query, Beth seemed to be ready for this question. The furrow on her brow suggested she was organizing her thoughts into a precise order. She didn't use her normal tone as she explained the situation to me. Her reply sounded . . . rehearsed.

"My brother is adopted. When he was twelve, his great-uncle tracked him down. His uncle was very sick and didn't have any blood relatives, but had knowledge of Jonah's existence. He had had been searching for Jonah for three years before he found him. His uncle died only a few months later, and left him everything. He was very wealthy. A trust account was set up.

When my brother turned eighteen, he signed over half of the account to my parents. My parents actually work for free and the money he gave them pays for everything. Jonah bought this house for them. They would have never picked such a fancy home."

I didn't notice I was standing there with my mouth hanging open until it started to feel dry from the breeze. I snapped it shut and looked away from her, pretending to focus on something I saw in the ground. I dug my toe in the sand. Beth stood silent, biting her lip in anticipation of my reaction. She looked uncomfortable.

Did she think I didn't believe her? Was her dad really a mob boss and this was the front story she had to tell everyone?

"Wow! Jonah's uncle must have really been loaded!" *Ugh! Foot in mouth, again!*

She let out a sigh of relief that I didn't think she meant for me to hear. "Jonah is the sweetest, most generous and caring person I've ever known. Well, next to my parents. He loves us all very much. He didn't even want a house of his own when we moved here. He wants to stay with us. He's paying for his own college education *and* mine, though he really doesn't need to go to college to earn a living, being that he's set for life and all. But he loves people and wants to help as much as he can, so he's going to medical school. He plans to go to third-world countries and practice his medicine there to develop vaccines for malaria and stuff like that."

He was gorgeous, generous, kind and smart; the perfect package and definitely out of my league.

Beth and I didn't talk much after that. I didn't want her to ask me any more questions and she must have felt the same. To be in the same vicinity as her and not hear her constant babble was odd. I was beginning to actually like her continual chatter. It meant I didn't have to do the talking. She led our conversations easily, which allowed me to simply follow along. She kept my attention so I wasn't always lost in my own thoughts. When she talked, it distracted me from the issues that usually sucked me into one of my daydreams.

As the sun began to dip below the horizon, Beth waved me over to the stairs. Each with a handful of shells, we headed up to the house.

The peaceful afternoon was broken when Beth stopped in the middle of our ascent. She looked right into my eyes and held my gaze intensely. "My brother is . . ." she paused for a few breaths. " . . . special. We all want what's best for him, even though I disagree with my parents on what that might be."

I gave her a confused look. Was this her way of warning me to stay away from him?

She shot me a quick smile, turned abruptly and started back up the stairs.

I shook my head. She was cute, but odd. Her little speech was completely lost on me. Only time would tell what she meant.

I followed her down a short path and passed a beautiful black bottomed pool as we headed toward a pool house. Floor-to-ceiling windows graced the west-facing wall, just like the main house. As we entered, the air hung heavy with the smell of the sea. The entire surface of a glass dining table was covered with towels and washed shells.

Beth walked over to the sink and put her newly found treasures in a strainer. Grabbing the handle of an industrial-looking faucet, she started to rinse them as I added mine to the pile. The strainer overflowed with shells and tipped to the side, threatening to dump our findings down the drain. As we both reached out to catch it, she dropped the faucet, sending water spraying all over us. She let out a scream.

"Oh, it's on," I announced, through giggles. She shot a quick squirt my way and I retaliated by cupping my hands under the running water and flinging it back at her. By the time the shells were clean, we were drenched and so was the kitchen.

Mrs. Gwenaël came running frantically toward the pool house. She laughed when she walked in the door. With guilty looks on our faces we stood in the middle of the kitchen, dripping wet. We did our best to hold back giggles.

"I was worried when I heard screams." She eyed us up and down, and ended her observation with an amused smirk. "Too bad you girls don't wear the same size. Anna, I think I have a box of Beth's outgrown clothes around somewhere. I'll rummage through it and grab a few things that might fit you. You can wear them while I put your clothes in the dryer. Dinner will be ready in about ten minutes. I'll leave the clothes for you on Beth's bed."

She turned to Beth. "There are some towels under the sink that you can use for the floor in here. I'll send Leah in to finish cleaning this mess when she gets in tomorrow," she said, then turned and walked back up to the house.

I looked at Beth, puzzled. "Leah?"

"Yeah, Leah is our housekeeper. It kills my mom to need help. She's used to doing everything herself, but she can't take care of this big house on her own *and* work full-time. My parents pay her way too much, but she's worth it. She's really nice. You'll meet her."

She eyed the shells and jerked her head toward the dining table. We spread them out on a clean, dry towel, arranging them by size. My fuzzy little sand dollar looked different all clean. It looked unique among all the other shells on the table.

"We'd better hurry up and get changed. These wet clothes are making me cold and I'm hungry! I think my mom is making spaghetti for dinner. Her spaghetti's the best!"

We raced into the main house, hurried up the stairs and into her room. Beth pointed to a door I hadn't seen before. "You can change in there," she said.

I walked over to the door and opened it slowly. It was a bathroom. *Nice!* She had her own suite! Decorated in the same beach theme as her bedroom, a framed picture of sand dollars hung over the toilet, giving the bathroom unique flair.

Shrugging off my wet clothes, I glanced at myself in the mirror. Oh, beautiful. My formal introduction to Jonah and Beth's dad was minutes away, and I looked like a drowned cat. I wrapped a towel under my arms and poked my head out of the bathroom. "Beth, do you have a hairdryer I can use?"

When I didn't get an answer back, I ventured out a little farther. No Beth, but there were muffled voices coming from the hall.

I tiptoed closer toward the door and a deep voice reverberated through the wall. I cracked the door open, hoping to catch Beth and ask about the hair dryer when I noticed Jonah standing just a few feet away, talking to her. His back was to me. Wanting to go unnoticed, I closed the door slowly, only to announce myself as the hinge creaked at the last second.

"Do you need something, Anna?" Beth asked innocently.

"Uh, yeah, I was wondering if you have a hair dryer I can use."

Jonah turned slightly and caught sight of me out of the corner of his eye.

I instantly felt self-conscious. My hair was dripping all over the carpet. I grabbed it and pulled it around to one side and held my hand under it to catch the drips.

"Sure, under the sink. You can use anything in the bathroom you need. Just make yourself at home."

I nodded to her before darting back into her bathroom. I was so glad Jonah hadn't turned around completely to see me standing there in a towel.

I rummaged through Beth's cabinets and drawers and found a round brush, the hair dryer and some makeup – all I needed to make myself look presentable. I only had ten minutes. I had better get this done in record time. I dried my hair, swiped on a little mascara and lip gloss, then threw on the jeans and an oversized T-shirt Mrs. Gwenaël had left out for me, so quickly that I didn't even take notice in the mirror of what I looked like in my borrowed threads.

Emerging from the bathroom, I found Beth sitting at her desk typing something on her laptop. She had French braided her wet hair and had changed into jeans and a T-shirt. She turned to look at me and let out one sharp laugh.

"What?" I asked.

"We're wearing the same thing," she giggled.

I looked down. We were both wearing jeans and the exact same UCSD T-shirt.

I didn't know what to say. I didn't care if we were wearing the same thing. Actually, I sort of liked the idea of being Beth's twin. It made me feel like I might possibly belong in her world.

"Twinkies!" she shouted and beamed a smile. "Now you look like you belong here."

My thoughts exactly.

"Dinner!" rang out from downstairs.

She grabbed my hand and pulled me out the door. As we descended the back staircase, two male voices echoed up to us. Beth bounced into the kitchen as I lagged behind, pausing a moment while still concealed behind the safety of the secret wall. I drew in a deep breath and prepared myself for the unknown. Emerging timidly, I took a few steps into the room. Standing directly in front of me was Mr. Gwenaël and behind him, Jonah.

"Dad, this is Ananiah Immaculada, but you can call her Anna," Beth announced joyously.

Mr. Gwenaël reached for my hand before I had a chance to offer it. He shook it enthusiastically. "Very pleased to meet you, Anna, I'm Isaac. Beth doesn't bring many friends home. You must be special." His expression was one of pride and satisfaction.

My face flushed. I wasn't special. I was a normal teenager who had just lived through some nasty tragedies. Did Beth bring me home because she thought I was a charity case? Now I felt awkward.

Tension and hesitation consumed me, as Jonah's eyes met mine. I searched each of the Gwenaëls' faces. Could they tell? Did it show that I felt caught in a lie? Could they see the how I longed for him?

His chin rose with confidence and his expression softened as he stepped around the kitchen island. "What my dad means," he said, as he patted Isaac on the back, "is that Beth only brings friends home she feels are worthy of becoming a part of the family. You're only the third friend she's ever brought home."

"Ever?" I mumbled.

"Yes," Rebekah chimed in, "Beth had two close friends back home, but you're the first friend she's introduced to the family since we moved here."

My heartbeat increased as Jonah's distance closed in. He was a mere two feet from me, now. He tilted his head down and looked straight into my eyes. "You *are* special."

A sweet, clean scent whirled into my face, wrapping itself around my body as he stopped in front of me. But there was something more this time. Something laced within the sweetness. I had smelled something similar to this before. It was an otherworldly scent, but it wasn't the dank, musty smell I was used to catching whenever I had an encounter. No, this scent was comforting, but definitely not of this world. My heart pounded. What did that mean?

He raised his hand out for a handshake. "Hello, Anna."

I took a small step forward, closing the gap between us and put my hand gently in his. His hand enveloped mine and a jolt of electricity hummed through my arm and completely filled my body. My knees wobbled. I reached out with my free hand to brace myself, leaning on the counter as I struggled to catch my breath.

"This is my brother, Jonah," Beth introduced proudly.

"Hello, Jonah." The words came out just above a whisper. It was all I could muster. All of my concentration was focused on the electricity surging between us. I locked my eyes on Jonah's strong hand still holding mine, and wondered if I might see the energy emanating from our touch.

He didn't let go.

"Your hand is freezing, Anna," he stated in a concerned tone.

I finally looked him in the eye and unwillingly choked in a sharp breath. His eyes were glittering, luminous and *so* green.

Collecting myself took all of my concentration. "B-between picking shells out of the cold, wet sand and washing them in the cold water, my hands haven't gotten a chance to warm up yet."

Still holding my hand, Jonah guided me over to the sink and turned on warm water. I fumbled and tripped my way behind him as I followed.

He grabbed my other hand, put both of them under the water and started rubbing them between his. The water dulled the sensation of the current surging between us, but only a fraction.

"Let the warm water run over your hands for a few minutes. That should warm them up," he said softly.

Under the running water, he inspected my hand carefully, turning it over to expose the very cut he had bandaged only a few days earlier. He raised one of his wet hands up to his mouth, kissed his thumb softly then placed it on my wound. I looked at him in shock. A warm smile moved across his face as he peered into my eyes.

Mrs. Gwenaël walked in from the patio. "Ready to eat?" she asked.

Jonah quickly let go of my hands. The electricity stopped instantly. I unwillingly let out an exaggerated exhale when his skin left mine, and braced my hands against the sides of the sink to steady myself. He grabbed a towel and vigorously dried off his hands.

Jonah snuck a look at Beth. She bit her lip, and held back a grin. Did she notice what happened when Jonah touched me? He gave her a sly nod.

"Yup, I'm starving!" he answered, turning his back to me.

Mr. Gwenaël echoed him.

I rubbed my hands together under the water until they warmed up, all the while surveying my surroundings for signs that anyone else noticed what had just happened. I hoped Beth was the only one.

I bit the inside of my cheek to make sure I was still awake. Maybe I had imagined it? Sneaking deep breaths, I struggled to return my pulse to normal.

Mrs. Gwenaël nudged me with her hip as she passed by. "Anna, would you mind bringing out the salad?" she requested, as she gestured toward a wooden bowl. Her hands were full.

"Sure, Mrs. Gwenaël," I replied.

"Anna, it's sweet and very polite of you to call me Mrs. Gwenaël, but please, call me Rebekah. I insist. We want this to feel like home to you, dear."

I nodded and grabbed the salad.

A feast of spaghetti, colorful garden salad and a wonderfully soft-looking loaf of bread filled the table. Jonah balanced a tray of crystal goblets filled with red juice on his arm while he unloaded each of them carefully onto the table. This didn't seem like a meal millionaires would eat. There were no chefs in the kitchen; Rebekah cooked it. There were no servants catering to us; we handled the meal ourselves.

Then I remembered that both Isaac and Rebekah were in public service. Not too long ago they were most likely struggling to pay the bills and make ends meet. They weren't the typical millionaires, they were real people. And they were my friends.

Chαpτξr 12

"Oh, my gosh! You'll never believe what happened to Anna and me today!" Beth blurted out as she interrupted the dinner conversation that, until that point, consisted of benign questions directed toward me about music and my favorite foods.

Beth's ability to explain our confrontation with Professor Dhampir in meticulous detail fascinated me. She recreated the scene so dramatically that I felt as if I were there all over again.

One thing I couldn't get out of my mind, though, was her apparent draw to him. When he was near, she couldn't help but want to get closer, while I felt almost physical vibrations from him pushing me away. How could she find him remotely attractive? I didn't get it.

Isaac and Rebekah seemed enthralled, hanging onto her every word. When she described her unfortunate flip-flop blow-out, their boisterous laughter consumed the conversation before they were able to calm down enough to begin eating their meal again.

"And Professor Dhampir didn't send out a posse to hunt you down? It sounds like he may have some unfinished business you girls ran out on," Isaac commented innocently.

Jonah shot Isaac a stern look.

"Beth paints that professor as a bit strange to me as well," Rebekah interjected.

Jonah's glare turned to her.

Rebekah back-pedaled. "Well, you know the literary type. They're usually very involved in the drama of it all . . . especially a Humanities professor who teaches mythology! Unfinished business or not, yelling after the girls like that sounds a bit unnecessary, doesn't it?"

Beth's eyebrows raised high as they disappeared under her side-swept bangs. "And the basis for that conclusion is . . ." she challenged.

"I'm sorry, am I stereotyping him? I guess my training doesn't safeguard me against the protectiveness that a mother feels for her children. Grouping your professor in a category of 'the literary type' could be completely wrong. His description just seems so textbook narcissistic that it's hard to detach my personal feelings from someone who has the potential to have such a profound influence over you girls."

You girls . . . Rebekah made it sound as if she was feeling protective of me as part of her family. The way she spoke so easily of me as an instant part of her worries sent a warm feeling through me.

I scanned each face, memorizing their features, making mental notes of their expressions, how their faces changed and what their eyes told me. I ended my gaze across the table. Jonah studied the tablecloth intently. His stern expression had turned inward and he looked . . . worried. What could he possibly be so concerned about? Beth's story was funny. And Professor Dhampir, well, *he* wasn't anything to worry about. He was just a big bully. He used his good looks and position of power to intimidate. His motive wasn't even a factor to me. He was probably used to getting his way all the time. If he had unfinished business with me, I would face it head-on.

I was more worried about Jonah. Not once had he looked at me. Not once had he included himself in the conversation since Beth began telling her tale. Simultaneous relief and discouragement flooded over me. Why was his interest in me, or lack thereof, so important? And what had just happened between us in the kitchen? When I touched Beth, or Isaac, or Rebekah, it didn't shock me and leave me dizzy.

I'd never been boy-crazy as a teen. It seemed backward, but maybe this was my atonement for sticking to the books instead of dating around and falling crazy head-over-heels for some guy against my will.

I reminded myself that Jonah was off-limits. Beth was my friend. The thought helped ease my obsession to find the reason behind the electric handshake and the emerald green eyes that made my heart pound.

I was going to start a new life and Beth was the friend I wanted to start it with. I wasn't going to mess it up over a boy.

"Oh, I almost forgot," Beth said to Jonah gleefully. "We're gonna to watch *Clash of the Titans* after dinner. Do you want to watch with us? I know you love that movie."

Jonah shot Beth a kind smile, mixed with exasperation and defeat.

"Thanks, but I need to study," he said, in a monotone voice. He immediately excused himself from the table, gathered up the empty plates and carried them into the kitchen. The sound of running water and clanking china lasted for only minutes before it was silent.

Beth scooped up the empty salad bowl and pasta platter in her arms. "Ready to watch the movie?"

"Sure." I grabbed the empty bread basket and headed into the kitchen.

When I had left the kitchen before dinner, the usual signs of a meal that had just been prepared covered every surface. The pot the spaghetti had been cooked in was still on the stove, the cutting board that was used to slice the bread was covered in crumbs.

The kitchen was now sparkling clean.

"Wow," I exclaimed.

Beth snickered. "Yeah, Jonah's never left a dish unwashed or a single piece of dirty laundry sitting around. He's annoyingly perfect like that. It's a hard act to follow."

"That makes it easier on your mom though, right? You know, not to have to get after him about things like that."

"He's not the typical guy," she replied.

"I guess not."

Beth led me to the family room we had passed on our first trip up the back staircase. It was decorated in earth-tones with deep brick red accents. I sat on the couch, sank down and caressed the fabric. It felt like velvet. It must have been filled with feathers and down because it was extremely soft and cushy.

As Beth loaded in the DVD, I noticed that the books in the bookshelves were all leather-bound and looked almost exactly the same. They must be her dad's law books.

"Want some popcorn?" Beth asked.

I patted my tummy. "Are you kidding? I'm totally full from that awesome dinner. You were right. Your mom's spaghetti is delicious."

She plopped down into a large leather chair and pushed "Play" on the remote.

The movie began. As I watched, I realized how comfortable I felt in this house. Everyone was so inviting. Even though the house was huge, it was warm and full of love. This was the dream family every kid wanted. I found myself longing to fit in and become a part of it.

Only a few minutes into the movie, I noticed a difference. I'd seen *Clash of the Titans* before, but this time the gods, Giants and the mythical aspect to the movie took on an entirely new meaning. The research I had been doing tied in with what I was watching. It made the movie so much more interesting! I even took notes.

Surrounded by the comfort of the deep, soft sofa, combined with a full tummy, my eyelids soon became very heavy. I hadn't been sleeping very much, or very well. Having the house to myself was cold and lonely. With the recent noises and odd occurrences, sleep was something that frequently eluded me. I hadn't gotten used to living alone. Maybe I never would.

I felt myself nodding off, but I don't remember actually falling asleep.

When I woke up, it was dark outside and a plush red blanket covered me. The TV turned off, I could only assume Beth had finished watching, only to find me asleep. Good thing Jonah had decided to pass on watching with us. It would have been embarrassing to fall asleep with him next to me on the couch.

Muffled voices caught my attention from the other room. I sat up, wrapped the blanket around my shoulders and staggered toward the sound.

I found Beth and Jonah in the front living room, lounging comfortably on the leather couch, gazing out the open French doors into the warm, starry night. Beth spoke in a hushed tone.

"She almost stopped breathing, of course she felt it. She probably felt it all the way up her arm!" Beth said, excitedly. "She's sweet and broken, but I can tell she's starting to heal already. It's as I suspected, Jonah. You tested her, yourself. She's Pure! You haven't found a Pure Blood in over ninety years. She's all alone. She's worthy. Please consider it." Her tone had turned pleading.

"I admit, I feel a draw to her that I haven't felt since I arrived, but you know I can't, Beth." Jonah's soft, low voice resonated through the room, sending goose bumps down my arms.

Inching secretly into the room, I accidently bumped into a side table. They bolted up, turned and looked at me as if they'd been caught.

"Sorry I fell asleep. It's late. I can call a cab to take me home," I said, apologetically.

"Of course not!" Beth practically yelled. "I'll take you home. Or you can stay here tonight . . . like a slumber party! Tomorrow's Saturday and the weather is supposed to be beautiful. We can spend the day at the beach!"

"That's really nice, but I don't have a swimsuit with me or anything, and I can't leave Nicodemus alone all night."

She looked disappointed. "Oh, right. No problem. I'll get my keys."

"Thanks," I muttered.

Beth dashed by me on the way to grab her keys, avoiding my gaze by paying particular attention to the floor.

Jonah shot a calculating glance my way from under his thick eyelashes, then without saying a word, he flew up the wide, curving foyer stairs and ducked into the first door on the right.

The same sweet, clean scent followed behind him. I inhaled deeply, trying to memorize his smell. I was on the verge of placing the indescribable scent when Jonah's bedroom door closed loudly.

They had both avoided my gaze as they fled the room. Had they been talking about *me*? I didn't get it. The first time we met,

Jonah was utterly charming and so gentle as he bandaged my wound. The second time, he was at the right place at the right time, saving me from . . . who knows what. But tonight he was totally confusing. He introduced himself as if we'd never met, then kissed the cut on my finger confirming that he knew who I was, then avoided me the rest of the evening.

Standing alone in the front room, I peered out the open doors and stared at the stars. *It doesn't matter*, I tried to convince my heart. I was fooling myself. Every night since we met, he had been in my dreams.

Beth hadn't returned yet, so I made my way back to the soft, red couch. I folded up the blanket and laid it over the back.

"Ready?" Beth asked as she padded into the room in her bare feet.

I picked up my book bag and slung it over my shoulder. "Ready."

The car ride home was quiet, mostly because I was half-asleep. I fought against my heavy eyelids just long enough to get home.

Beth pulled up to the front of my house and hung her head. "I'm pretty sure you overheard what I was talking to Jonah about. I don't want you to think I was talking about you behind your back. I'm just so excited about our friendship I wanted to share my excitement with him. He's my best friend."

Her words made sense, but it felt like there was something missing from her apology. I distinctly heard her say "pure" and "worthy." Why would I need to pass some sort of character trait test to be her friend or spend time with her family? And that comment her dad made about being special and Beth only bringing home three friends her entire life? She was eighteen, pretty, bubbly and outgoing. Surely she has had dozens of friends through the years.

But I couldn't think about it now, I was too tired.

"I don't really have any plans this weekend so if you want to hang out or study, give me a call, okay?" she pleaded.

"Okay," I said, as I held back a yawn.

I got out of the car, said goodbye and gently shut the door. When I entered the house, Nicodemus meowed at me angrily. I dumped some food in his bowl and dragged myself up the stairs, barely brushing my teeth before I lay down and fell asleep as soon as my head hit the pillow.

Chαρτξr 13

In a vast sea of night, bright light shone down on only me. With it came an invisible breeze that chilled every part of my body. I searched out an end to this night, running until my bare feet were numb. Crumpling to the ground, I wept and shivered in the cold.

I couldn't find it. There was no end to this solitude. Every part of the world I knew had vanished, replaced by a vortex of nothingness, where even the souls that made up the human race had abandoned me. Hours passed, or maybe days, as I sat alone in this new, unchanging and unending world.

Then, a slow, methodic swishing began in the distance. As it came upon me, brisk air licked at my skin in swift gusts. It had finally happened. The spirits that haunt me had finally found me here in this empty place. I couldn't look up; I just waited for whatever it was, to devour me.

But instead of perishing, a luxurious warmth met me there in the darkness and swaddled me in a satin softness, unlike anything I had ever felt before. As this cloak enveloped me, it sent heat coursing through my veins, replacing the consuming chill of the world of midnight around us. Overwhelming love emanated from the cocoon that was my new home and filled every empty facet of my being. I could not place the source of this comfort that embraced me, but as I explored its silky surface, my fingers laced through long, down-soft feathers. I held tight to them, squeezed them in my fists and wrapped them snugly around me.

"I'm sorry it took me so long to find you, but now that I have, I will never leave you," a deep voice whispered into the wind. The voice was accompanied by an image of a face that appeared in the fringes of my mind. The image connected me to the velvety warmth somehow. As it slowly materialized, I looked into the face of my protector. Piercing green eyes stared at me through the darkness.

My heart launched into a gallop, awakening me with a jolt as bright morning sun glared into my eyes. But, I wasn't alone. The warmth from my dream had followed me into my bed. I frantically searched between the covers to find whatever it was that had saved me from the darkness, until I discovered I was holding a handful of long, white feathers.

I had never experienced this side of the supernatural before. I was connected with this spirit so closely that I brought part of it back with me. As the warmth faded, empty sadness filled my chest. I longed to be reunited with the spirit that loved and protected me.

As I examined the feathers in my hand, they passed through broken sunlight cast by the window shutters and gleamed an iridescent flash that shimmered on the wall. These feathers were the first real evidence that the otherworld and I were joined.

With no pockets available, I tucked them into the waistband of my pajamas and sighed as I ran my fingers through my hair.

I organized the day in my head. It was going to be another hot one.

The beach sounded like a good idea. I could spend a carefree day with Beth lying in the sand with the sun on my skin. Maybe I would even catch a glimpse of Jonah and those beautiful green eyes. Green eyes? The same green eyes from my dream?

My heart palpitated as bits of the night before came rushing back.

"Pure, worthy?" I whispered to myself.

Spending time with Beth was the best thing I had going in my life right now, but her friendship came with a lot of questions.

I let my eyes close and rubbed at my shoulders, trying to clear my head, but one thought persisted. It was time to live my life instead of crawling into a hole. I was past that. Living meant feeling. Feeling meant experiencing happiness, excitement, anxiety, curiosity – all emotions I hadn't touched in a long time – until I met Beth. I needed to start *feeling* again, no matter which feeling it was.

I lifted my chin, confident in my resolve. I wasn't going to sabotage my friendship with her because of my curiosity about her brother. The best friendships I ever had were based on trust. Trust is a feeling . . . a very vulnerable feeling, but it's also a decision. I had decided. I would trust her.

I rubbed my eyes and looked around. The early morning sun shining through the cracks in the shutters, cast sharp yellow lines across my bed. My room looked cheery for the first time in months. "It must be the sun," I whispered to Nicodemus. The paint looked fresh and the black and gray flowers on my white comforter seemed to bloom in the strips of sunlight cascading across them.

My mother and I had redecorated my room just two years ago, removing all of the childish drawings and stuffed animals, replacing them with refined contemporary artwork. The pink walls were now covered with a somber shade of gray paint. The only item left that reminded me of the way the room had been was my fuzzy pink alarm clock. When I looked at it now, I often caught glimpses of happier memories.

I felt distant from my parents during the time of the redecorating and the mood of the room showed it. I knew the project was my mother's way of attempting to stay connected, but I fought her on the cheery color palate she picked out and insisted on this dreary choice. One I now regretted. It made my room feel even more depressing now that she was gone.

Despite the bland color and the memories it brought with it, the room held a new liveliness this morning. Usually when I thought of those things I felt cold and alone, but this morning the load of emotional baggage didn't seem quite so heavy. Being around Beth's cheery disposition brightened my outlook.

Maybe a day on the beach would be a good idea. Beth had certainly made the invitation clear. I picked up my cell phone and dialed her number.

Chɑpτξr 14

I didn't have a "green" car like any of the Gwenaëls. My burgundy Nissan 240 was old, but it had never let me down before. At least it had a decent sound system and a moon roof.

I was glad my last trip to Beth's house wasn't long ago. My memory was still fresh as I navigated the confusing residential streets close to the beach. I managed to find my way easily, parking along the curb outside of the massive iron gates. I walked up a short path to a keypad and entered the code "737." A soft click unlocked a small walk-thru gate to the side of the driveway.

As I climbed the steep hill, my eyes wandered to the shimmering sea as endless facets of sparkling liquid diamonds rolled onto the shore. I stood for a moment, taking in the beauty of the ocean.

Music drifted in the air as I meandered closer to the house. I passed the front door, opting to walk around the side, following the music. The shade of the house hid me from sight as I rounded the corner. Beth was already in her swimsuit, sunning herself on a lounge chair as she sipped a tall glass of the same strange red juice we drank with dinner. I emerged into the sun and she peered over her sunglasses. She squealed loudly as she jumped up, sending her cup tumbling to the ground, spilling the juice.

Just then, Jonah emerged from the kitchen door. I stopped in my tracks and took a small step back into the safety of the shade. My pulse increased at the sight of him, which warmed the feathers that rested against the skin around my waist. I just couldn't leave them at home. Somehow the feel of them against my body gave me a sense of security.

Unaware of my presence, Jonah headed toward her with a towel in one hand and a fresh glass of juice in the other. "What's gotten into you, Bethie?" he remarked in an upbeat tone. "It's a good thing I gave you a plastic cup this time!"

My heart hammered in my chest at the sight of him. His well-defined muscles flexed with each movement, and the board shorts and tank top he wore never ceased to stun me. Peeking out from the arm holes again was that tattoo scrawled across the back of his shoulder blades. I recalled my first glimpse of it numerous times, trying to figure out what it was, by piecing it together as I connected the lines in my mind, only to fail miserably, leaving me more curious about him than ever.

He handed the cup to Beth and gave her a loving nudge on the shoulder. "This is the last of the tea. I'll have to go get some more ingredients. Is there anything you want from the market?"

I stood silently, holding two styrofoam cups in my hands like a fool. I'd stopped at Jamba Juice on my way and bought Beth and me breakfast. Beth peeked around Jonah's brawny arm.

"Anna, do you want anything from the store?" she voiced loudly so that I could hear, while trying to suppress a grin.

Jonah whipped his head around so fast his sunglasses flew off his face. In a swift motion he caught them in mid-air and tensed at the sight of me.

I forced myself to put one foot in front of the other and strolled over to them as casually as I could manage. "No, I'm fine. But thanks for asking."

I made my way around the pool to Beth and handed her one of the smoothies. "Hi Jonah," I said, trying my best to put on a cool façade.

He nodded and shoved on his sunglasses, quickly covering his surprise.

"Beth asked me over for a girls' day. Sorry, I didn't know you'd be here, or I would have gotten you something from Jamba Juice, too."

The laid back attitude and conversation he was just having with Beth turned hard and business-like as he addressed me. "That's quite alright," he said, in a deep, formal voice.

I shifted the cup I was holding into my other hand and struggled to take off the heavy bag slung over my shoulder. Jonah grabbed the straps and lifted it off of my arm gently and set it on the ground. My heart pounded.

"Th-thanks," I stammered.

He gave me a nod, turned briskly and paced away.

I watched him until he disappeared into the blackness of the kitchen doorway, then turned to Beth. I caught her overdoing an exaggerated eye roll. "Always torn," she scoffed.

I felt like an intruder stifling their conversation by my arrival. "I'm sorry, did I interrupt something?"

"Nah. He knew you were coming over today. I just didn't tell him when, so he was surprised, that's all."

That's all? He just turned from cute, fun Jonah into hard, businessman Jonah at the sight of me. He must think all of Beth's friends are hot for him, thus the evasive disappearing act he seemed to have down so well. Whatever. I tried not to let it bother me. Yet something grappled inside of me, begging me not to let it go so easily.

"Did you bring your swimsuit?" Beth inquired, worriedly.

I slid my thumb under the shoulder of my tank top and pulled out my suit strap, snapping it back onto my skin.

"Excellent," she declared. "Whatcha got in the bag?"

Being the studious geek that I am, I brought some of my text books, a towel and sunscreen.

Beth poked around in the bag and pulled out one of the Nephilim books I'd checked out from the library. "A little light reading?" she asked, with a laugh.

"It's just some research for Prof. D's paper," I defended.

"He's got a nickname now?"

"His name is a pain to say, plus, did you know 'Dhampir' means 'child of a vampire father and a human mother'?" Dhampirs are supposed to have vampire-like powers, but without the usual weaknesses. They're supposed to be able to kill other vampires. That is, if you believe in vampires in the first place," I laughed. "I stumbled across the definition while doing my Giants research. Every time I say his name, it gives me the creeps, so I've just think of him as 'Prof. D'."

"Wow. How could someone so hot have such a creepy name? What a shame," she sighed. "Well, Prof. D works for me!" Beth eyed the many books that filled my bag. "You aren't actually planning on reading that while you're here, are you? We're supposed to have fun today!"

"I wasn't sure how long we'd be lying around, so I thought I'd make good use of my time. I did bring another book to read that's not for school, so it's not like I planned on studying all day."

Beth bounced around the lounge and plopped down, grabbing at her toes to inspect them.

"Good. We have pedicures at two o'clock. I thought we could get some sun now, have lunch before our pedi's, then just hang when we get back."

"Sounds like a perfect day to me."

Lying in the sun next to my best friend and a glistening pool with the sound of the ocean in the background was paradise. I was deep in serene thought when I heard a splash and felt a spray of water across my legs.

"Not without me, you don't!" I yelled, following after her.

We paddled around the pool, periodically splashing each other and giggling. I hadn't felt this comfortable with another human being in a long time, not even my own parents.

"So what's the deal with your brother?" I blurted. My face turned hot with embarrassment. I wanted to sink into the water and never surface again. Anna's famous foot in mouth disease had just reared its ugly head again!

"What do you mean?"

How could I back-pedal and cover up my brazen question with something benign? "I mean, you're always so nice to each other. How do you pull it off? I haven't seen you bicker even once with him, or anyone else for that matter. No family can be that perfect."

It wasn't a question, really, it was a jealous statement. Not having a sibling, I didn't have this issue to navigate, but the relationship I had with my parents was constantly full of tension. The ease between the Gwenaëls just didn't make sense to me.

I secretly hoped that their family was flawed in some way that would satisfy my own insecurities about not being as perfect as they were.

"We didn't always work like this. Jonah and I fought sometimes, as most kids do, I guess. Things changed when his uncle found him. He had to do some deep soul-searching at a very young age. When you're forced to see the world for what it really is, it changes you.

After a few months, our entire way of living transformed into what you see today. He simply told us that the ultimate way to live is to be devoted to one another in love, and honor each other above yourself. Every time an argument would start, he would remind us of that and our frustrations with each other would disappear. We've been working this way for such a long time now, I haven't heard him say it in years.

We mesh well together. It's all about trust. Jonah and I trust my parents without question. We know they guide us out of love and knowledge. And they trust us right back. They know if we do something it's because we know it's for the best. It's not a common arrangement, but we've got some major celestial muscle on our side to cement our bond. It comes easy for Jonah, but I have to work at it every day." She pulled at her chin. "I've been finding it harder lately for some reason," she mumbled. She looked confused.

"It must be nice to be you," I said, with sarcasm – a comment I instantly regretted. *Ugh, that was mean.*

"We work at it, Anna," Beth said, taking in my tone and diffusing it with kindness. Most people don't put forth the effort. My dad, for instance, used to be a big-shot defense attorney. He always took the cases no one else thought they could win. He defended and won legal battles for hardened criminals, even making the victims pay a lot of the times. He was really good and made tons of money. He ran in the fast lane when he was practicing in Manhattan, schmoozing with all of the mucky-mucks and all."

That didn't sound so bad. Being good at what you do can be very rewarding.

"He was once the spearhead attorney for this huge case. Some old guy was accused of murder and my dad got him acquitted after three months of trial. In some ingenious twist, my dad even made the victim's family pay for the murderer's legal fees, which ranged in the hundreds of thousands of dollars. The poor family lost their daughter to this criminal and then went bankrupt from the legal fees. The case made his firm really famous. A month later, the guy raped and killed a five year old little girl."

Beth held her breath and winced, waiting for a negative reaction from me. I tried my best to keep a straight face and not judge as she had been so kind to do for me, but I had to snap my mouth shut and hold back a "no way."

"That was when my dad went berserk," she continued. "He quit his job, sold his Maserati and his multi-million dollar Park Avenue apartment and started working in public service. His story was in the papers and everything. He gave away so much of his money to the needy that he was even homeless for a while. That's when he met my mom."

"Dang, you can't write that kind of stuff!" I exclaimed, embarrassed as soon as the words came out. I covered my mouth with my hand in a gesture of apology.

"It's okay, Anna. It's a really crazy story. Anyone who hears it is shocked. Anyway, my mom was the director of a homeless shelter in Manhattan and that's where they met. He had a place to live at the time, but he was volunteering there and approached her about offering his legal services free of charge to the people who needed it at the shelter.

They fell in love and were married only four months after they met! They've worked in public service ever since.

For a really long time they were so poor they rented a studio apartment that they said was no larger than a big closet, but they were happy. Eventually, my dad got hooked-up at the Legal Aid Center and they were able to afford a small two bedroom apartment. They tried to start a family. After two years, they were told by the doctors that they only had a three percent chance of conceiving. That's when they adopted Jonah."

Beth's tone was matter-of-fact now, not apologetic or timid as when she began her story. She swam off, leaving me there with my mouth hanging open, again. She mounted a raft and paddled around the pool.

I couldn't figure out what was more staggering: Isaac being a nasty lawyer, being homeless, or marrying Rebekah after only four months of meeting. The story was so . . . wow!

I had to physically shake my head to knock loose the images of what Beth had just told me. I pushed off of the black pool floor, launching myself onto my back and floated peacefully. The cool water supported me from beneath, while my skin drank in the warm sun from above.

I closed my eyes, setting a calm stage for my brain to process the story I just heard. It seemed almost tragic. Isaac had what everyone dreams of . . . power, influence and stature. He was revered. He gave it all up to help others and now look at him. He lives in a mansion on the beach, surrounded by an awesome family that adores him. Would he have all that if he had stayed on his prior course? The mansion, yes; the adoring family, probably not. Which was more important? Isaac seemed to have figured it out early enough to save himself a lifetime of loneliness and regret.

I peeked through my eyelashes into the clear, blue sky and caught movement from an upstairs balcony in my peripheral vision. A flash of green eyes disappeared as soon as I turned my head. "What the . . ." I whispered to myself.

"Time to dry off and go grab some lunch," Beth announced. "C'mon, we can change in the pool house," she said, waving for me to follow.

"Actually, do you mind if I grab a Vitaminwater out of the fridge in the kitchen? All this sun is making me thirsty."

"Sure, no problem," Beth said, as she headed off for the pool house. I walked the opposite way toward the kitchen.

I wrapped my towel around my waist, leaving my torso exposed. It felt inappropriate walking into the house dressed in only a towel and a bikini top, but I knew if I put on my clothes, they would be wet the rest of the day.

Before I entered, I twisted my hair to wring it out so it wouldn't drip all over the floor, then let it fall against my back. It always seemed so much longer when it was wet. It brushed against my waist.

The sun was high and glared into my eyes until I stepped through the door. It seemed dark as a cave inside as my pupils took time to adjust. I padded slowly on the marble floor, trying not to slip, made my way to the fridge and pulled open the door. I grabbed a Vitaminwater and closed the door, to find Jonah standing behind it.

"Oh, my gosh!" I said, as I jumped back, thrusting my hand to my throat in reaction to his sudden appearance.

"Sorry to startle you, Anna," he said smoothly, with an admiring smile on his face. Every time he spoke my name my heart pounded.

He deliberately reached around me, and grabbed for an apple out of a fruit bowl on the counter, his proximity so close I had to lean back. My heart thudded impatiently in my chest at the thought of him brushing against me.

"Oops," he whispered. His breath was warm against the wet skin of my shoulder.

I craned my neck around to see what the problem was. As he brought the apple back to him, the stem had caught in my hair and become entangled.

He bobbed his head from one side of me to the other, trying to view the stem that had knitted itself into the wet web of my hair.

I reached around the back of my neck and brought all of my hair around to the front in order to view the fiasco. Jonah gently held a mess of knotted hair and apple stem in his hand. As I tried to untangle the stem, our fingers brushed several times, sending a lightning bolt into my body with each touch. I inhaled sharply, holding my breath each time, in an attempt to hide it. Jonah searched my face in reaction to the sound. His eyes lingered on my lips. The silence of the empty room produced only echoes of my erratic breathing. I was sure he heard my breath quicken; my heart pound. How could he not? A mere graze of skin led to such an intense exchange of power. Seemingly I was the only one experiencing it.

His calm demeanor unsettled me and my face flushed with embarrassment. I felt an instant rush to flee. I grabbed the apple abruptly out of his hand, twisted the stem off and tossed the apple back to him before turning and marching away with the stem still caught in my hair.

He was hot one minute and cold the next. Was he teasing me? Why? Nothing seemed to make sense when I was around him!

The short walk to the pool house did nothing to calm my irritation. I changed hastily and did my best to ensure my mood was visibly upbeat.

"I'm starving, what's for lunch?" I asked enthusiastically.

Beth bounced off of the couch, swinging her wet ponytail as she bopped along beside me. "Hmmm. I know of a perfect place," she said, as she gave me a wink.

"Oh, I get it. You need a partner in crime to visit Islands again, right?"

"You got it, babe!"

"So, I'm just a chaperone to this stalking event, then?"

She looked at me and her face fell. "Oh, Anna, please don't think that! More than anything I want to spend the day with *you*. Seeing Zech was an afterthought, really!" She hooked her arm through mine and gave it a squeeze.

I sighed, dramatically wiping the back of my hand across my forehead for flair and shot her a sly smile. "Okay, I'm game. Let's go!"

She clapped her hands furiously and pulled me along to the car.

Chαptξr 15

Waiting for a table on a Saturday at high noon was torture. The lobby was standing room only. Backed against the adjoining wall of the bar, we stood beneath the grass hut of the bar façade. Multi-colored lights hung over our heads, casting red and blue hues on our slightly sunburned faces. It was far too loud to hold a conversation, so we stood and stared at the TVs that showed the same surfing videos looped over and over again.

Beth caught sight of Zech from across the restaurant and gave him a little wave. He delivered a handful of drinks to a nearby table and walked up to the hostess, never taking his eyes off of Beth. The hostess was a shy-looking girl, no older than sixteen, who blushed when he rested his hand on her shoulder to get her attention. A whisper into her ear was all it took. She nodded to us and thankfully sat us at a table outside on the shaded patio, away from the noisy dining room.

Zech walked briskly behind her, carrying fresh strawberry lemonades in his hands. In one fluid movement, he set them on the table and bent down to give Beth a kiss on the cheek. A dark red blush started at her forehead and ran all the way down her neck.

"Hi," he said softly in her ear. She reached up and patted his cheek a few times, never taking her bulging eyes off me. I could sense her hesitation to look at him. I imagine she was about to burst at the seams, too excited to even glance in his direction.

He stood up abruptly. "Ahem." He tapped the end of his pen to his tongue and poised it over the pad of paper in his hand in anticipation.

"What can I get for you lovely ladies this fine, warm afternoon?" he said sarcastically in his deepest, most formal voice.

As he stood behind Beth, his hip brushed against her shoulder. Her eyes bugged out of her face as she bit her lower lip. She jerked her chin at me to order first.

"The Yaki please, no cheese. Oh, and thanks for the lemonade!"

Beth's face was three shades of scarlet and her lips were tucked firmly between her teeth.

Rescuing her, I added, "uh, we'll be sharing that . . . and a basket of fries, too, please."

"Got it. I'll be right back with the fries."

Zech strutted away, his head held high. As soon as he was through the door, Beth let out an enormous gust of air.

"Good grief, Beth, I thought you were going to pass out!"

"Me too! I didn't know I'd be so excited to see him. His soul is just so transparent, I feel totally connected to him and we've only been on one date."

"He has a transparent soul?"

She looked like a deer in the headlights. "Oh, uh, I mean," she sputtered.

"Don't worry about it. You can explain later. No big deal. I know you're just really excited to see him," I interjected.

"Right!" she shouted, relieved to have been let off the hook. She took a few deep breaths, trying to prepare herself for Zech's return.

He breezed back through the door carrying a huge basket of fries and an entire tray of assorted sauces.

"You look like you're a dipper, Anna, so I brought you one of everything . . . ranch, honey mustard, teriyaki . . . and your Yaki will be up in just a few minutes, ladies."

"Nice!" I exclaimed. "I'm totally a dipper! How thoughtful of you, Zech, thanks!"

This time he stood between us, in plain view of Beth's face. She had calmed herself enough to be able to look up at him. "Thanks," she said, in a small, shy voice. He reached over and squeezed her shoulder.

Trying to give them a moment of privacy, I looked around at my surroundings, when my eyes met Mara's. She was ogling out the window with squinted eyes and pursed lips, watching Zech touch Beth.

"Uh, I think we have a problem, Zech," I said, in a calm voice that was filled with just enough concern to get his attention.

"What's up, Anna?"

I shifted in my seat uncomfortably. "Well, the last time we were here, you went on break and Mara, there," I pointed toward the window, "assisted us for the remainder of our meal. She was very unpleasant and even mean to little Bethie here. She's burning a hole in the back of your head with her eyes as we speak. You're not going on break again while we're here, are you?"

Zech's eyebrows pulled together. He let out a sharp breath and turned around, catching Mara's face practically pressed against the glass. Without breaking eye contact with her, he stepped to the side so Beth was in her full view. He put his hand on Beth's shoulder and motioned to her and then to him and then did the most romantic thing. He slid his hand in the neck hole of his shirt and pumped it in a bom-bom, bom-bom motion over his heart.

An audible shriek cut through the thick glass of the window as Mara whipped her black, pouffed ponytail around and stomped off.

Beth's face swooned as she reached up to her shoulder and rested her hand over his.

"That was uncomfortable," I stated plainly.

Both Beth and I looked to him for an explanation.

"I apologize for Mara," he said, in a soft voice. "She's had a crush on me ever since I started working here. It's always been annoying, but I haven't had a girlfriend or anything since I've been here, so she's never had to face the possibility that there's no real chance for her and I, even though I've explained it to her many times. I'll make sure you never get seated in her section."

He looked at Beth's sweet face and caressed her cheek with his palm. "Don't worry about her, Beth." He gave her an affectionate smile and walked back inside.

"Okay, was that weird, or is it just me?" I shot the question to her rhetorically.

"He's sweet and nice and HOT . . . why would that be weird?" she said, defensively.

I put my hands up in surrender. "Whoa, there. Yes, Zech is all those things. I was talking about Mara. Don't you find her a little . . . disturbing?"

She took a deep breath, then blew it out hard.

"Of course. Sorry, Anna. I've never really had a boyfriend before, so I'm not really sure how to do this. My excitement seems to get in the way."

"I know how you feel," I muttered under my breath.

"What?" She'd heard me.

"Oh, nothing, I just mean, I know what it's like at the beginning of a relationship. Everything is new and exciting and confusing. At least you know Zech is totally into you now. Did you see the thing he did with his hand over his heart? That was precious!"

She snapped out of her worries and glowed. "Yeah!" she practically squealed. "How sweet was that?"

"That was one of the most romantic things I've ever seen. You sure know how to wrap people around your cute little pinky!" I said, affectionately.

She bounced up and down in her chair, clapping her hands together silently.

Beth had paid. Again. And left Zech an embarrassingly large tip. Knowing he would have to share at the end of the day, she shoved a one-hundred dollar bill in his back pocket. "Spread the wealth, babe!" she giggled.

As we walked across the parking lot to the nail salon, I couldn't help but wonder what the tip meant. Mulling the thought over in my head, I gave her a sarcastic, judgmental look.

"What?" she challenged.

"A one-hundred dollar tip?"

"It's the only way I can think of to help him out with dignity. He busted his butt to get a full scholarship for his undergrad work and then busted it again to get a grant for his Masters. He lives in a tiny one-bedroom apartment and barely has enough money to get by. Someday his hard work is going to pay off and he'll be in a totally different place. I don't mind helping him along until that happens!"

My head bobbed unconsciously. "That's ingenious, Beth. You can fund your own dates!"

She stopped in her tracks. "Oh my gosh, I never thought of it that way. In that case, it sounds horrible of me, doesn't it?"

"No. As long as Zech doesn't mind."

"He refuses to let me pay for anything, so leaving him a huge tip is the only way I can think of to give a little extra. He has to share it at the end of the night with the bus boys and all, so it's not like I'm paying him for going out with me or anything."

I patted her on the back. "Of course not, Bethie, no one would ever suspect anything like that from you. I was just making a joke."

It occurred to me that I had used Jonah's pet name for her repeatedly. "Sorry I keep calling you Bethie. I heard Jonah call you that this morning and I don't know, I picked up on it. It's cute. Do you mind?"

A smile brightened her face. "Jonah's the only one who calls me that, but it's a good nickname for a sister, isn't it? You can call me Bethie anytime!" She linked her arm through mine.

During our pedicures, Beth complained of a headache. She was uncharacteristically quiet, sitting back and relaxing while resting her eyes.

As soon as we arrived back at her house, she went upstairs to lie down. I propped up a pillow under her head. "Can I get you anything? Aspirin, water, anything?"

"No. This happens sometimes, no big deal. I'll just take a little nap. When I wake up I'll feel totally fine. You don't mind, do you? Please stay! There are tons of movies downstairs, or you can bust out your books and get some homework done. My dad is barbequing tonight. You can't miss it, he makes the best barbeque! Promise me you'll stay!"

"I promise," I reassured her. "I can read here just like I could at home or the library, and the view is exponentially better here! Take a good nap and feel better. I'll be here when you wake up."

I draped a throw over her, tiptoed out of the room and down the curving front staircase. I found myself standing in the middle of the living room of the big beach house. My breath echoed off of the high ceiling and the marble floor. The house looked different now that there was no one chaperoning me along. It felt wrong to be standing in the house all by myself. The Gwenaëls had so much trust to let someone they'd only met a few times ramble around in their home alone. Where was everyone, anyway?

I sighed. I promised Beth I'd stay, so now I just had to find something to do until she woke up. Movie? Study? Swim? Read! I brought a book I had started devouring last week and couldn't wait to continue.

The double-wide lounge by the pool was a perfect place to settle in with my book. The sun warmed my skin like a blanket and the heat from the lounge cushion on my back soothed my muscles.

I had read about three pages of my book when Rebekah walked out of the kitchen door, holding a beach towel.

"Well, hello, Anna." She looked around curiously. "Where's Beth?"

"She has a headache and is taking a nap. She made me promise to stay for dinner. Apparently, Isaac is barbequing?"

"Hmm, another headache. She's been getting a lot of those lately. I had better go check on her."

"Actually, I think she may already be asleep." I would hate for Rebekah to wake her up when she said that the nap would be the best cure for her pain.

"Oh, good. She'll be fine when she wakes up." She nodded with a smile and continued out the door toward me.

"I'm glad you're staying, Anna. Beth's right. Isaac makes wonderful barbeque." She stopped at the foot of the lounge and tilted her head to the side. "What are you reading?"

"Oh, it's Anne Rice's latest novel, *Of Love and Evil*. It's fantastic so far, I can't put it down!"

Rebekah chuckled and slipped her hand in between the folds of her towel, pulling out her own copy of *Of Love and Evil*. "I was just coming out here to soak up some vitamin D and finish my book."

I let out a roll of laughter. "No way, that's too funny!"

"Mind if I join you?" she asked with an amused smile.

I scootched over and patted the other side of the lounge next to me. "Of course!"

Rebekah set down her towel and book. "Would you like anything from the kitchen? I'm going to get some iced tea."

"Tea sounds wonderful, thank you!"

Rebekah's movement was lyrical as she walked back into the kitchen. She had such a serenity about her that I imagined she was ingenious at her job as a social worker. It takes someone with unsurpassed patience and compassion to shoulder the woes of others and help them work through their troubles.

She was back in no time, carrying two sparkling crystal goblets filled to the brim with . . . red juice? She handed me the goblet and silently floated down on the lounge next to me.

"I hope you like sweet, herbal tea. It's Jonah's secret recipe. Sometimes he overdoes it with the sugar."

"It's red."

"That's part of the secret."

Well, that explained the strange, red juice they kept drinking. It's not the juice after all, it's tea. The taste made much more sense now.

I sniffed it, then took a sip. This wasn't overdone as Rebekah said. It was the perfect blend of crisp, fresh white tea with a hint of jasmine and . . . I sniffed deeply . . . something I didn't recognize, sweetened with just the right amount of sugar, a drop of honey and . . . mmm . . . a flavor that eluded me. I closed my eyes and rubbed my fingertips together trying to grasp it. I took another sip, savoring it on my tongue. My body warmed. My heart thudded an extra beat and my eyes shot open. Jonah! His crisp, sweet scent smelled almost like this tea tasted. Like summer and spring with a nip of fall in the air mixed with the warm honey of a sweet embrace. And that scent that eluded me . . . it was almost spiritual. It reminded me of the ancient smell that accompanied the unwelcome cold that followed me; except this was its opposite.

I took a few more sips. Each swallow tingled as it went down, giving me an almost blissful feeling.

I'd forgotten for a moment that Rebekah was sitting next to me. My eyes slid stealthily her way, checking to see if she had noticed the strange reaction the tea gave me. Her nose was already buried in her book.

I leaned back, letting the sun-drenched cushion melt around me and form to the shape of my body. I picked up my book and began where I had left off.

> Of course it had been foolish for me to think that I might see angels and not demons.
>
> "After all, I'm your guardian angel. My assignment is simple. You are my charge."
>
> "And Malchiah?"
>
> "Again, you know the answer to your own question. He is a Seraph. He's sent to answer the prayers of many. He knows things I can't know. He does things I'm not sent to do."
>
> I was in the presence of a visible angel and I felt fear. It wasn't overwhelming, but it hurt, as if someone were subjecting me to an electrical current just strong enough to burn.

I'd never doubted the existence of a supernatural world. These passages brought to light the origins of the encounters I'd dealt with my whole life. Between Anne's words and the research I had been doing the past few weeks, my world was reshaping itself before my eyes. It was turning into something where the earthly dimension and the spiritual dimension were melding into one. I couldn't see it, but I could feel it, little by little, more and more each day.

Rebekah startled me as she commented aloud on the book.

"Isn't it amazing how Anne's entire way of writing shifted from dark characters, embodying and romanticizing evil, to these new characters hunting down and destroying evil? Her early books were heavily about vampires, their triumphs and cheating death. This one is about love and good overcoming. What a life journey she must have been on for her outlook to change so drastically and yet still write with such beauty and passion."

Rebekah's words were profound.

"I've never thought of what would be going on in an author's life to inspire them to write their stories," I replied. "You must think about the 'story behind the story' all the time in your line of work."

She nodded and appeased me with a smile before bringing her book back up to her face to continue her own journey into the story.

Reading always made the time fly by. A breeze had picked up, pushing a high fog over us raising goose bumps on my arms and legs with each flurry that passed by. Rebekah flung one of her fluffy towels over us and we snuggled close to keep warm. The thought of going inside was appealing, but the beautiful scenery and comfort of Rebekah's proximity gave me a cherished feeling I hadn't experienced in a long time. I was enjoying sitting in silence next to her. Our arms pressed against each other and after a while that was the only part of my body that was warm.

As the ocean breeze grew more insistent, I started shivering. The temperature couldn't have been cooler than seventy-two, but to my slightly sunburned skin and the lack of warmth from the sun, it felt brisk.

"Anna, honey, if you're cold, one of Isaac's sweatshirts is folded up on my bed. I just washed it. Feel free to go put it on if you're chilly, dear."

Rubbing my arms, the thought of a thick, fuzzy sweatshirt enveloping me was just what I needed. "Thanks, I think I'll take you up on that."

The warm concrete beneath my feet made the contrast to my cold skin more pronounced and goose bumps flared up all over my body. I raced through the kitchen and up the stairs, creeping past Beth and Jonah's rooms, and headed straight for the sweatshirt. It was on the end of her bed, right where Rebekah said it would be.

I threw it on hastily. It hung down mid-thigh, the sleeves so long that not even my fingertips poked out. As big as this sweatshirt was, the neck was choking me. I looked down. I had put it on backwards.

"Dang it!" I practically shouted. All I wanted, was to burrow into the sweatshirt and hug it around me until the shivers went away. I pulled it off over my head, accidentally pulling my outer T-shirt off with it, leaving me in only a tank top and shorts, prancing around Rebekah's room to keep warm. I yanked at the two tangled shirts, which only snarled them together worse.

"Argh! How big is this thing anyway?" I huffed out an exaggerated sigh. Shivering and standing practically naked in the middle of Rebekah's bedroom, I hugged myself tightly to keep warm for a moment before attempting to untangle the shirts again. I was tempted to jump under the covers of their bed to stave off the shivers.

"Hrm," came from the doorway.

I looked up to find Jonah leaning against the doorjamb with a smirk on his face, watching me tug at the frustrating labyrinth of fabric. His half-smile, sad puppy dog eyes and a pouting bottom lip patronized me. He drifted forward, smoothly reached behind his head and pulled off his sweatshirt. In only a few strides he was standing directly in front of me.

We gazed into each other's eyes steadily. I flinched and choked in a gulp of air when he ran his hands down my arms. He grabbed my wrists, lifting them over my head. My heart had only seconds to break into an electric sprint before he slipped his sweatshirt on me and our skin contact was broken. A ragged gush of breath hissed out from between my teeth as my jaw clenched and my nose flared – a reaction to his touch that was embarrassingly obvious.

"Am I hurting you, Anna?" he asked with full concern in his voice.

I glared at his shoulder, not wanting to look into his face as I growled my admission. "Not now, you're not."

He reached for my hand. I pulled away. Was he *trying* to test his effect on me?

Breathing in slow, silent breaths, my jaw was held together tightly with tensed muscles. My eyes found the floor as I concentrated on the fibers of the white carpet.

My shivers stopped as the lingering warmth from his body radiated through my new layer of protection from the cold.

The goose bumps were stubborn though, not budging under the pressure my hands made as I rubbed them over my arms. I gave up and reached down to rub the tops of my thighs, hoping that I could create enough resistance on my bare skin to melt them away.

"I'm sorry about getting the apple stem caught in your hair today." Jonah's voice was deep and gentle. He reached out and stroked my arms rapidly, increasing the friction enough to dissipate the goose bumps. His warmth encircled my torso and wound its way down my legs. Shivers gone, goose bumps vanished, my body was calm and warm again. I breathed in deeply, my eyes closed unwillingly. He held my arms in his strong hands, waiting patiently for me to reply.

"I'm sorry I stormed out on you," I said, with closed eyes. It was easier to talk to him if I couldn't get lost in his emerald gaze. The truth was, I wasn't sorry I'd walked out on him at all. I was sorry I couldn't handle being so close to him.

"I was out of line, I apologize," I whispered.

His posture stiffened and he began to pull away, but I didn't want him to leave. The calm he brought to me by simply being near me was amazing. I didn't want it to end. I flung my hand up and grasped his wrist, keeping his hand on my arm. My breath quickened at the touch of his skin. My pulse pounded through my veins. He turned his hand over and wrapped it around my wrist. Only a few seconds passed before the electric dizziness took over and I wobbled where I stood. He was holding my wrist so gently it was almost a caress. Wait. Was he taking my pulse? I opened my eyes and took a step back breaking his grasp.

"Thanks for the sweatshirt," I whispered, out of breath. I stared at the floor. I couldn't look at him, afraid I would lose myself in his eyes.

He cleared his throat. "Anytime."

A flurry of his scent surrounded me. When I looked up, he was gone.

It was five o'clock and Beth was still asleep. Isaac was wearing a "Kiss the Cook" apron while scrubbing down the grill, readying it for the feast he was about to prepare. Rebekah had me in the kitchen shucking corn, while she measured and whisked a special sauce for the homemade coleslaw she was making from scratch.

"Anna, would you be a dear and fetch Jonah, please? I bought a sack of carrots today at the farmers market, but left it in the trunk of my car. Would you ask him to get it for me? I'm up to my elbows in cabbage here."

I rose from a stool along the edge of the massive kitchen island and brushed the corn silks from my hands. "I can get the carrots for you. No worries." Another awkward encounter with Jonah was *not* what I needed right now.

"They're in the trunk of my car." She smiled at me with her eyes and promptly returned to shredding a large head of purple cabbage.

I wound my way down a wide hall toward part of the house I'd never been in before. Directly in front of me was a heavy metal door. On the other side, I assumed, was the garage. Heaving the door open, I stepped down three shallow stairs. Rebekah's car was the second to last. The massive garage was deep enough that I had no problem getting around the cars without having to shuffle sideways as I always had to do in my own garage at home.

I stood for a moment, not remembering how to open a car trunk without the key. My car was so old, everything required a key. Luckily, the driver's side door was unlocked, but when I searched for the lever to pop the trunk I came up short. It was usually on the floor next to the seat, wasn't it? I climbed in and started patting around the cockpit feeling for anything that would pull or give and found nothing.

My head was under the steering wheel, searching for a visible lever when the passenger side door opened. It startled me so badly that I smacked the back of my head on the underside of the dash in my haste to sit back in the seat.

Jonah was wiping black grease from his hands with a rag as he slid into the seat next to me. He must have been tinkering with his vintage contraption that rested next to Rebekah's car.

Flustered, I blurted, "the carrots are in the trunk. Where's the dang button?"

He reached over me, pressing his arm against my hips and the tops of my thighs and gently touched a button on the interior door panel. There was a tiny click and the trunk whirred open slowly. The top of his head directly under my nose, I breathed in the fresh, sweet smell of him.

As he sat up, he wore a small grin and flashed his jeweled eyes at me. He had a small smudge of grease on his chin.

My hand was drawn to him. Forgetting the jolt I was about to receive, I found myself caressing his jaw as I wiped the grease off with my thumb. For a second, his shock spread into my body like a web of adrenaline, before I yanked my hand away.

"Uh, I'm sorry." I let go of him and hung my head, embarrassed. "You had a smudge on your chin." My words ran together hastily as I shoved my thumb up to his face to show that it was now blackened with grease.

He purred a cool, "thanks" and floated out the door, tapping it shut with one finger.

Anna, you're such an idiot! I thought to myself as I smacked my face into my hands. Oh, right, carrots. I pouted out of the car, shuffled around the back and pulled the bag out of the trunk. I wanted nothing more than to vent my frustrations, but I couldn't take them out on Rebekah's beautiful car. It took all my might to resist slamming the trunk down as hard as I could.

A ratcheting sound came from the direction of the antique automobile. I peeked around the open trunk to find Jonah's head hidden under the hood of his car. The fact that he couldn't see me didn't make a difference. I shot him a dirty look, turned my back to him and stalked out of the garage, letting the heavy door close loudly behind me.

Inside the hallway, I burned with frustration and welcomed the lack of light as the darkness concealed the irritation on my face. *How does that man-boy get me so unglued? He's just a guy! He's my best friend's brother! Brothers are off-limits, plus, I don't want to start anything right now with a boy anyway. How can I even think that? My boyfriend only died a few months ago. I should be mourning, right?*

My aggravation wasn't with the timeline of the situation. It was with the pull I felt to Beth as a friend and the magnetism I felt to Jonah as what . . . a brother? That didn't feel right. A friend? That seemed so impersonal considering how he made me feel when we touched. I knew the right word that would connect what I felt for him, but I couldn't even think it.

My struggle seemed to lie between accepting or denying that Jonah stirred my soul in a way I'd never felt before. At the present moment, I chose denial.

I need to focus on school, I tried to convince myself with loose determination. I would just avoid him. But how could I? Every time I was near him I felt drawn to him in a way I couldn't explain – like as soon as we were in the same vicinity of each other, an invisible bubble formed around us, contracting its elasticity, pulling us together with such force I found myself unwillingly reaching out to him.

Each time we had any interaction he was cool and aloof. I was deranged and barely in control of myself. I tried my best to hide it, but I knew he had noticed.

What did his opinion of me matter anyway? I was here for Beth, my new best friend.

A loud huff came barreling out of my mouth, puffing out my cheeks, sending flyaway hairs fluttering around my face.

I wasn't pulling off the denial thing so well, I thought as my body slumped in failure.

Standing in the dark hallway, I forced an admission I'd been suppressing. If Beth was going to be part of my new life, then her family came along with it. Take the good with the bad. In the short time I had known Isaac and Rebekah, I'd already grown to love them. I would hate to give them up because I couldn't control myself around their son. I would just have to try harder.

Chαρτξr 16

Monday in class was lonely without Beth sitting next to me. Her headache had turned into a bad case of the flu. She had never made it down to dinner, so Isaac went to check on her and he found her in her bathroom, beside the toilet. She was asleep on the floor, wrapped in the throw I'd draped on her before her nap. After carrying her back to bed, Jonah and Rebekah took over, acting as nursemaids through the dinner hour, leaving Isaac and me eating in uncomfortable silence.

I called first thing this morning and begged Rebekah to let me come and see her and bring her some fresh chicken soup, but she insisted that I stay away, for fear of catching it myself.

I'd be flying solo today. In the short time I had known Beth, my dependence on her had gone unnoticed . . . until now. It had always been *my* choice if I wanted to see her at any given time, but without the possibility of her presence at my whim, I felt desolate and edgy.

I settled into my usual seat in myth class. The lack of chatter and emptiness next to me was so barren I had to forcibly distract myself. I checked my phone at least ten times already this morning, hoping for news of Beth's condition. All I got was radio silence . . . her phone must be turned off.

I opened my book and engrossed my thoughts in the text, only looking up when Professor Dhampir entered the room.

He skipped the usual introduction of today's lecture and promptly began listing the mythological Giant races and their associated characteristics and legends. I quickly became so absorbed in the lecture, hoping to grasp what little he covered about my theory, that class was half over before I discovered a tall muscular blond sitting next to me. He was doodling a beautiful pencil drawing of a dragon, seemingly not paying attention to the lecture at all. His steel gray eyes bore into the paper as he drew the intricate details of fire blowing out of flared reptilian nostrils. Deep dimples appeared in his cheeks when he licked his lips in concentration.

Professor Dhampir called out a question to the class. The blond spoke up without even lifting his eyes off of his paper.

"The Jötunn were a race of Norse Giants, residing in Scandinavia. They were romanticized as heroes, like Thor or depicted as barbarians like the Vikings," the boy said, through an Irish accent.

I had researched this. I hadn't found that Thor and the Vikings were directly connected to the Jötunn, but there was a general overtone that all of the Norse figures were Giants and Thor was thought to be a demi-god.

He looked up and paused his doodling when he noticed he had the full attention of the class. Expectant eyes were on the mysterious blond next to me, craving more explanation. A short grunt of agitation echoed from him. Had he forgotten what else he wanted to say?

My voice sounded off unexpectedly, adding to his description. "Thor was the god of Thunder, Lord of Asgard. Asgard was the heavenly dwelling of the Norse gods and slain soldiers. The Vikings believed that if they were courageous and died in battle, they would spend their afterlife in Asgard."

"Exactly!" Professor Dhampir boomed from the front of the class. "Finally, two people who have done their homework!" He gave us a thank you nod, before continuing the explanation of the Norse Giants.

The blond leaned over to me. "Great save, thanks. I blanked out when I saw all those eyes on me . . . guess I'll never be a teacher, will I?"

He held out his hand for an impromptu handshake. I reluctantly lifted my hand into shaking position. He gently grabbed it and gave it a few light shakes. "I'm Cain," he whispered.

I nodded.

"Hrm." A deep voice grumbled from the front of class. Cain and I twisted in our chairs toward the front of the class. Professor

Dhampir stared at us as a creepy smirk spread across his face. He gave Cain a sly raise of the eyebrow, and turned away.

"Excuse me . . . Miss . . . hello!" Cain's voice grew louder as I dashed toward my next class. A tap on the shoulder froze me mid-stride. I didn't have my Beth buffer with me. It felt like the first day of school all over again; my nerves were jumpy.

"You left your phone on the desk," Cain's voice rang behind me.

I started to say "thanks" but it came out as "thu" as I turned to find my eyes at his chest. His height shocked me. Sitting next to me in class he was big, but standing next to him, I felt like a child. I had to practically look straight up to meet his eyes. His hand was outstretched, holding the phone as he smiled down at me.

My heart sped lightly as I reached out to take the phone from his fingers. Somehow I felt like I was cheating on my feelings for Jonah by simply talking to him. He was tall, superior looking to most males and he was showing me an act of kindness which should have made me soften a bit; instead I felt guilty.

"It was really nice of you to rescue my phone. Thank you."

"A save for a save, eh?"

I shot him a wary glance.

"You saved me in class . . . I saved your phone. We're even."

"I didn't know we were keeping score." The words came out hostile.

Cain flung his hands up is surrender. "Hey, sorry, just gathered you might not want to lose it, is all."

Anna, where are your manners! I screamed to myself in my head. "I'm sorry. I appreciate the gesture, thank you. I'm Ananiah Immaculada. Anna for short," I said, sheepishly.

"Ananiah Immaculada. That's a mouthful. Where'd that lovely name come from?"

I hadn't explained the origin of my name in years, it always made me uncomfortable. The least I could do was appease him and try to make up for my rude behavior. I decided to explain the origin, not the meaning, the lesser of the two embarrassments.

"I was named after one of my family's ancestors, Anna Katharina Schönkopf. Apparently, she had a love affair with some famous writer, slash politician, slash lawyer back in the seventeen hundreds, which produced a child. My lineage comes from that relationship."

My tone was matter-of-fact but I found myself wincing, ready for a response to my questionable origin.

Cain's face was expectant. I guess he didn't connect those dots. I don't know why it mattered to me so much; maybe because Anna's lover was in the public eye, You never know when something like that can come back to haunt you, make you a target.

"Ananiah was also some sort of biblical figure, oh, *and* it's also a man's name. My mom thought it would be cute as Anna. I've never really liked it much."

"Well, I think it's a beautiful name, doll," his accent thicker now. His alluring smile sent a shot of adrenaline down my spine. Was it anxiety from attraction or fear, I couldn't quite decide. The last time I felt this way, I was trying to size up Professor Dhampir.

"Well, thanks again, Cain. I appreciate the phone rescue. See you around." I turned and started on my way, leaving him standing in the middle of the quad. He was good-looking, distant, yet somehow intriguing. I weaved through the oncoming students and when I thought I was out of sight, looked back. He was standing in the same spot, staring after me.

Talking to him was a rush. Why, though? He *is* hot and I *don't* have a boyfriend. Maybe I should consider Cain, the blond hottie?

A lump rose in my throat at the thought . . . Jonah. Even though every encounter with him was awkward, he was home somehow. My consuming fiery attraction to him was nothing like this tepid feeling I had toward Cain. Cain was the sort of guy that would have to grow on me. There was something there, something exciting, but nothing like my pull to Jonah – intense, undeniable . . . and forbidden. I had to keep reminding myself he was Beth's brother.

Cain wasn't attached to anyone I knew, making him instantly more attractive.

The week passed sluggishly and nothing seemed as cheery and colorful without Beth around. The only bright spot in my day was the library I was headed for. My Giants research was always interesting, despite Prof. D's lack of enthusiasm for my thesis. Lately the subject intrigued me immensely. I never knew what astonishing fact might lie around the next corner. My findings always surprised me.

> Azazel taught men to make swords, knives, shields, breastplates and introduced them to the metals of the earth and the art of working them. He taught how to make bracelets and ornaments out of all kinds of costly stones, how to beautify the eyelids, coloring tinctures and the use of antimony.
>
> Semjaza taught enchantments and root-cuttings. Armaros taught the resolving of enchantments. Baraqijal taught astrology, Kokabel the constellations, Ezeqeel the knowledge of the clouds, Araqiel the signs of the earth, Shamsiel the signs of the sun, and Sariel the course of the moon.
>
> And there arose much godlessness, and they committed fornication, and they were led astray, and became corrupt in all their ways. And as men perished, they cried and their cry went up to heaven.
>
> —Enoch 8

The Angels that came to Earth and taught men these revelations were not human, they were not animal, they were new creatures on this planet. They were the Fallen. Their offspring were abominations, another new breed on Earth who were hailed as demi-gods; half human, half god. In those days, who wouldn't think a Nephilim half-breed was a god?

I found so much evidence in so many different books about the Nephilim, each of which boiled down to the same source: Enoch. Who was Enoch, anyway? I felt uneasy referencing a source I had no knowledge of. I scrawled his lineage in my notebook.

> *Enoch — the seventh generation after Adam and Eve (Adam · Seth · Enos · Kenan · Mahalalel · Jared · Enoch · Methuselah · Lamech · Noah). He was Noah's great-great-grandfather. The Book of Enoch was found among the Dead Sea Scrolls and is considered a sacred text. He was believed to be the recipient of secret knowledge from God. Enoch is also mentioned in Jude 1:14 and Genesis 5:24.*

> And Enoch walked with God; and he was not seen again, for God took him.
> —Genesis 5:24

The Dead Sea Scrolls, really? I saw the Dead Sea Scrolls at the San Diego History Museum when I was younger. Could I have actually seen with my own eyes, physical evidence of the existence of the Nephilim? Did the very answers to all of these questions still exist today?

> *The Scrolls were ancient texts, thought to be mostly written by prominent figures in biblical times. Many religions still use them today.*
>
> *Though Enoch is mentioned in the Bible, his own work was not included. There are many works that were written and thought to be informational about the ancient times, but not divinely inspired by God. These books had been left out of the Bible.*

My early teachings guided me to believe that the Bible ended up exactly the way God wanted it. If He didn't want us to know about the Fallen Angels and the Nephilim, He wouldn't have allowed the passage in Genesis 6 to be included. Enoch's writings were more detailed explanations of what happened.

The Angels fell during the time of Enoch. That meant they had six generations to grow their race before the Flood came, plenty of time to create a race of monsters. My belief in them solidified.

My stomach growled loudly. I pulled a granola bar out of my bag and nibbled on it until it was gone, but that seemed like hours ago.

Feeling satisfied with my progress, I couldn't stand the hunger any longer and decided to call it a day. I stretched my arms over my head as I slowly brought myself out of the world of the Giants and back into reality. The action increased the blood flow into my atrophied muscles, sending a tingling sensation all over my body.

I squinted as I scanned the room. The heavy tint on the windows did little to subdue the intense setting sun. The cavernous library was void of any other students, except for one girl sitting three tables down from me. The place was practically empty.

It was a Friday night after all. Most people had a social life that started right about now. I guess it was only fitting that I was one of the last left studying and not out having fun.

My stomach growled again, breaking my thought. It was late. How many hours had I been here anyway? I checked the clock on my cell phone. Seven thirty! I'd been here almost seven hours. The entire day was gone.

I leaned back in my chair running the list of restaurants in the food court through my head, when a clean, sweet smell trickled its way to where I was sitting. My heart sprinted into a gallop. Jonah was near. I scooted back from the desk and stood up to find him walking toward me with a backpack slung over his shoulder. My heart jumped up into my throat. I slowly began to sit back down, hoping the partition that separates each computer station would conceal me from view before he saw me, when our eyes met.

Jonah strode to me with cool confidence. A coy smile revealed the dimple in his left cheek.

"Anna," he said, with a nod.

His voice was so inviting, I felt myself lean forward uncontrollably. "W-working tonight?" I stuttered. I could never get out a coherent sentence in his presence.

He shook his head. "No."

"Studying?" I prodded.

He shook his head again.

Was I supposed to *guess* why he was here? My heart pounded harder. Was he watching me? Why? An inner struggle welled up again, warring inside me between conceding to my attraction to him or denying it. So what if he was watching me, right? Beth's brother is off-limits.

"Get much work done?" he cooed. His crooked smile smoldered, melting me where I stood.

I nodded clumsily, just as my stomach growled so loudly it echoed off of the far wall. I grabbed at my belly as if it would muffle the sound. My face flushed with embarrassment.

Jonah chuckled. He set his backpack on the desk opposite me and pulled out an Asian apple pear.

"Would you like this? I picked it off of the tree in our yard just this morning." He stood with an outstretched arm as he leaned over the double-wide desk that separated us.

"Uh, sure. Thanks," I said, shyly as I reached for the fruit. I grasped it delicately as not to touch him. An electric shock from him would be all it would take right now to collapse my weak knees.

"Uh . . . how's Beth?" I blurted. "I haven't heard from her all week."

"She's doing much better, thank you for your concern, Anna. Actually, I thought she would have gotten in touch with you by now."

Just then my phone vibrated on the desk. I snatched it up and stared at the screen, relieved to have a reason to look at something other than Jonah's beautiful face.

Anna, sorry for the silent treatment. My mom and dad had me on lock-down. That was the nastiest flu I've ever had, but I'm totally better now. We're having a bonfire at sunset. I miss you so much! Please come!—Bethie

"Speak of the devil. It looks like I'll be at your house tonight." I tried my best to sound cool about it, but there was no way to hide the shaking in my voice. Every time I saw Jonah I felt as if I would pass out, my palms turned sweaty and my heart raced faster than I thought was possible.

"Of course. We're having a bonfire this evening. I'm on my way home, now. You're welcome to join me if you would like."

Oh, crap. There's no way I could survive a ride in the car with him. I'd pass out for sure, or do something totally embarrassing.

His gaze was hopeful as he waited for my answer. The library air conditioning blew his sweet scent to me. I fought everything in me not to jump over the desk and kiss him right there.

"Actually, I need to go home and feed my cat. I'll be over in just a bit, okay?" I shifted my weight nervously.

"Certainly. I look forward to our evening together, Anna. It should be fun." With a debonair nod, he walked with a poised stride toward the exit.

As soon as he was out of sight, I let out a huge gust of air. I had been holding my breath. What was wrong with me? No person on Earth had ever made me react this way!

I gathered up my notes and books and threw them into my bag. I really wanted to make it to Beth's house before the sun was totally gone.

Jogging home only took a few minutes. Nicodemus jumped into my arms as soon as I walked through the door and smothered me with nuzzles. I felt bad for being gone so long today. Owning an animal was still new to me. He missed me when I wasn't home. I took a few unplanned minutes to give him a good ear rub and a quick brushing before slopping some stinky wet food in his bowl. I bit into the apple pear Jonah had given me and rushed upstairs to change my clothes.

My first instinct was to wear something cute, but I didn't want Jonah to think I'd changed my clothes just for him. Normally I would don shorts and a tank top for a bonfire, so I grabbed the first ones I found and hastily threw them on.

I looked in the mirror and didn't bother with my hair. It had been twisted and up with a pencil all day. Taking it down now would mean that brushing and straightening would be required. I swiped on some lip gloss and grabbed my keys.

Chαpτξr 17

By the time I reached Beth's house, the blood orange sun was just about to dip into the ocean. It cast long, gangly shadows and covered everything in an ominous orange hue.

I reached the top of the cliff and looked down. Flames were roaring in the fire pit on the beach. *Dang it, I missed the lighting of the fire.* At least I'd made it before sunset. Squinting through the smoke and heat waves, I vaguely made out three people around the roaring flames.

Chunks of black soot floated up the cliff side, along with smoldering orange embers. Tongues of heat conjured an unnatural breeze that swirled around my face, forcing me to turn away to protect my eyes from rising traces of the blaze below.

There were only three blurry figures on the beach, so I knocked on the door, hoping I'd find Beth inside. When no one answered, I walked around to the side of the house to find the French doors wide open.

"Hello?" I called softly. No answer. I took a few tentative steps inside and tiptoed slowly toward the kitchen, trying my best to muffle the annoying echo of my flip-flops off of the marble floor and vaulted ceiling.

From the kitchen, I heard the refrigerator close. Oh, good, someone was inside. I rounded the corner through the doorway when Jonah crashed right into me full-force. I blindly grabbed at anything I could grasp and caught hold of Jonah's shirt as we both went down. Jonah slipped his arm around my waist, catching me just before I would have landed flat on my back with him on top of me. Our bare arms pressed against each other, sending his electric surge up my arm and through my heart as it filled my entire body. My eyebrows uncontrollably pulled together as I inhaled a series of sharp breaths.

He stood me up. On my feet now, I held my breath in an attempt to cover up my reaction but it came out in a gush through my teeth.

He held me in his arms. I fought to control my breathing as he stared into my eyes, holding my gaze for a long moment before breaking into deep chuckles.

Panicked, words raced out of my mouth. "I'm so sorry, I didn't mean to startle you . . . I, I knocked and no one answered. I was looking for Beth."

"Slow down, Anna. It's okay. No harm done."

He looked me over slowly. "Well, except for your clothes."

I looked down and salsa was splattered all over both of us. The smashed jar looked like blood against the white marble floor and chips crunched under my unsteady feet.

My eyes bulged at the sight of the mess. "I'm sooo sorry!" I whispered as I struggled to mask my rapid breaths.

He tilted his head down slowly as he gazed straight into my eyes. Electricity hummed between our arms . . . my knees gave out.

"Whoa." His deep voice was mesmerizing. "You okay?"

Half of his face crept into a smile while the eyebrow on the other side lifted.

I shook my head, squeezing my eyes open and shut a few hard blinks as I tried to control my reaction to the current surging between us. "Yeah. I think I just slipped on the salsa," I lied, through racing breath.

The smile fell from his face and the muscles in his arms tensed as he promptly let me go. He looked down at the floor with a scowl. "I should clean this up," he stated abruptly.

"Beth was hoping you'd stop by tonight. She's down at the beach, why don't you go and join her?"

The electricity gone, cold emptiness permeated from within me. Shivers ran down my arms.

I shifted my eyes to the floor. "I should help clean this up."

Still looking down, he quickly replied, "really, there's no need. I can handle it."

I breathed deliberately, concentrating on slowing my speeding heart rate before I spoke again. "I was the one who snuck in the house unannounced and slammed into you. I'm helping!" I retorted fervently.

He reached over to the counter and grabbed a roll of paper towels, ripped off a chunk and handed it to me. I started for the sink to moisten them when I wiped out, landing on my butt. This time I really *did* slip on the salsa.

"Ow!" I exclaimed.

I couldn't control myself. Laughter shook my entire body. Lying on the kitchen floor, the pain I felt was overcome by consuming hilarious convulsions.

I looked to Jonah. From across the kitchen, he noticeably sniffed the air and faced me with wide eyes. A drawn-out hungry, guttural moan escaped from his throat.

Exhilaration and fear stirred from within the deepest part of my being. What was this look on his face? Concern? Desire? Fear. He masked his expression and leapt toward me, slipping on the salsa and skidded into the cabinet door. Hurriedly, he knelt down and thrust his hands toward my arms to pick me up, but paused just before he touched my bare skin.

"You're hurt," he said, panic erupting in his voice.

Intense pain was coming from the left side of my lower back, but I wasn't really hurt, was I? I had only a second to assess my condition. I shook my head.

Our eyes locked. He was hovering so close to my skin that I could feel heat radiating out of his hands. He froze there for two breaths. Suddenly seeming to realize that he was about to touch me, he flared his nostrils and pulled his eyebrows together, let out a gust of a breath and turned his head away. Before I could blink, he was clear across the room.

At that same moment, someone called his name. I scrambled to my feet just as Rebekah walked in.

"Oh my goodness, what's all this?" she mused, with laughter in her voice.

I gave her a sheepish smile as I turned to Jonah, hoping he would explain, but he wasn't there. I peered around the island to find him knelt down, wiping the floor.

"Beth texted me and invited me to the bonfire tonight. I was looking for her when I came in unannounced. I crashed into Jonah and made him drop chips and salsa all over the floor."

Jonah spoke from his crouched position, his eyes focused on his task. "Actually, it was my fault. I was in a hurry and not paying attention."

Rebekah tucked her lips in between her teeth. Her shoulders began shaking, holding back a giggle. She crossed her arms and pulled her eyebrows together sternly to cover up her amusement. "Every time we meet, Miss Anna, you're having wardrobe issues. Maybe I should start stocking some clothes in your size in the guest room?"

My cheeks turned hot. I looked down at myself. Not only was I splattered with salsa but now I was covered in it.

"Well, I'm glad I didn't put that box of Beth's old clothes away yet. It's in my room. Come on upstairs and we'll get you changed. I'll put your clothes in the wash – again," she said, with a smile.

I followed her up to her room. Double doors opened into an expanse of white carpet. The last time I had been in this room, I was freezing cold and on a mission to find a warm sweatshirt. Running into Jonah had stripped me of all my cognitive abilities to notice the room's grandeur.

In front of me stood the largest mahogany sleigh bed I'd ever seen. The furniture matched the bed, beautiful rich wood, massive in size but simple in style. The bedding was a luxurious white and yellow floral tapestry pattern with matching accents throughout the room, including the drapes framing a wall of windows that faced the ocean. The rest of the room's décor was sparse, save for two walls completely covered in framed pictures of the Gwenaël family.

Rebekah handed me a pair of jeans and a snug pink T-shirt. I felt bad that she had to keep rescuing me from my unfortunate clothing disasters. "I'm sorry I'm so much trouble, Rebekah."

"Oh, Anna, you're no trouble at all. Beth just adores you and it's so nice to have you here. You're welcome here anytime you'd like, day or night," she said, with a smile. "And thank you for calling me Rebekah, sweetie," she said, as she gave my cheek a little pat.

"Day or night? Really? I, I mean, thanks," I mumbled as I focused on the floor. I didn't want to seem anxious. People say things like that, but rarely mean them.

"Of course, dear." She pointed toward the bathroom. "There are towels in the cabinet you can use to clean up with. Come and meet us down at the bonfire when you're ready."

She disappeared, closing the doors behind her and I was left in her ginormous bedroom alone. I gravitated toward the photo walls and examined them carefully. Snapshots covered the walls with a few formal portraits mixed in.

A happy lifetime was spread out in front of me. Half of them were baby and toddler photos of both Jonah and Beth. Even as a small child, those green eyes dominated Jonah's face. None of the pictures seemed to be taken in extravagant or far-off places. Most were photos of the family laughing, hugging, throwing snowballs at each other or messing up each other's hair. I'd never had a sibling to mess up my hair or throw snowballs at. I didn't know families actually lived like this. I longed to be a part of their fairy tale.

I sighed and grabbed the clothes off the bed, found my way to the bathroom and began to undress. As I pulled off the salsa covered tank top over my head, a sharp burning sensation slashed across the left side of my back. I turned to look in the mirror and gasped. A chunk of glass from the salsa jar was lodged deep in my skin.

I had felt pain when I landed on the hard marble floor but contending with Jonah and his strange reaction had distracted me from it. The salsa smeared across the back of my shirt covered the blood oozing through the fabric.

Standing in the middle of Rebekah's bathroom, I was unsure of what to do next. With my shirt off I could now feel the blood trickling down my back, pooling at the waistband of my shorts.

As I twisted to view the gash in the mirror, a loud moan of pain escaped my throat.

"Anna?" Jonah's voice was anxious through the closed bathroom door.

I'd never been good around blood. Bandaging Beth's heel had almost done me in. This was so much more blood than that.

Lightheaded, I squeaked, "uh . . . I think I need a little help in here. Can you go get Rebekah?" The words came out slurred, as black spots appeared before my eyes.

I reached for the counter to brace myself, but missed and landed on my knees.

"Aaahh!" I cried out.

Jonah burst into the bathroom to find me crumpled on the floor. He rushed to my side, quickly assessing the wound and my condition. In any other instance I would have been mortified for him to find me shirtless and only in my black lace bra, but I was so glad someone was there to assist me; the thought was fleeting.

"This is going to need attention," he said, all business.

He was the med student. If anyone was qualified in this house to deal with this, it was him.

He was out of the bathroom and back in a fraction of an instant. My head turned faint and fuzzy, but noticing Jonah moving so fast that he became a blur was something I didn't miss.

He returned, holding a massive first-aid kit, his hands already covered with surgical gloves. He wrapped his arms carefully around me and helped me to the bench. "I'm going to put a topical anesthetic on this so it won't hurt so badly. I'll get the glass out, clean the wound and adhere a few butterfly stitches," he said, in a soothing bedside manner. "Are you with me, Anna?"

I nodded, not saying a word, afraid that something incoherent might slip out in my woozy state. I closed my eyes and let him work, trying to forget how embarrassed I would feel about this when my head cleared.

His hands moved over me so whisper soft I wasn't quite sure when he was done. When I finally looked up, he was gone and a glass of orange juice sat on the counter next to me.

My frustrations with him from the day completely evaporated. He followed me . . . saved me . . . took care of me.

I sat stunned for a long while before staggering to my feet. Sipping the juice helped the dizzy spots to disappear. My energy returned and the task of washing off my salsa-covered arms and clothes lay ahead of me. A shower seemed like the best course of action, but then I thought of the bandage on my wound and how it probably shouldn't get wet for a while. The sink would have to do.

I washed off every bit of salsa I could see, then quickly pulled on the clothes Rebekah had given me. Jonah did a good job of fixing me up. When I moved nothing pulled in a way it shouldn't.

Feeling almost myself again, I sauntered over to the wall of windows overlooking the ocean. Isaac, Rebekah and Jonah sat around the fire, laughing on an otherwise deserted beach. Didn't any of the other houses privy to this private paradise ever use it?

Just then, I heard Beth's voice calling for me.

"Up here," I yelled back.

In my borrowed attire, I hurried out of the room and met her on the foyer stairs.

"Oh," she said, with a giggle. "My mom said you spilled something on yourself. My old clothes look cute on you. That shirt used to be one of my favorites. I'm glad she kept it. C'mon. We were waiting for you at the fire but you were taking so long, I got worried."

I followed her out the French doors, down the white, wooden staircase and stepped into the still-warm sand. The sun had set, but the sky glowed a faint orange along the horizon where it had disappeared into the sea not even ten minutes ago. Pink wisps of clouds cut through the dark purple sky and beyond them, the first stars of the evening shimmered in the twilight. Beth linked her arm through mine and led me to the fire.

Mr. Gwenaël's voice cut through the crackling of the timber flaming in the pit. "Hello again, Anna."

"Hello, Mr. Gwenaël."

He smiled at me and rested his hand on my shoulder. "Please call me Isaac. We're all family here."

Family, I thought to myself. I smiled and gave him a nod.

There were five chairs arranged in a half-circle around the fire. Beth dragged the last empty chair over next to her, sat down and patted the seat.

"We were just roasting marshmallows. Want one?" she asked with a hopeful grin.

As soon as I sat, she held out an almost empty bag of marshmallows. I reached into the bag and took only one.

Across the fire, Isaac and Jonah were having a contest to see who could get their marshmallow closest to the flames without catching it on fire. Shoving each other teasingly, Isaac caught the brunt of a powerful wallop from Jonah and almost fell out of his chair.

"Oh, it's on now, Kid," Isaac laughed.

"Bring it, Daddy-O! My marshmallow's gonna beat down your marshmallow!" Jonah challenged.

Isaac stared at the smoking ball of marshmallow on the end of Jonah's fork, not paying any attention to his own when his burst into flames and dripped into the fiery pit below. It hissed as it hit the hot coals. With a defeated look, he pulled his fork out of the flames to reveal an empty skewer.

"Victory! I am the marshmallow king!" Jonah bellowed as he stood up and raised both arms into the air.

"You just wait Kid-O. I'll get you next time," Isaac declared.

Beth shoved a fork into the marshmallow I held in my hand and handed me the long wooden handle. Roasting marshmallows was something I had only done a few times at summer camp, over hot coals from a small hibachi. Toasting a marshmallow over huge open flames of the bonfire was completely different. I quickly learned that the flames didn't even need to be near for it to work. The heat alone turned the marshmallow from white to a deep, golden brown.

"Anna, you're a pro," Isaac commented as he stared at the perfectly toasted marshmallow on the end of my skewer.

Beth took the fork from my hand and sandwiched the steaming marshmallow between two graham crackers. She handed me the sandwich as she retracted the fork from in between the graham crackers, accidently pulling everything with it. We watched it fall into the sand.

Beth gasped. "Aw, man!"

Jonah stood and brought his winning, golden-toasted marshmallow to me. The way he moved as he walked in the sand was fluid, graceful. Anticipating his intention, Beth quickly prepared another graham cracker and pulled the smoking morsel off of his skewer. As Jonah handed it to me, white goo seeped out from the edges. He put his hand under mine to steady the sticky mess that entwined its way around our fingers. I flinched at his touch. His grasp on my hand was just enough to keep the evening snack from toppling to the ground.

"It's the last one," I said, meekly. "I can't take it."

"What's mine, is yours." He said, as he looked at me with expectant eyes. I took a bite. It was delicious.

Chαpτξr 18

Rebekah straightened her back, scooted forward in her seat and sent a dashing look around the circle, while Isaac and Jonah stood up and brought their chairs closer to Beth and me.

When everyone had settled, Rebekah began. "Anna, we're so glad that you and Beth have become friends. Beth tells us that you've had some hardship in your life recently, but she's given us no details. We would love to really be here for you, honey. We all very much want you to feel like a part of this family."

Although I felt welcome, I also felt ambushed. They were so nice, but this seemed like too much too soon. Something felt urgent.

Isaac cleared his throat. "There's something very important we need to discuss with you, Anna, but we need to know that we have your trust first."

Isaac's formal tone made me feel uncomfortable. My mind raced. What could this possibly be about?

The circle was silent as they stared at me in anticipation.

Did it matter? I liked them. I could let them in or I could run. It seemed as though I had to decide right now. It had to be all or nothing. I didn't want to lose the only friend I had. I didn't want to lose the chance to find out what was going on with the rush of power Jonah gave me when we touched.

I breathed in deeply, letting my chest rise as far as it would go, held it there for a second and blew out slowly.

All in.

I opened my mouth to speak but nothing came out. I was lightheaded at the thought of completely opening myself up.

Beth knew everything. I remembered how good it felt to tell my story and get it out in the open. It felt good to share some of the burden with someone. I had trusted Beth with my tragedies before I'd met her family, or even really knew who she was. She didn't judge me. I would have to trust that they wouldn't, either.

They wanted me to be a part of the family. They wanted to love me.

The only genuine love I had ever felt was from my parents and in the last few years I had spent with them, they had grown paranoid and distant. I hadn't felt real love in a long time, not even with Seth.

Tears welled up in my eyes.

"I'm sorry, did I say something to upset you?" Isaac looked at me with concern.

"No. I . . . I." *Deep breath, Anna. All in, remember?*

"I apologize. Beth's right. I've had some tragedy in my life this last year and it's a part of me now. Even in the short time I've known you, you've welcomed me here as a part of your family, and for that I am deeply grateful. You have no idea what your kindness means to me. But I think before you invite me into your family, it's only fair that you know my story. What I mean is, how can you really know a person if you don't know what's happened in their life that makes them who they are?" My eyes focused on the sand. "I still struggle with some of the issues left over from what's happened to me in the last year," I admitted meekly.

I lifted my eyes and looked around the circle. This would be *so* much easier if Jonah wasn't here. My feelings for him were so confusing. I was even confused about having feelings for him in the first place.

He is part of the family, I forced myself to admit. I mentally pushed my invisible bubble of trust out as far as I could, until he was safely inside.

I stared into the fire and began telling them the events that had taken place in the past year of my life. As I spoke, I realized that it was a lot easier to talk to them about this than I thought it would be. Surprised, I determined that the raw emotions, exposed for so long since my parents' death, must be healing. Even the loneliness after Seth's death seemed to have lifted.

A feeling of security washed over me. I started to speak my feelings aloud. I expressed that all the mess in my life seemed like it was long ago and really the only thing that was holding me back from being *me,* was that I was alone.

A log in the fire popped, startling me out of my story. Their faces were enthralled. I glued my stare again to the sand as I felt tears well up in my eyes. I held back a silent sob. "I've said too much. I'm sorry," I said, as smoothly as possible to cover up the lump in my throat.

Rebekah spoke softly. "Anna, you've trusted us with your tragedy and all of the feelings and insecurities that go along with it. It has been a very long time since I've heard someone open up like that. I'm very proud of you. That is a very hard thing to do, honey."

Beth put her arm round me and gave me a little squeeze before letting go quickly.

I reached down and drew lines in the sand with my finger, an attempt to distract myself enough to pull it together before a tear escaped down my cheek.

A breeze blew across my shoulders, sending a shiver down my spine. I hadn't brought a sweater. The warmth and protection of my hair would have to do. I pulled the pencil out of the twisted maze I'd created this morning to keep it out of my face and shook it gently, letting it fall to cover my bare neck and arms. It gently blew in the ocean breeze.

I looked up to meet Jonah's clear emerald eyes staring at me with a wide expression. His lips were parted and glistening as if he had just licked them. His face was hungry, longing.

His eyes darted away.

My heart raced as I struggled to heave in a steady breath. I hung my head, desperate for my hair to hide the difficulty I was having merely breathing at the sight of Jonah's concerned eyes searching me.

Moments later, Isaac's voice snapped me out of Jonah's spell. "You're absolutely right, Anna. Really *knowing* one's friend is crucially important to the development of that friendship. You have been wounded by the recent happenings in your life, but wounds heal and scars fade. There's no doubt in my mind that we have your full trust now. You have let us in. It is time."

Each member in the circle straightened their posture, readying themselves for what Isaac was about divulge. They all knew something I did not. This bonfire . . . this very meeting had been planned.

"Our family is unique, Anna," Isaac stated proudly. "We have the honor, privilege and ability of helping those in great need. It is our passion and our duty."

Great. I'm a charity case.

"Beth has spoken to us about your mythology assignment regarding the Giants of old. There is some very current truth in those myths and legends."

He exhaled out a long breath and searched the circle for approval. I had never seen hesitation in his eyes until that moment. "Have you heard of the Nephilim?" he asked clearly.

"Y-es," I answered hesitantly. I was stunned. Why would he be interested in my research paper? "My search of mythological Giants led me to the Nephilim. I've been doing extensive research on them. My findings have been . . . intriguing."

If I continued, I would be airing out my entire theory of the Giants for everyone to see. It seemed so far-fetched; humans and Angels procreating a race of half-breeds. At the same time, it made perfect sense to me. The very existence of such creatures and their resulting deaths connected the ancient supernatural world to the present. And it was here, in the present that I was being followed by spirits.

Writing a paper about it was one thing, but to discuss my own thoughts about the subject made it seem so close and real. I hoped my understanding of the Nephilim was right, or this was going to be humiliating.

"I've researched far enough back, to connect ancient races like the Titans . . ." I said, as I gestured to Beth, she nodded, " . . . as stemming from the existence of the Nephilim. Most of the legends of these Giants and world wonders like Stonehenge and the Pyramids have Nephilim origins. Even legends of vampires began with the Nephilim.

The Nephilim were around during the time of Noah. After they had consumed everything on the land, they turned on humans.

Some of them had ferocious bloodlust, eating the humans and drinking their blood. Over the years, the ancestry of the vampire has changed and the true origin has morphed into something much more . . . Hollywood. My research turned up so much evidence as to the true birth of the vampire existence, it baffles me how skewed it has become and how no one else seems to know this."

Isaac nodded in agreement with me. "Many Nephilim do have the bloodlust you spoke of, and most of the vampiric legends do indeed stem from that bloodlust. You're also correct that the vampire origin has been pulverized by so many fantasy versions that the truth has been buried very deep. But those fantasies are art imitating life. Many of those stories come from true events."

My eyes grew wide. "Did you say that they *do* have bloodlust, as in *present tense*?"

Rebekah patted Isaac on the knee and changed the subject. "You mentioned that you're acquainted with the story of Noah and the Great Flood."

I nodded toward Rebekah hesitantly. "I thought I knew the story well. It's one of the staple Bible stories learned as a child. Then in my research, I found the whole version. The one that's not sugar coated by our parents and Sunday school teachers to keep us innocent.

Apparently, God wiped out everything on the entire Earth except for Noah and those inside the ark because the Fallen Angels with wicked hearts, along with the Nephilim, began to oppress the human population and teach them to do evil. They were gaining power over the humans. Everyone became consumed with wickedness, due to the Nephilim seed spreading throughout humanity. God regretted creating man. He was so angry with the Fallen Angels who mated with the humans that He locked the worst of them in a dark prison in the otherworld, and left the rest to die in the Flood. The Greeks called the prison the Tartarus. It's the lowest region of the world; a dank, gloomy pit, surrounded by a wall of bronze and beyond that a three-fold layer of night. It's a place for sinners that resembles hell. They're still awaiting Judgment."

Isaac looked at me, perplexed. "You have a very good grasp of this history. You gained this knowledge just today?"

"Well, over the past few study sessions," I replied.

Beth turned to me. "It took me over a year to fully understand all of that and what it means for us today. You understand this stuff a lot easier than I ever did."

The circle was silent, as if waiting for me to fit pieces of a puzzle together before their eyes. But hadn't I already figured this out?

When I didn't respond, Beth turned to me and put her hand on mine. "If Angels came down before the Flood and mated with the daughters of men, is there any reason to believe they wouldn't, or couldn't do it again? Could they have somehow given up their free will, or gained some sort of super restraint that caused them to never love a human again?"

I scanned the circle suspiciously. "I guess not." I'd come to the same conclusion, ironically basing this exact principle as the thesis of my entire research paper.

I fidgeted in my chair. "I read that there are people who believe that some of the Nephilim survived the Flood. Others believe more Angels fell after the Flood or that Satan started an entire new race of Nephilim, using his own army of Fallen Angels. You know, the ones that he took with him when he fell from heaven initially."

Jonah spoke through his teeth. "The Nephilim did *not* survive the Flood. God's plan worked."

He leaned forward, rested his elbows on his knees and stared at the fire blankly. The muscles in his jaw clenched. Frustration filled his face. Deep breaths expanded his entire torso as he searched for control. He spoke again. "Those who believe that more Angels fell after the Flood are correct. There *have* been more Angels, rogues, who have come in search of earthly pleasures. When they find it, new generation Nephilim are born. An entire race has been bred, but this time the Angels knew the consequences of their actions. They keep close watch over their offspring until they can be bred as a weaker species. That's when they are released into the general population.

There have also been other Angels that have been sent to Earth as Watchers, but only in very special circumstances and not many, considering how many humans are on the Earth now. Of those, only a few completed their tasks and returned to heaven. Unfortunately, the others let the evil of the world penetrate them, let temptation overcome them and they fell. Some of them have created new Nephilim."

I understood the words he was speaking, but my mind simply couldn't grasp the full concept and consequences behind it. "But the Angels who created the Nephilim in the time of Noah were locked up in the Tartarus and are still awaiting Judgment, right? If I were an Angel, I wouldn't want to get locked up there. That would be enough incentive for me to stay away from the temptation of a mere human woman. We can't be *that* tempting," I joked nervously.

"So, you're telling me that there are Nephilim on Earth today and if you're telling me this, it's because you're involved with them somehow, right?" My voice reeked with sarcasm.

Everyone sat silent. Then Jonah gave me a single and determined nod.

A shot of adrenaline surged through me. "What? I was kidding!" My adrenaline wasn't from excitement, but from fear. I'd seen Jonah move supernaturally fast when he thought I wasn't looking. The family must be talking about him. No! Not the beautiful boy with the mesmerizing emerald eyes that made me weak in the knees! Jonah, a Nephilim . . . the evil spawn of a defiant Angel? Not him! Anyone but him!

Should I hold him close and not care about his bloodline, or flee?

I knew I couldn't possibly escape Jonah's speed, but the urge to run overwhelmed me. Paralyzed with fear, I sat, unmoving.

"Put your head between your knees, Anna," Beth said, as she rubbed my back. I shooed her hand away, but did as she said. No one spoke while I calmed myself. I slowly raised my head and peered at Jonah from under my eyelashes. He looked . . . hurt, like someone had just broken his heart.

I was the first to break a long silence. "Are the Nephilim nice?" I whispered.

Jonah sat up straight in his chair. "She believes," he said, in a grave tone. His comment was directed toward Isaac, but he was staring right at me.

Why would he think I wouldn't believe? Then the thought occurred to me . . . I hadn't even doubted the truth of what they were saying. I had immediately jumped to wanting to know the consequences of my knowledge.

Rebekah spoke in a soft, kind voice. "Some of them are nice. Some of them are very evil. Most of them don't even know they're Nephilim."

"Most of them?" I squeaked out a whisper.

"Anna, please don't be frightened. Most people have no idea about the existence of any of this," Beth said, lightly.

"What do you mean most of them?" I asked again as a lump rose in my throat.

They traded glances at each other. "Almost everyone has Nephilim blood in them. In fact, there are only a few Pure Bloods left on the Earth," Beth stated, matter-of-factly.

"Why are you telling me all of this?"

Jonah stood up and walked toward me. He crouched in front of my chair and took my hands, not hesitating as he had after my fall. My body tensed at the surge of electricity that flowed between our skin. I gasped unwillingly.

He looked straight into my eyes. "We're telling you this because you're one of the only Pure Bloods left on Earth, Anna. And now that we've found you, we're here to protect you. Part of protecting you means you need to know the whole truth."

My heart felt like it was going to pound right out of my chest. I was beginning to pant. My hands shook fiercely.

"Can you feel a tingle in your hands right now?" he asked as he peered into my eyes.

A tingle – seriously? Try an electric shock! Of course I could feel it! His electricity throbbed through my entire body.

I held back the rush of emotion that I wanted desperately to shout out. "Yes." I whispered, out of breath. "Why?"

"Anna . . ." Jonah shut his eyes tight for a long pause.

"I'm a Fallen Angel. I fell almost two hundred and fifty years ago. Only Pure Bloods can sense that I'm a celestial being. The energy you feel through our touch can only happen between an Angel and a Pure human. It's one of the pleasures an Angel can give to a human. It's one of the reasons why the lure between Angels and humans is so strong. I can't feel it; only you can."

Did he say pleasure? This wasn't pleasure, this was torture! I was hyperventilating; could he not see that?

He lifted his hands and caressed my cheeks. My face pulsed with his power. With a soft touch, he lifted my chin, forcing me to look into his eyes.

The look on his face was one of adoration. "You're one of the last humans on Earth that is a direct descendant of Noah. You have *no* Angelic blood in you. You're Pure human."

My eyes filled with tears as they overflowed and streamed down my cheeks. I was breathing so rapidly at Jonah's continued touch that I was starting to see spots. I reached up and grasped his wrists to steady myself as I gazed at his perfect, beautiful face. Then everything went black.

Chαρτξr 19

I was awakened the next morning by noises coming from downstairs. I cracked my eyes open to find my pink alarm clock glaring a bright green seven a.m. in my face. Rolling over slowly, my skin tugged against the bandage Jonah had adhered after stitching me up the night before. I found it strange that I didn't feel any pain, only the pull of the tape on my back.

I patted the blankets around my body. Nicodemus was nowhere to be found.

Pots and pans clanged from the kitchen below. I sat up, panicked at the thought of an uninvited visitor in my home. I snuck quietly out of bed and grabbed the only weapon in my house; an old baseball bat that I discovered in the attic when I was a child. I retrieved it shortly after my parents died, but hadn't brought it out from under my bed until now. I knew that it wouldn't have defended me from any of the other intruders I experienced in this house recently, but this uninvited visitor seemed like it might be flesh and blood. The bat in my hand gave me a sense of security. All I had to do was swing. The bat would do the work, smashing and bruising the soft flesh it connected with.

My heart raced as I tiptoed to the top of the stairwell. The smell of breakfast, mingled with soft music, wound its way up to me, mixing with my fear, confusing my perception of the situation. Creeping stealthily down the stairs, I avoided the creaky sixth step and stopped when I heard a female voice humming along with the music. I peeked around the hallway wall to find Rebekah in my kitchen, making breakfast.

"Oh, good morning, Anna," she said, innocently, as she caught me spying on her.

I loosened my grip, letting the bat slide to the floor and rested it behind the stairwell wall.

"Uh, good morning Mrs. Gwen . . . I mean Rebekah," I stammered. "Did you bring me home last night?" I ambled toward the kitchen and sat down at the counter across from where she was standing.

"Isaac and Beth brought you home. Beth stayed here all night, but I came to take the morning shift."

"The morning shift? Am I under surveillance or something?"

"No, dear," she said, as she eyed me up and down.

I looked down at myself. I was still in Beth's clothes from the night before. I looked like a rumpled mess. Suddenly the sand from the beach last night felt hard and crusty between my toes.

"Why don't you go get cleaned up. Breakfast will be ready in about twenty minutes."

I wasn't ready for whatever was going on here. A shower sounded good. It would give me time to try and wrap my head around what might happen next. After last night, I needed to try to piece things together.

"Yeah, good idea," I sighed. I rose from the barstool and padded back up to my bedroom.

Once in my room, I closed the door softly, shrugged off Beth's old jeans and shirt and headed for the shower. The scent of salsa still clung to my hair and skin which made me acutely aware of the wound brought on by being impaled by the broken jar.

I spun around to view my back and carefully peeled off the gauze and tape that covered the gash in my skin. Two butterfly stitches rested over a deep, pink scar. Tracing the line of the cut with my finger I felt no ragged flesh. It was sealed. There was no scab, only a fresh scar.

How could this have healed so quickly? It only happened last night, right? My mind searched the last twenty four hours to make sure I didn't have my days mixed up.

As the bathroom filled with steam, frustration filled me at the fact that, yet again, more questions were arising from the Gwenaël family. I stepped into the shower and let the hot water run over my shoulders, begging it to ease my tension and wash away the doubts bouncing around in my mind about my new friends.

I washed carefully, but protecting the wound from getting wet wasn't an issue any more. There was no wound. Maybe it wasn't as bad as I had thought. That had to be it.

Rebekah said breakfast would be ready in twenty minutes. I hurriedly finished, wrapped myself in a towel and headed for the dresser. I tugged open the stiff drawer then wrestled on a pair of denim shorts and a white cotton peasant blouse, brushed my teeth and threw on some makeup. I'd let my hair air dry today. It was so warm already it would be dry in under an hour.

"I hope you like pancakes," Rebekah said, as I entered the kitchen. She pushed a plate of beautiful, warm, blueberry pancakes toward me. After hardly eating at all yesterday, I was famished. Scrambled eggs decorated half of the plate in a bright, cheery yellow. I started on them first.

"Anna, you must be confused after last night. If you don't have any plans today, I would like very much to spend the day with you so we can talk about all of this."

Her invitation was intriguing, but I couldn't get past the elephant in the room. "Rebekah, why are you here, in my house, making me breakfast?"

"Sit down and eat your pancakes, honey. Maybe you should get some food in your tummy before we start talking about this again. You seemed to have a hard time with it last night."

I rushed to swallow a mouthful of eggs. "I had a hard time controlling the electric *shock* Jonah was surging through my entire body when he was touching me last night, that's what I was having a hard time with! When he does that I can barely breathe. My heart races and I can't think."

I shoved a bite of pancake into my mouth.

Rebekah's eyebrows raised into high arches. "You feel all of that when Jonah touches you?"

I nodded vigorously, eyes wide, chewing. Was my reaction overzealous? I assessed it in my head. Maybe part of it was because I thought he was so beautiful. Every time he looked at me with those clear, green eyes I lost the strength in my knees.

"Jonah has never come across a Pure Blood that feels more than a slight vibration or tingle from his touch."

"When he touches me it feels like an electric shock. It feels . . ."

I searched for exactly the right word to describe the energizing, intense feeling Jonah's touch gave me. I gave up and went with . . .

" . . . strange. But a good strange, I guess. It's hard to take for very long, though."

Rebekah walked over to Nicodemus, picked him up and scratched behind his ears gently. "I think we need to talk about what has happened in your life. It will give you a much better understanding of what the future holds for you. Why don't you finish your breakfast and we can take a drive to the beach house. Do you have anything you need to accomplish today?"

I smirked. "Actually, this conversation could probably be used as research for my Giants paper."

Rebekah rushed back over to me and sat down, resting Nicodemus in her lap. "You must not tell anyone about this knowledge you have of Jonah or yourself. We're pretty sure you're being hunted and if the Dark Ones find out that you have understanding of your . . . situation, they could break their traditional intervention of infiltration and attempt to end you."

"Wait a minute, what? Infiltration? Who are the Dark Ones?" My voice cracked.

"Anna, now that it's been confirmed that you're a Pure Blood, your tragic past makes sense. You have no doubt been targeted for many years by the Dark Ones. Your safety is very important."

"Do you have some special orders to protect Pure Bloods or something?" I snapped at her. My tone was sharp and Rebekah was undeserving of it. Ashamed, I felt my cheeks blush.

"Do you remember much of what was said last night?" Rebekah asked.

I took a deep breath to calm myself. "I think so. I remember everything up until Jonah told me I was a Pure Blood."

Rebekah's next words sounded cold and distant as she spoke in a tone I was unfamiliar with. "Nephilim blood runs through every human being's veins, except for a very special few. Some Nephil bloodlines are very strong, which indicates that a new

Fallen Angel recently began a new bloodline or that they have bred themselves to be such. The Nephilim blood in most people is weak and diluted by Pure human blood. These people are the vast majority and have no idea about any of this. They live their lives unaware. They aren't breeding for bloodline, they're marrying and reproducing out of love.

In your studies of the Giants, did you get any further than Genesis 6 in your research about the Nephilim?"

My voice waivered. "I'm not sure what you mean."

She shifted in her chair. "After the Nephilim consumed all of Earth's resources, they turned on humans. God chose one family to survive this bloodbath. That's when Noah began building the ark. In it, he took with him his wife, his three sons and their wives. They essentially started the human race over. God chose Noah not only because he was the last person on Earth that truly loved Him, but Noah and his family were the last intact family left on Earth whose blood wasn't tainted. They were the original Pure Bloods.

Noah and his family were able to repopulate the Earth through many generations. When they multiplied and humans started to grow in numbers, the Angels came into play again. Over the centuries, new Angels have fallen in love with human women and bred with them producing new Nephilim; we call these "New Generation Nephilim." Beth likes to call them the NG's. She says it sounds more ominous," Rebekah chuckled sarcastically. "The breeding of a new Fallen Angel with a human woman is not as it was in Noah's time, though. Angels today are much more careful with the Nephilim they breed. They are aware of the consequences of their actions and conceal their offspring or hide them in plain sight, using the sheer number of humans on Earth to cloak their existence. This has become increasingly easier over the years as the human race has become more outwardly violent and easy with their virtue. We as a people have become much more open to embrace our dark side and express it outwardly. This is a huge advantage to the Nephilim who are aware of what they are. They blend in much easier today than ever before.

From what Jonah tells us, God has put an Archangel in charge to oversee that the punishment for this sin is carried out. These new Fallen Angels are sought out one by one and sent to the Tartarus."

I remembered this part. "The prison I was talking about last night. Where they're still awaiting Judgment?"

"Yes, that's the one."

"If an Angel falls and the Archangel sends them to the Tartarus, why is Jonah still here?"

"I'm glad you asked that, Anna. Jonah was sent to Earth as a Watcher almost two hundred and fifty years ago to protect a man whose work would become very influential over generations. During his assignment, he lived among humans. His love for our race grew so deep that he didn't want to leave the Earth. He wanted to live as one of us.

When his assignment was over, instead of returning to heaven, he chose to remain on Earth with the humans he so deeply cared for. He turned his back on God and in that decisive moment his wings were stripped, along with his celestial connection to heaven. He immediately realized what he had done and was deeply remorseful.

He could not get back into heaven and floundered about for years before deciding to continue his original mission and protect any Pure Blood he found. He believes this continued heavenly service, combined with the fact that he has not succumbed to mortal lust, is the reason he is still here on Earth and not in the Tartarus with the other Fallen Angels."

"So, if an Angel falls and mates with a human woman, the resulting birth of a Nephilim is the cause for being sent to the Tartarus?"

"That is exactly what Jonah believes, yes."

A long, uncomfortable pause filled the room. I took another bite of the half-eaten pancake on my plate.

"You see, Anna, Jonah has been on Earth for centuries, but he has been in existence since the beginning. He watched man's history transpire, and knew where many of the great treasures of the past had been hidden or lost. He lived as an archeologist and antiquities dealer for many decades and amassed a great fortune selling the great relics he unearthed.

He loved working beside the humans, but he never let himself get too close. He realized after a great many years that the Archangel had not come for him. He figured that was because he had not fallen in love with a woman and mated with her, producing an offspring.

But he grew distraught with the realization that after all the time he had spent with the humans, loving and caring for them, he would never know the romantic love and companionship of a human woman. Since he could also never return to heaven, he hid his fortune and secluded himself for forty years."

The story played out in my head like a movie; one of those movies I always had questions about. Luckily, Rebekah was here to answer the one question that seemed to ring out louder than all the others.

"Jonah's been on Earth for almost two hundred and fifty years?"

She smiled and chuckled.

"I'm sorry, is that question funny?" I asked defensively.

"No honey, it's just that in all of the information I have just given you, you want to know how old Jonah is. I just find it amusing, that's all."

Okay, so that did sort of sound like a superficial question. But I reasoned with myself, justifying the question so I wouldn't feel like such a teenager, but an intellect. Age is important. Age is attached to wisdom and power, both of which I knew he possessed now, even if he did look like a tattooed, surfing college student. His age changed him somehow.

Rebekah continued. "After being alone for all that time, his guilt overwhelmed him. He loved and cared for the humans around him, but the fortune that waited for him made him realize he had fallen victim to the selfishness and greed of humanity.

As much as he wanted to, he could not escape and go home to spiritual world he came from. And as much as he desired to live as a native of this world, he could not because he's not from this world. So he decided to reenter society; but not as before.

Though experiencing the love of a woman is what he desired most, he resolved that the next best thing would be to live as a human from beginning to end. He wanted a family to love and belong to, so he searched out the most deserving humans he could find. He morphed his appearance into an infant and that's when he came into our lives.

You see, Isaac and I could not have a child, so we adopted a baby boy. Jonah was that baby. To our shock, four years later we conceived Beth. Jonah was overjoyed to have a sibling to be able to experience that human connection with.

As the years went by, we noticed Jonah wasn't exactly . . . normal. He rarely disobeyed and he greatly excelled in his lessons. When he was twelve, he told us about his past. He gave us most of his fortune and told us he desired to stay with us forever."

"So the story of his uncle finding him and leaving him a fortune?" I asked.

Rebekah sat tall in her chair. "I apologize, Anna. That's the cover story the family came up with. Beth mentioned to me that she told you. She has had to choose her friends very carefully over the years. We have a lot of important secrets to keep, which makes it hard for her to get too close to anyone. She has very acute intuition. She told me she was drawn to you for your pureness of soul. She could sense that from the moment she met you. She told you our cover story simply so that she could develop a friendship with you, before she even knew what you are."

I lifted my head and smiled widely at Rebekah. "She chose me as a friend before she knew about my past *and* before she knew about my blood? She was willing to keep up that complicated story just so she could be my friend?"

Rebekah gently touched my knee. "Yes, dear. Her intuition is usually very accurate. Jonah has been working with her on developing it for many years now."

I tilted my head to the side and wondered aloud. "I don't get Jonah. He's nice to me one minute and ignores me or disappears the next."

Rebekah reached across the counter and dragged a glass of juice toward her. She took a sip and sighed. "Jonah has a great passion to help humans. He loves our race very much. Over the years we've learned that he still desires one thing above all . . . the love of a woman. He dreams of a human family of his own. But he knows he can never have these things. He's torn every day between letting himself love and keeping his distance."

Rebekah pulled her eyebrows together. A troubled look filled her eyes. "Anna, there are very evil Nephilim that have been hunting Pure Bloods for centuries, tainting their bloodlines. There are only a handful of Pure Bloods left in the world. Your parents were Pure Bloods, that's how they made you. Single Pure Bloods are the most common, but a bonded Pure Blood pair is very rare.

You see, Pure Bloods are drawn to each other. The draw is so strong that when they find each other, they stay together for their entire lives unless forced apart by evil. Each Pure Blood pair forms a very special bond that's unique only to them.

My guess is that it was the Dark Ones that led to your parents' death."

Sadness filled my chest at the mention of my parents. I had wondered for almost a year exactly what happened on that day. Now, facing the possible answer to that question, I wasn't quite sure I was ready to hear it.

"Are you all right, Anna?"

Though my eyes welled up with tears, I was able to hold back a sob. "Yes. I want to know what happened to them."

"You see dear, the Dark Ones are being watched by the Archangel. They have to act in very secretive and manipulative ways that are not obvious. Their goal is to taint Pure Bloods, not kill them, but it does happen. If they cannot break the bonded pair, they resort to death. If they choose to murder a Pure Blood, they sacrifice themselves. The Archangel will come to cleanse them from the Earth, so they leave death as a last resort."

"So you think my parents were killed by a Dark One?"

Rebekah avoided my gaze as she spoke. "If the Dark Ones find a bonded Pure Blood pair, they do anything they can to break them apart. They get close to them, using vanity as the key to open the door to tempt them with fame, fortune and infidelity.

They confuse their minds with alcohol and drugs. They inundate them with sin to harden their hearts. This hardening dulls their sensitivity to evil. This evil is corruption in its simplest form. Most people don't even see it for what it is.

Have you noticed that the media shows more and more skin on TV? They use worse and worse language? Movies and video games include so much violence these days, most people aren't shocked by it anymore. This is the most obvious form of premeditated evil, even if the ones producing this media are unaware. This constant flood of savagery numbs us. The Dark Ones use this and anything else they find effective, to destroy the bond so that the Pure Blood pair cannot produce any new Pure children. The reach of this Dark evil is so long, that it touches every human on Earth. Not only does this evil break apart the Pure Blood pair, it corrupts society and the humans on Earth so much that most don't even see it anymore. It has become a way of life.

If the Dark Ones are successful in breaking the Pure bond, it causes each Pure Blood intense pain and sadness to be separated from their mate. The cunning ways of the Dark Ones make sure that they are unaware that this separation is the reason for their despair.

The Dark Ones work within their Clans as a team, one wedging in between the pair to tear it apart and another coming alongside the newly single Pure Blood, comforting them and complimenting their strength and choice to forge ahead a new life. This is when they strike, using lust and false security to taint the bloodline."

"So, if Pure Bloods find each other they bond for life?"

Rebekah nodded gently.

"What about the Pure Blood children that are conceived like me? It obviously happens; I mean, I'm here. But you said the Dark Ones are hunting me, so they must know about me. I'm not bonded with anyone. What's going to happen to me?"

Rebekah's eyes quickly averted mine and she directed her attention to a photograph of Seth and I on the refrigerator. "Your late boyfriend . . . he was a basketball player and very tall?"

"Yes." It sounded like she was avoiding my question.

"Interesting," Rebekah whispered.

"You don't think he was a . . ." I couldn't even imagine Seth connected with the evil she spoke of. He wasn't perfect, but a Dark One? I'd known him for years; since we were practically kids.

She shrugged, uncertain of him as well.

A dizzying shiver ran through me at the possibility of being so close to such great darkness and not even knowing it. I took in a deep breath and sighed loudly.

My future was uncertain, or worse, bleak. If Seth was involved with the Dark Ones, that meant they knew I was here.

I looked around the kitchen and things looked different. My world had changed. The beautiful granite countertops seemed to swirl and tease my eyes with their confusing patterns. The morning light coming in through the window cast an eerie shadow on the wall.

Rebekah sat silent for the first time in over an hour.

"Rebekah," I repeated gently, "what's going to happen to me?"

A muffled sigh escaped her throat. "We suspect that the Dark Ones were part of your parents' death, but we don't think they have a current connection to you.

You don't have any family and you have very little contact with your previous friends, correct?"

"Yes," I whispered, as I hung my head. I was embarrassed by my circumstantial abandonment.

"We may have found you at just the right time. Surely the Dark Ones are aware of your existence because of your parents, but they don't seem to have any current infiltrators attached to you right now. We will do our best to protect you. You must be wary of any new people or friends from this point forward, Anna."

"Great," I sighed.

Chapter 20

I jumped at a knock at the door. I walked slowly to the entry and turned the doorknob, not knowing what to expect. I never had visitors.

Beth was standing on the other side of the screen. With her hands behind her back, she was rolling back on her heels and then forward onto her toes. "It's Sunday and it's *gorgeous* outside! Shopping, anyone?"

I opened the door just wide enough for her to slip through. She immediately walked to the couch and made herself comfortable.

"Thanks for the invitation," I replied hesitantly, "but I've got to be in a certain sort of mood to subject myself to a crowded mall. I don't think I'm up for that right now. Maybe I'll go for a walk."

Beth shot Rebekah a concerned look.

Rebekah rose and walked up behind me. She laid her hand gently on my shoulder. "Anna, we don't mean to be intrusive into your life, but nothing is the same now. You need constant protection."

I took a step backward and stared at her. "I'm never going to have a minute to myself again, am I?"

"Of course you will," Beth chimed. "But one of us will always be close by."

"What makes your presence so protective? I mean, you seem like normal people to me."

Rebekah sighed. "Jonah has trained us for years in self-defense and evasive techniques. He's worked with us to strengthen our God-given Gifts. We are fairly good at using our Gifts for the purpose of protection. We can add a layer of protection to you, simply by being near. And we will only be a short phone call away from Jonah at any given time."

"So it's actually Jonah that will be protecting me, but with your help?"

"Pretty much," Beth said.

I plopped down on the couch and let my new life marinate in my mind for a moment. "If God sends Watchers to protect the important humans and I'm so precious, where's *my* Watcher? Why isn't God protecting *me*?" I asked innocently, but it was a heavy question.

"God uses the tools on Earth for His good," Rebekah said. "You're here, alive, thriving and under our protection. And you *do* have a Watcher, Anna, your own personal, devoted and lifelong Watcher."

Right. Jonah. My heart raced as this realization surfaced.

"It is difficult to see God's plan through the evil of the world, but it *is* there and it shines when we use our free will to push the evil aside and strive for the Truth."

It seemed unfair that I was now protected, but my family lineage had perished, and for what? My thoughts turned angry. "What about my parents? Where was God when *they* were killed?"

"God does not intend for us to be harmed, dear. He loves us, but evil is very cunning. It turns the will of the faithless to darkness. God does not command our free will and sometimes the darkness that controls so many, wins."

"How can Jonah protect me? I mean, he's *Fallen*. He's not even a real Watcher anymore!"

Beth scooted next to me. "Even though Jonah was stripped of his wings and hasn't been allowed back into heaven, he is still more powerful than any Nephil! He's susceptible to exertion and pain, not that it would slow him down any. He hasn't used his powers for a long time, but he's still very skilled with them. He'll use them to protect you when he needs to. That's what he was sent to do initially. Protect Goethe."

"Wait. Did you say Goethe?" I was stunned. How did they know about my ancestor?

"Yeah. He was the human Jonah was sent to protect almost two hundred and fifty years ago. Johann Wolfgang von Goethe.

Jonah had a very powerful connection to him. Apparently it's the most effective way for an Angel to protect a human. Goethe is the one who wrote Faust, the famous poem that was turned into the Opera. Do you know it?"

I had to sit down. I rested my head in my hands and let my hair spill around me, blocking the view of my face. This was hitting too close to home.

Rebekah sat next to me immediately. "Anna, what is it?"

"Really?" I said, sarcastically. "Goethe? Might this explain the zap I get every time Jonah touches me? Or why I feel like there's a magnet pulling us together, even when I try to ignore him?"

"Anna, you're not making any sense," Beth said.

"Johann Wolfgang von Goethe is my ancestor . . . like my great, great, great, great, great, great, great grandfather or something like that. Before he was married, he had a child out of wedlock with his mistress, Anna. It was very secretive back then, but someone along the way took notes. My mother's bloodline comes from them. I only know because my mom and dad did a genealogy tree when I was younger. It was framed and on our wall for years, before it disappeared when I was about thirteen."

Beth was texting rapidly. "Jonah's got to hear about this. It could explain so much!"

"Jonah was sent to protect Goethe like, forever ago. Even so, wouldn't he know about my lineage?" Frustrated, I put my head in my hands.

Nicodemus promptly jumped into Rebekah's lap. She rubbed his ears as she spoke. "Jonah lost touch with everything during his seclusion, including an entire generation of humans he was close to. That must explain why he doesn't know you're the descendant of Goethe."

"Ugh, what makes me so special, anyway?" I asked rhetorically from beneath my fingers covering my face.

"If it was important enough for God to cleanse the Nephilim from the Earth and keep Noah's family safe, it is equally as important for us to keep today's Pure Bloods safe and help them to find other Pure Bloods to keep the bloodline going."

My head popped up. "This is all about breeding?" I screeched, furious at the thought. "Am I supposed to *breed* with another Pure Blood? Is that your reason for protecting me?"

Rebekah stroked the hair out of my face. "I know this is hard for you to understand, honey, but imagine if there were no Pure humans back in the time of Noah. There would have been no one to start the human race over again. The Rephaim Genocide would have been the end of humanity. The Flood was God's last resort to keep a Pure bloodline on Earth, while wiping out the evil of the Nephilim.

I slumped back into the couch, utterly overwhelmed. "Why do the Watchers protect the Pure humans, anyway? I mean, I get that we have Pure blood and all, but what is it about us that really needs protecting, other than our reproductive abilities, apparently?" I said, sarcastically. Neither Rebekah nor Beth deserved my hostile tone.

Beth put her head on my shoulder. "Because, silly, God gives Pure Bloods amazing Gifts. They do things that benefit mankind according to His purpose, even if they're unaware of it. If Pure Bloods are important enough to God that He risks the Fall of his Angels to protect them, then we will risk what we have, too."

"You see, dear, the world is so inundated with Nephil blood that the few Pure Bloods that are left have great power over them. The Gifts God gives to Pure Bloods have the ability to greatly strengthen the war for human souls. A great battle is raging. It is the battle for these souls. Jonah tells us that the Pure Bloods will be the key to winning over these souls from evil. Today there are millions of humans with very diluted Nephil bloodlines. They have turned from their wicked ways and have become faithful to the Truth."

"Diluted or not, the world seems to be doing pretty good with all the Nephils in it."

Beth grunted sarcastically. "Glossing over images you see and words you hear to make things "seem fine," is an illusion the Dark Ones work very hard at. There is great evil in the world, but because of the few Pure Bloods, there is hope for great love and peace as well. We don't always understand everything that's happening around us, but we need to have faith that we're doing the right thing."

"Beth's right," Rebekah added. "We're not sure what is going to happen tomorrow, or next month, or next year, but we do know that if we forge ahead, keeping mindful of the good things we can do to help others and the love we can give to one another, a time will come when our efforts will be rewarded and our sacrifices will become evident.

I'm going to tell you something that helps ease my mind in times of uncertainty. It helps me to remember that we are not always the ones in control.

> There is a time for everything, and a season for
> every activity under heaven:
>> a time to be born and a time to die,
>> a time to plant and a time to uproot,
>> a time to kill and a time to heal,
>> a time to tear down and a time to build,
>> a time to weep and a time to laugh,
>> a time to mourn and a time to dance,
>> a time to scatter stones and a time to gather them,
>> a time to embrace and a time to refrain,
>> a time to search and a time to give up,
>> a time to keep and a time to throw away,
>> a time to tear and a time to mend,
>> a time to be silent and a time to speak,
>> a time to love and a time to hate,
>> a time for war and a time for peace."

This was not my life. I'd always been so blah and so normal. I didn't have any God-given Gifts. I wasn't special. Why me? Wallowing in self-pity and complaining wasn't my usual M.O., but all of this war for human souls talk had my head spinning. I needed to get out of the house.

I turned to Beth. "Give me ten minutes. What are we shopping for?"

Her face lit up.

Chαpτξr 21

Beth didn't take me to a mall to shop, she took me to Seaport Village. I'd been here many times before with my parents, but it seemed totally different now.

The wooden planks of the boardwalk taunted me as if they would cave in and swallow me up at any moment. The Spanish style, cream-colored buildings of the village, with their orange terracotta roofs, seemed like perfect dwelling places for evil. As I looked out at the bay, the breeze licked at the surface of the water. A thousand eyes seemed to be staring at me as the sun glinted off of their peaks.

People passed by and I wondered how much Nephil blood they had running through their veins. I wondered if they were unaware, as Rebekah said most were, or if they were evil, cloaking themselves under the façade of human skin.

I felt all their eyes on me. Could they tell just by looking at me that I was a Pure Blood?

Beth bounced into an oceanic novelty shop. "There's something I saw here a few months ago that I think my mom will just love."

Baskets of shells and things from the sea lined the walls. Wind chimes hung from the ceiling and blew gently in the ocean breeze as it whisked in through the open doors.

"Here it is!" she squealed. Beth walked over to me, carrying one of the more elaborate wind chimes. The silver chime tubes were accented by delicate baby starfish and a large sand dollar that hung at the bottom as the wind catcher.

Her smile beamed. "Isn't it beautiful? Seaport Village was one of the first places my parents and I visited when we arrived here. When we walked by this store, my mom said that the sound of all the wind chimes playing together sounded like Angels singing.

She never buys anything for herself and I've been meaning to come back here to buy it for her. Do you think she'll like it?"

The music it made was enchanting. "I think it will make her very happy that you sacrificed a shopping spree to drive to a special store just to buy something for her."

Beth bounded up to the cash register and I was left standing next to a rack of handmade recycled paper cards. I casually browsed through them when a card with a single sparkling oval on the front caught my attention. A halo, I thought. I read the inscription.

> *Your sacrifice may be great, but my gratefulness will last forever. Thank you for loving me enough to risk everything.*

Wow. Hallmark never carried cards like this.

Just then Beth was standing next to me. "Hey, do you want some salt water taffy?"

I glanced out the window and saw a fresh batch just coming off of the taffy pull as the shopkeeper began to wrap it up. "Why don't you go get in line? I'll be there in a minute."

"Sure thing," she said, and dashed out the door.

I purchased the card and tucked it into my purse. It was ironic how at home the card with the gold halo on it, looked, next to the long, white feathers I always carried with me.

An ocean breeze gently blew the many wind chimes hanging in the shop. I let the air swirl around me as I listened. Rebekah said that the music sounded like angels singing. I imagined the tattoo on Jonah's back as beautiful wings, spread wide as he soared over the glistening water and wondered if I would ever have the courage to give the card to him.

I found Beth at the order counter, fidgeting and trying to seem indecisive. I walked up behind her, laced my arm through hers and nudged her hip with mine.

"Thanks for stalling," I whispered. "How about a bag of whatever is fresh, please," I kindly asked the man behind the counter.

"Perfect. I couldn't decide what flavor to get." She gave me a wink. "On me."

"What's with always buying me snacks? First the latte, then the smoothie, now taffy?"

"If you've got it, use it for the greater good!"

"My snacking habits are the greater good?"

She snickered. "Babe, everything about you is for the greater good now."

We sat under a tree on a blue, mosaic-tile bench looking out at the bay, picking various flavors of taffy out of the bag.

"Beth, how many Pure Bloods has Jonah known during his time on Earth?"

She had just popped an entire piece into her mouth. "Seven," she mumbled through a mouthful of taffy.

"That's it?"

I had to wait for her to swallow before she could reply. "Yeah. I don't think you realize how rare Pure Bloods are. He's been on Earth for almost two hundred and fifty years, and you're only the seventh one he's ever met."

She paused and looked at the ground. "He's having a hard time with this, you know."

I gave her a concerned look. "What do you mean?"

"He knows your safety is the most important thing to any of us now."

I remembered that we had all just started college. Beth and I were freshmen and Jonah was a first year med student. Protecting me was going to take time away from his studies.

"He's worried about having to babysit me all the time, isn't he? He's worried about not doing well in school."

She giggled. "No, silly, he'll barely have to crack a book. Attending med school is just a formality. He'll get his degree, no sweat. He's afraid he'll fail you."

I scoffed. "Fail me? How could he possibly do that?"

She got up without answering and headed for the trash can to toss her taffy wrappers.

"Beth, what are you not telling me?"

"Nothing," she shot back.

She quickly changed the subject. "I'm really excited to give this wind chime to my mom. Want to come with me? I can't wait to see the look on her face!"

I wasn't going to get the story out of her. I'd never been one to drag things out of people. "Sure," I sighed.

The howl of a dog in the distance caught my attention. It sounded like a big dog. The howling grew louder. As I stood up, I saw a man chasing after a massive beast running wildly toward me.

Beth screamed. "Get up on the bench! Don't let it touch you!"

I stood up on the bench, then climbed into the tree behind it. The dog jumped on the bench, howling loudly. The dog's owner was not far behind. He looked like a Viking. He was huge, with long blond dread locks pulled back, massively broad shoulders and huge arms. He had a square jaw, high cheekbones and a huge Adam's apple that bobbed in his throat. He looked like he should have had a dragon as a pet, not a dog.

I looked anxiously at Beth. She had her phone in her hand.

"I'm sorry, lass." The man shouted in an Irish accent, over the dog's deafening howls. He held up a broken leash and grabbed the dog by the collar. Holding the dog at arms length, he held out his hand to help me out of the tree.

I shook my head, denying him the chance to touch me, then climbed down on my own. As soon as my feet touched the ground, Beth bounded over to me and yanked me away, running.

"What the heck was that?" I yelled as we sprinted for the car.

"A Hunter! A NEW GENERATION HUNTER!"

"The dog or the man?"

"Both!" she screamed.

We ran as fast as we could, pushing our way through crowds of people. As we reached the car, she fumbled with the lock.

"They're following us! Hurry!"

"This stupid key!" she grumbled loudly as she pushed the unlock button on her car alarm repeatedly. She had forgotten to change the battery in the key remote. She frantically shoved the key in the lock and turned it hard.

"There! Get in!" she yelled.

We got in and slammed the doors. She started the car, floored it and screeched out of the parking lot.

Beth was trying to call someone on her phone. "Stupid, friggin' thing!" she snarled. Her hands were shaking so badly she could barely hold the phone.

"Give it to me. Who are you trying to call?"

"Jonah," she replied sharply.

My heart pounded at the thought of talking to him.

I studied her phone closely. It was much fancier than my own. There were no buttons to push, only a touch screen I had no idea how to work. I couldn't figure out how to get to the phonebook. "What's his number?"

She rattled off seven numbers in a shaky voice. I dialed, then put it on speaker. Her fingers drummed loudly on the steering wheel, impatient for Jonah to answer. She spoke frantically once he did. "A Hunter found Anna. He had a bloodhound with him. We're safe in the car for now. They were following us, but I don't see them now. What's the plan?"

Jonah's answer was cryptic, but simple. "To the water. You know where to go. I will get to you within twenty minutes."

She looked at me. "I hope you don't mind getting wet. We're going to have to ditch the car and go for a little swim."

"What?" I shrieked.

She was breathing rapidly. "The dog was a bloodhound."

I gave her a "yeah, right" look.

She huffed and rolled her eyes. "How do you think that breed of dog got its name? The Dark Ones have been breeding them for centuries to find only one thing, PURE BLOOD! When they find a Pure Blood, they become insane with blood thirst, like they turn rabid or something. For the rest of its life that dog is going to hunt you down. The only things that can destroy our trail are fire and water."

It was scary how easily I believed her. "How did you know that was a New Generation Nephil? And what did you call him? A Hunter?"

She took a few deep breaths and started an explanation that left me dumbfounded.

"God gives each human a Gift. Some Gifts are external. They masquerade as talent, like people who are really good singers or actors. Most Gifts are of the mind. They come in the form of knowledge or wisdom . . . the mathematician, the brilliant business man. Finely tuned intuition or incredible compassion are Gifts of the soul. When the Gift of healing is given, people usually end up as doctors or therapists, or a social worker, in my mom's case. People with Gifts of the spirit often see ones that are not of this world, or can see into the future. The fewest Gifts are of the heart, like the ability to give pure love.

When you mix these Gifts with new Nephil blood they can become amplified or go haywire.

Fallen Angels were never *meant* to breed with humans. New generation Nephils are more powerful than Nephils with a diluted bloodline. A lot of them breed for the sake of combining powers. New Nephilim are born with immense power that can be used for great good or great evil.

Did you see that guy? He was huge! I could feel his dark presence as he ran toward us. He's a Hunter!"

My hands shook uncontrollably. "They've left me alone until now. Why is the Hunter suddenly after me now? What changed?"

As she swerved her little car between the lanes, the Prius suddenly performed like a sportscar. I white-knuckled my handle as she swerved smoothly toward the exit ramp. I looked over and expected to see James Bond sitting in the driver seat next to me, not sweet little Beth. Where did she learn to drive like this, the Autobahn?

She shot me an impatient look and continued to speak frantically. "You HAVEN'T been safe until now, you just didn't know it. Think about all the tragedy in your life over the past year. They must have been watching you all along, but since you withdrew yourself from everything they probably couldn't get a Dark One close enough to infiltrate your life. They've assigned a Hunter to find you. They're officially after you now."

"Infiltrate?" I squeaked.

"Yeah. They get one of their spawns to get close to you. They get you to fall in love with them, marry them and have Nephil offspring. If they can get to you before you bond with another Pure Blood, they keep you from birthing any Pure children before you die. That way they don't have to kill you and risk being punished by the Archangel for murdering a Pure Blood, they just get you to breed with one of their Clan members, instead."

"So, I haven't been infiltrated yet?"

"I don't know, are you still a virgin? You don't have any kids, do you?"

I hesitated. Telling someone you're a virgin is personal.

"Anna!"

"Yes, I'm a virgin!"

Beth's face looked grim. "*And* you're over eighteen, which means you're Pure *and* of age. No wonder they're after you. Right now you're the hottest item on Earth."

I brought my knees up to my chest and rested my chin on them. "This is just the beginning, isn't it?" There was fear in my voice.

"I think so," Beth answered, as she gave me a grim look.

The car swerved through a maze of confusing streets until we hit the ocean. "You can swim, right?" she asked frantically.

"Yes, but ocean swimming is different than taking a dip in the pool!"

We arrived at a small boat launch. She drove the car halfway down the boat ramp and put it in park, then pulled out a plastic dive bag, a screwdriver and a small bottle of liquid from the glove compartment. She put her cell phone in the bag and handed it to me.

"Put your phone in here if you want to save it from a watery grave," she stated abruptly, as she shoved the bag at me.

I plunked my phone in the bag, zipped it up and got out. She followed, quickly unscrewed her license plates and threw them into her backpack. She grabbed my purse off of my arm and shoved it into the bag as well, then secured it on to her back, clipping it around her waist and chest.

Cris L. P. Olsen

She put the car in neutral and gave it a push, sending it rolling into the water. I didn't have time to ask questions. She grabbed my arm and pulled me, running across the sand.

She took off her shoes, shirt and pants, then stuffed them into the trash can. She stood there in her tank top and underwear.

"Your clothes will weigh you down as you swim. Put everything except the essentials in the trash can. We need to burn them."

I stood there, dazed, looking back at the water. "You just killed your car!"

"Anna, now!" she ordered.

I shook my head to clear the disbelief and shoved my shoes and shorts into the trash can. She took the small bottle of liquid and sprayed it into the garbage, struck a match and threw it in. The trash can went up in a blaze. I shielded my face with my hand. She grabbed my arm and ran for the water, spraying a trail of lighter fluid on our tracks in the sand, then lit a match and tossed it on the wet trail. A small line of flames lit the sand on fire.

"Why are we doing this?" I screamed, running from the lighter fluid nipping at our ankles.

"Fire and water, Anna. We're covering our trail. As soon as we get into the ocean, the bloodhound will lose our scent and as soon as we get out of sight, the Hunter won't be able to find us, so MOVE girl! C'mon! We've got to swim! Concentrate!"

I swam furiously, following as best I could. Fifteen minutes of fighting the ocean waves, exhausted me. I was about to ask her to take a break, when I saw something coming toward us. There was such a flurry of water surrounding it that it took me a moment to realize it was a person. Then I saw green eyes.

Jonah swam by Beth and tossed her a life preserver, before heading toward me. As he drew closer I could tell that he had one of those red lifeguard foam things strapped to his back. He reached me, put it under my arms, and clipped it around my back.

"Are you okay?" he asked, with serious concern in his voice.

I was breathless. "We're in the middle of the ocean; I'm terrified, exhausted and confused! Does that sound okay?"

A brilliant smile crossed his face. "Here, hold this and try to relax."

I held onto the white rope that was wrapped over one of his shoulders and under one arm. He towed me while he swam. When we reached Beth, he grabbed the rope floating off of her life preserver and began towing both of us. We swam for at least an hour. Beth and I tried to help by kicking when we could, but we were tiring much faster than he was.

Finally, we came to a cliff I recognized. We were almost to the beach house. The cliff looked like a caramel-colored castle bursting out of the water soaring hundreds of feet into the air. It looked impossible to swim around.

Jonah stopped for the first time and turned to us.

"Beth, you know what to do. Anna, we're going to have to ditch the life preservers and duck under the waves when they come. I'll hold onto both of you and keep you from hitting the rocks, but you need to do some hard-core swimming to get around the cliff because there's a strong rip current today."

"A rip current?" Beth screeched. "Great, this just got ten times harder!"

I could swim, but this was crazy. Memories of getting pulled under the waves when I was a little girl flashed in my head.

Jonah constantly had his arm around both Beth and I, helping us navigate the waves and stay clear of the rocks. Every few seconds Jonah's skin met mine, the sporadic electric surges helping to keep my strength up, but it wasn't enough borrowed energy to sustain me.

As we made it through the worst part of the breakers, we found ourselves on their private beach. There wasn't a single muscle in my body that had an ounce of strength left in it after vigorously fighting with the sea for close to two hours. Jonah had lost his grip on me, leaving the waves to carry me to shore. I washed up on the sand and lay face down, unable to pull myself out of the water.

Jonah ran in the water behind me and dropped to his knees. He slipped his arms under me, turned me over and dragged me to the dry sand. My eyes stung from the salt water crashing into my face. I was unable to open them. He hovered over me, casting a dark shadow that blocked the harsh sun through my closed eyelids.

"Anna, open your eyes," he pleaded, as he brushed the hair out of my face. His hand caressed my forehead and my cheek. I gasped as his voltage raced over my skin. I found just enough energy to peek through heavy eyelids.

Jonah was breathing rapidly and smiling down at me. "You did great, Anna!" he complimented, between gasps of air. "Just lay here and rest. Isaac and Rebekah should be here soon to help us."

"Water," I heard Beth huff.

He turned to her. "I put the towels and water over by the stairs. Don't get up, just rest, I'll get them."

I turned my head and squinted in the direction of Beth's voice. She seemed to fare the torrential swim much better than me. Crawling toward me with her head hung down, she reached out and put her hand in mine and gave it a squeeze. She lay with her arms out to her sides, fighting for breath. Behind her, I watched Jonah dash toward the stairs and grab something. He returned to us with towels and water bottles.

He spoke softly to Beth. Through my lashes I saw him lay a towel over her and hand her a bottle of water. I closed my eyes and concentrated on getting enough oxygen to my lungs to keep from passing out.

Jonah lay down next to me in the sand. He slid his hand under my head. The electric power of his hand on my bare neck swirled under my skin and into my muscles. My sheer exhaustion dulled the usual intensity of his touch and gave me a feeling of dreamy exhilaration.

"Open your mouth," he whispered.

I licked the salty water off my lips and opened my mouth slightly. He trickled water over my tongue. I managed a few swallows before he laid my head back down. He sat at my side as he sipped on the bottle.

He lay down beside me, and rested his head in the sand within an inch of mine. His steady breaths brushed against my ear.

With all my effort I hovered my arm just above the sand and searched for his hand. I found his leg instead and gave it a squeeze. He jumped.

He rolled onto his side and cupped my chin. "What's wrong? Are you okay?" he prodded, frantically. I cracked my eyes open and watched him as I nodded. In a raspy voice, I managed a whisper. "Thank you."

He wrapped a towel around me and hugged me gently. Our cheeks touched, sending his surge down my neck. His embrace comforted me until a small giggle broke the silence. Both Jonah and I turned our heads to see Beth eyeing us with a brilliant smile on her face.

She turned her head toward the sky and closed her eyes. "Finally," she whispered.

Just then I heard clomping coming from the wooden staircase. The cavalry had arrived. Isaac and Rebekah were running as fast as they could toward us, with Zech not far behind.

"What is *he* doing here?" Jonah asked. His gaze bore into Beth.

"Zech is here?" She shot Jonah a wide-eyed stare. "What? I don't know why!" she said, defensively.

"I'll take Beth," Jonah said, as he moved toward her. "Isaac, I don't think Anna can move. You'll have to carry her."

"I've got Beth," Zech offered, eagerly.

As Zech picked her up and cradled her, a lovesick glow burned through her exhaustion.

Isaac knelt down beside me and blocked the sun out of my face with his hand. "How are you? Can you move?"

I tried with all my might to sit up, but I could barely even lift my head.

"Just take it easy, Anna. I've got you."

He gently slid his arms under me and picked me up. I couldn't find the strength to put my arms around him. He carried me like a rag doll up seventy-three stairs.

My mind rolled in and out of consciousness as I lay in an unfamiliar bed. Nico's soft meow's resonated just loudly enough, that they stirred my awareness and I had to force my eyes to open through the grainy crust that had formed over them. Blurry shadows slowly came into focus.

Sheer curtains covered French doors and beyond them, bright stars illuminated a night sky. In this strange room, many familiar things caught my attention. My floral comforter lay lightly over me and the open closet door exposed my own clothes hanging in tidy rows.

A light tapping came from the bedroom door as Rebekah peeked her head in. "Hi, honey."

She walked over to the bed and grabbed a glass of water from the nightstand, held it in front of me and put a straw into my mouth. "Drink as much as you can, and take these."

I tried to speak, but my throat was parched and burning from swallowing so much sea water. I moaned a few times and managed to clear my throat enough to whisper, "what is it?"

Rebekah brushed her hand across my forehead and pushed the hair out of my face. "It's just some aspirin, sweetie. Please take it."

She placed two pills on my tongue and I sipped some water to wash them down.

"Just rest, Anna. The sun will be up soon. You'll feel better once the aspirin kicks in. I'll be back in a little while to check on you. Just sleep, dear."

I nodded and closed my eyes. What happened yesterday? Why were all my things in this room? I didn't have the energy to ask the million questions swimming around in my head. Within seconds, I was asleep.

Chapter 22

When I awoke, the room glowed a dull green. I strained to focus through the sting that lingered in my eyes. Thick velvet curtains in a soft sage color were drawn over the French doors, now.

I had never seen this room before. Was I in the guest room? The black furniture was contrasted by the walls covered in designer black and white fleur-de-lis wallpaper. There was a grouping of live orchids in the corner of the room and a single French door on the other side to what I could only guess was a bathroom.

We swam forever yesterday fighting against the waves and rocks to get to safety. I lay there, assessing how much pain my body was in. My arms and legs felt like they weighed five tons. My eyes and throat burned. I remembered Rebekah coming in a few hours ago and giving me some aspirin, but it had surely worn off by now. The bottle sat on the nightstand, along with some eye drops and a glass of water. Using all my strength, I raised my head about an inch off of the pillow before plopping back onto the bed. Unable to reach for the relief that was a mere two feet away, I occupied myself by counting the hours I had slept. Almost twenty hours had passed since I washed up on shore and still, my body felt completely weak and sore.

"Anna?" I heard Beth's voice call out.

"Yeah," was all I could whisper.

She walked in timidly, the sunlight following her through the open door. Nicodemus walked toward her as she sat on the bed.

"How are you feeling?"

I cleared my throat a few times and managed to find a weak voice. "How are you up and walking around? Aren't you sore?"

"Yeah, I'm totally sore, but I'm on major aspirin and a muscle relaxer. Plus, we've all practiced that swim quite a few times.

Jonah and I swim in the ocean twice a week, so I guess I'm more used to it than you are."

I closed my eyes. "That was a pretty well-planned escape."

"Jonah made sure as soon as we got here we started practicing possible escape scenarios," she admitted quietly.

I chuckled. "You killed your car."

"I know. I'm totally bummed, but I'll get another one. Maybe this time I'll get one that can unlock itself!"

"Beth, would that Hunter have come after you if I wasn't there?"

"No," she said, meekly as she focused on the floor.

"This is all my fault. You put yourself in danger and killed your car for *me*?"

"Of course, silly. You're my best friend *and* part of this family," she said, it as if it had always been and will always be. "I'll kill a hundred cars if it means keeping you safe."

I managed a soft laugh. "No one has ever told me they would kill a car for me before."

I looked around the room. "Hey. Why is all my stuff here?"

Just then, Rebekah walked in. "Hi honey! How are you feeling?"

I tried to lift my head, but it felt like it was sewn to the bed.

"Oh, honey, don't try to get up. Just rest."

I looked at Rebekah and jerked my chin toward the bathroom.

"Oh," she said.

It took both Rebekah and Beth pulling and holding me up to make it to the bathroom. I guess they *were* really family now. They had just watched me pee.

They were able to hold me up long enough so I could brush my teeth, then barely got me back into bed before I collapsed. Beth collapsed with me, as we plopped down into the soft covers. I closed my eyes.

"I'll go make something to eat," Beth said, as she lay on the edge of my bed, dangling her legs off of the side. "What sounds good?" Beth turned her head and looked at me with far too much enthusiasm for someone who had just gone through the same thing I had. I felt like a fool lying there, helpless. I was jealous of her energy.

"Food. Yes. Anything. I'm not picky . . . oh, no dairy and organic if possible." The thought of food made my mouth salivate. I was starving.

She got up with much less bounce in her step than usual and slid out the door.

Rebekah put her hand on my cheek. "Is there anything I can get to help make you feel better?"

I lay there for a moment dreaming of a hot bath, and then I thought of something that could probably make me feel a *lot* better.

"Uh."

"What is it, dear?"

Should I tell her what I really thought would help? Life would be a lot easier right now if I wasn't bedridden. "You know how I told you that when Jonah touches me, it sends electricity through my body?"

"Yes," she nodded.

"When he was helping Beth and me swim through the waves, every time he touched my skin, it felt like I was borrowing energy from him. I really think it's the only thing that kept me going."

She smiled tentatively. "That's very unusual. Jonah has never met a Pure Blood who has such a strong reaction to his touch."

I closed my eyes in exhaustion. "I think if he touched me, you know, held my hand or something, the electricity might help give my body energy and make me feel better."

"Hmm. I didn't even think of that. Does that mean you want to try?"

"Would that be okay?" I asked. "I mean, would Jonah mind? I'd do just about anything right now to not feel so horrible."

Rebekah chuckled quietly. "Honey, if Jonah knew he could help you, he'd be up here in a flash. He feels so badly about the Hunter and the bloodhound attacking you and having to escape the way you did. I'll go get him."

"Thanks," I whispered.

I had almost fallen back asleep when I heard Jonah's soft footsteps on the floorboards. I peeked through my lashes, but he had turned to leave when he saw that my eyes were closed.

"Stay," I managed to get out in a scruffy voice.

"I'm sorry, I thought you were asleep," he said, softly.

"I was waiting for you."

He took a few steps into the room. "Rebekah told me about your idea. I really don't know how much it will help, but I can try."

I looked at him suspiciously. "Did Rebekah tell you how your touch . . . affects me?"

He shook his head as he stepped closer. "No. I suspected the first time we met, that my touch might have a stronger effect than I was willing to admit, but I thought I was just seeing something that wasn't there."

I exhaled loudly. "Sit," I ordered.

Jonah sat on the edge of the bed by my feet.

I smiled and let out a long sigh. "I think," I paused. "I'm embarrassed to tell you."

Words rushed out of his mouth. "Is it painful? If it is, I'm so sorry."

I shook my head, rolling it from side to side on the pillow.

"At the bonfire you asked me if I could feel a tingle when you were holding my hands. Well, I don't feel a tingle."

Jonah's face was full of concern.

"When you touch me it sends an electrical shock through my entire body. My heart starts racing, I have a hard time breathing, I get dizzy, my hands start to shake and a sort of power bolts through my heart."

He concentrated his gaze on the blanket. "I had no idea. No one has ever had that sort of reaction to my touch." He looked up at me. "Does it hurt?"

I took a deep breath and couldn't believe what I was about to admit. "No, it's not painful. It's . . ." I paused for a long while.

"It's okay Anna, you can tell me. I need to know so I don't hurt you."

I raised one finger an inch off of the blanket. I had to collect myself before admitting my reaction to him. "It's . . . it's the most intense thing I've ever experienced. But every time you touched me before, I thought it was either my imagination or something was wrong. I haven't been allowing myself to feel it for what it is."

Jonah's eyebrows lifted and he smiled. "This is interesting. And you think by me touching you, it will help your body to feel better?"

His expression mocked me. I would have to explain this better. He didn't understand. "When we were swimming against the waves, it felt like I borrowed some of your energy every time you touched my skin. It helped me immensely. I know I wouldn't have been able to swim for that long against the waves and rocks and find my way to shore without your, uh, help."

He scooted up on the bed closer to me, and leaned his head down toward mine. "Are you sure you want to do this?"

I nodded, and agonizingly tried to lift my arms toward him.

He noticed my suffering the second I moved. "Please don't move. I'm so sorry you're in such pain. Of course I'll do whatever I can to help. Forgive me for even doubting you. I just don't want to hurt you."

I bit my lip and closed my eyes. "When you touch me it's like raging heat that swirls through my muscles. The power you send to me penetrates every cell of my body. It doesn't hurt, exactly, although I don't know how long I can take it. It's almost . . ." Was I going to admit it? I closed my eyes and sighed out the word . . . "Euphoric."

I was grateful when Jonah ignored what was likely the most embarrassing thing I'd ever admitted to a boy. To admit that someone gives you pleasure is so personal, so raw.

He nodded briskly and stared down at my hands. His fingers hovered above mine. With a swift motion he brushed his fingertips against my hand for just a moment. I unwillingly took in a small gasp. The corner of his mouth turned up. He slowly brought his hand closer and hovered it above my shoulder then brushed his fingertips down the length of my bare arm and pulled his hand away.

I squeezed my eyes closed tight. "You're teasing me."

I opened my eyes to find his emerald gaze boring into me. My heart sped.

His smile faded and his brows furrowed, creating a wrinkle between them. A determined look settled over his face. "I've never had this effect on anyone before. I'm swimming in uncharted waters here. I'm not exactly sure how to proceed."

Frustrated and exhausted, I used all my strength to try to sit up. My struggle was apparent. He reacted, reaching out to help and grabbed my arms.

My mouth fell open in a gasp as my heart launched into my throat, pumping a rush of blood triple-time through my body. The electrical surge was so intense my eyes squeezed shut, tensing all the muscles in my face.

I didn't realize I was holding my breath until I heard him whisper in my ear. "Breathe."

His breath brushed through my hair and tickled my neck. I exhaled and opened my eyes, trying to control the sensation. His stare was intense, searching me as he watched me for the first time with full understanding of his effect on me. There were no words to say to him. All I could do was attempt to bear his electricity as it pulsed through me.

He moved his hand up my arm and slipped his hand underneath my hair to the back of my neck. I closed my eyes and slowly leaned by body forward against his chest while his current hummed down my spine. His other hand trailed down my arm and found my hand. He laced his fingers through mine. I squeezed his hand as hard as I could, hoping the reaction in my muscles would dull the sensation somehow.

We didn't sit there long before the dizziness began to consume me. I knew the black spots that were appearing before my closed eyes meant I was only minutes, maybe even seconds away from fainting.

He gripped the back of my bare neck and pulled me gently off of him as he laid me back onto the pillow. As he sat back his strong bicep brushed against my shoulder. A tingle spread across my collarbone and down my arm. He shifted his weight on the bed and lay down next to me. The only point of contact now, were our entwined fingers.

I laid still, my eyes closed, trying to gain control over the feeling of his touch. The centralized contact on my hand made it easier for me to bear the rush of energy. With each passing minute, I concentrated on my breathing. I was able to isolate it, slow it down. As the electricity thrummed through my body, I envisioned it as a white light filling each individual cell. Imagining it this way, I could almost control where it went. I mentally imagined pushing it down into my legs and felt a subsequent surge of strength in them. Then I worked the energy up my body through my torso and into my arms. Finally, I concentrated the energy into my back and shoulders, where I felt the most pain from the ocean escape.

The only thing I couldn't control was my racing heart. Surely Jonah could feel my pulse throbbing through our touch.

We lay there for what seemed like hours, not talking, not even acknowledging each other, just healing.

Rested, my eyes flitted open to find Jonah asleep on the pillow next to me. Reluctantly, I gently pried our fingers apart. I knew the cold emptiness would assault me as soon as the energy rush stopped. And it did.

Each time the frigid feeling devoured me, I had to fight my way out of it. Each time his touch left mine, tears welled up in my eyes. This time they were so voluminous they spilled over, running down my cheeks in waves. I was relieved Jonah was asleep and not able witness my lack of emotional restraint.

The emptiness faded as I wrestled it out of my system. It was getting worse though. Each time we touched, the withdrawal of his power left me feeling more and more empty, as if part of me was being ripped away. I was beginning to only feel whole when I was near him, touching him.

Cris L. P. Olsen

Only inches from my face, Jonah moaned in his sleep. My attention was immediately consumed with him. I rolled over onto my side to face him, tucking my arms tightly to my chest to keep from touching any part of him and just stared at him in amazement.

I marveled at the creature next to me.

There is an Angel sleeping in my bed, I thought to myself in awe. *He's here to protect me. I'm part of his family.* For the first time in a long time, I felt like I belonged to someone. And I liked it. I closed my eyes and dozed off.

When I woke up, Jonah was gone. My body felt completely normal; energized even. I couldn't believe that only an hour before, I was so sore and exhausted I could hardly even move.

The smell of food wafted up the stairs and into my room. My stomach growled after just one whiff.

The smell of the sea in my hair and the feel sand on my skin made me acutely aware that I was still in my escape clothes from yesterday . . . just underwear and a tank top. I looked around the room trying to familiarize myself with it. Oh, right, I had my own bathroom.

I quietly padded to the bedroom door and closed it, then rummaged through the closet and the dresser drawers to find that almost all of my clothes were here. Grabbing the essentials, I headed for the shower.

The plunking of the drops on the shower floor acted as a metronome to steady my thoughts as I worked through my memory to piece together the events that led up to this very moment. I had so many questions. First and foremost, why was all my stuff here? Even Nicodemus was here. Was this an extended vacation or a permanent thing? Either answer to this question was okay with me.

My fingers began to prune, so I twisted the handle until the water stopped flowing. When I stepped out, I felt different. I looked at myself in the mirror. Somehow I looked different. My eyes seemed a brighter shade of blue, my hair seemed shinier. My muscles felt toned and firm and my skin glowed with a radiance I'd never seen before.

∞ 186 ∞

Maybe it was just that I felt different, emotionally. Jonah's continued touch definitely made me *feel* everything. The texture of the towel was rougher than usual. The lip gloss sliding on my lips felt extra smooth.

I looked around the bathroom, taking it in and saw my purse sitting on the bathroom counter, unopened and still wet.

"Bummer!" I whispered, when I remembered the card I had bought at the shop in Seaport Village. It surely must be ruined. I unzipped the purse and found the card wet but still intact, the lettering amazingly unsmudged. I continued to pull out the few items still left inside and set them on the counter to dry.

The family seemed to come into my room a lot. I'd better hide the card until I decided if I was going to give it to Jonah or not. I opened up one of the cabinets next to the bathtub and placed it inside.

I quickly dressed and sat on the bed, preparing myself to face the answers to my questions. I wasn't sure how I would feel when faced with the reality of the truth, but I did know one thing to my very core. This was my family now. I completely trusted them. Whatever was happening was for my safety, for my future, for the good of mankind. Wow. I might have a stake in the future of every living soul on Earth.

I stood and bounced on my toes a few times, psyching myself up to leave the room and opened the door to an empty hallway. The smell of food drew me down the back stairs toward the kitchen.

At the bottom of the secret staircase, I peeked around the corner and found Beth pouring batter into a hot waffle maker.

The patio door opened, bringing with it a warm ocean breeze. Rebekah entered the kitchen, holding a bouquet of freshly-cut roses from the garden. "Oh, good morning, Anna," she said, with a smile.

"Anna!" Beth squealed as she dropped the ladle in the bowl of batter and bounced over to me. She hugged me so hard I thought my eyes might pop out.

"Careful honey, she's probably still very sore," Rebekah warned as she took over Beth's job and checked the waffle iron.

Beth dropped her arms and stood directly in front of me, her face only inches from mine.

"Are you okay?" she whispered with bulging eyes.

I threw my arms around her and squeezed her as tight as I could.

She exhaled under the pressure of my hug. "Ow!" she wailed.

I let go. "Are *you* okay?" I asked.

"Dang, Anna. Got muscles?"

Chuckles rolled through the kitchen. It wasn't so much Beth's comment that was funny, really, as it was the fact that I was energetically engaging her to everyone's astonishment. I suppose I should still be lying in bed hardly able to move.

"So Anna, feeling better?" Isaac asked, as he prepared a plate of breakfast for himself.

I drew in a deep breath and exhaled hard, as I ran my fingers through my hair. "Thanks to Jonah, I feel wonderful!"

"That's incredible!" Rebekah stared at me with honest perplexity. "Just an hour ago you could barely move. Jonah's touch seems to have healed you!"

She turned to Jonah. "Have you ever heard of anything like this? You've never mentioned having this effect on anyone before."

Jonah stared right at me. He slowly shook his head and radiated a warm smile my way. Tendrils of his spirit invisibly wrapped around me. A quick breath caught in my throat. A physical connection formed between us across the wide expanse of the room. Everyone else disappeared and I saw only him. The bitter, cold ache I felt each time our touch ceased was being filled by an unseen force. Part of him was filling my soul.

"Helloooo?" Beth voiced.

I hardly heard her.

"Anna!" She nudged my elbow.

I snapped out of the Jonah daze. "So, what's for breakfast?" I said, as I cleared my throat. I broke my eyes away from Jonah's and looked out the window. Breakfast time was clearly over. "I mean, for brunch?"

Beth bopped her hip against mine. "Waffles!" she exclaimed.

She turned her back to me and headed for a buffet of food, spread out on the counter that included quiche, fruit and steaming waffles, hot off the iron.

I shot Jonah a stern look. What had just happened? Our gaze created some sort of connection that no one else noticed. Jonah acted nonchalantly as if he had no idea why I was glaring at him.

Of all the things I accused my mind of conjuring up, I knew I hadn't imagined *that*! Everything seemed so unsure right now; everything except my growling stomach.

Chαpτξr 23

Beth walked over to her spot and sat down, just as Rebekah was rising off of her stool. "Sit here, honey. I'll put together a plate for you."

Half of the kitchen island was filled with platters of food. The other half was used as a casual table with barstools around it.

"Isaac, we only have four stools. We'll need to get another one for Anna."

"Good idea. I'll pick one up today," he replied on his way out the door.

"So, I'm staying for a while?" I asked tentatively. I had a million questions running through my head.

As I sat, Rebekah pushed a plate full of the most wonderful smelling breakfast in front of me.

"Why don't you eat some breakfast; then we can discuss this in the living room."

I nodded and took a bite.

Jonah had only taken a few bites before he pushed back from the counter and washed his plate. He walked out the door to the patio and disappeared out of sight. Isaac followed close behind.

Just Rebekah, Beth and I were left in the kitchen.

"Did I say something wrong?"

Beth gave me a little smile. "Do you remember what we were talking about at Seaport Village just before the bloodhound charged at you?"

I searched my memories of the day and was having a hard time recalling anything but our escape. I shook my head.

"I was trying to tell you about how Jonah's afraid of failing you."

"Oh, right. I asked if there was something you weren't telling me, and you brushed me off."

Rebekah patted Beth on the hand. "Beth is having a hard time with all of this. She wants so badly for Jonah to be happy, but she also knows that there are other things that are much more important now; things that require much restraint and self-control."

"I'm sorry, I'm not following."

Beth chimed in. "Jonah's main concern now, is protecting you. It's his job. It's what he was originally sent to Earth to do. He has protected other Pure Bloods before, but they were all men. He continued to protect Pure Bloods even after his initial mission was complete. He takes protecting them very seriously."

Beth looked at Rebekah, unsure of how to continue.

"Jonah's having a hard time separating his *job* from his *heart*," Rebekah said. "He cares for people and their well-being very much and he deeply loves this family. You are a part of this family now, but there *is* a distinct difference. You are a Pure Blood. You take priority over all of us, now. Jonah is drawn to you in many ways, some ways he's never felt before. No Pure Blood has ever had such a strong reaction to his touch. No Pure Blood he's ever protected before has been a part of his family. It's confusing him. He's afraid his feelings will blur his vision and he'll be unable to protect you as he needs to. He is also aware that he needs to help you find another Pure Blood as a mate. He's feeling very torn right now."

I heard a door open behind me. Jonah strode in and walked right past us before bounding up the stairs. I shifted in my chair uncomfortably as he passed, not knowing what to expect each time I saw him. We heard his bedroom door close, and everyone breathed a sigh of relief.

I looked back and forth between the both of them. "He doesn't know you're telling me this, does he?"

They both shook their heads.

Rebekah grabbed the empty plate from in front of me and took it over to the sink. "He's fine with you knowing about the protection part, but he's reluctant about you knowing how he feels. Now that you'll be living here, it will be much easier for him to protect you, but harder for his heart to draw a line between the job and his adoration for you.

Isaac, Beth and I think it best for you to know the entirety of what's going on, even if it means telling you about Jonah's struggles. We have agreed that you knowing his main source of weakness right now might help to protect you further. We're also hopeful that he will gain control over his confusion, and things will become clear to him so that he may continue his mission effectively. It will not always be so confusing to him. At some point he will have to make a decision one way or another. Until then, please be mindful of the fact that he's struggling right now, all the while formulating a plan for your protection."

"What decision?"

Rebekah shut off the faucet and dried her hands on a red and white paisley apron tied around her waist. "Anna, I know things are confusing to you right now, dear. We will tell you absolutely everything you need to know, but some things will need to present themselves in time." She gave me a nod, the kind of nod that ends a conversation.

I trusted her enough to know that whatever she was telling me, or not telling me, was for my own good. It was frustrating, but I put my faith in knowing she'd tell me what I needed to know when I needed to know it.

"I noticed most of my things are here, including Nicodemus. What does that mean, exactly?"

Beth bounced out of her chair with a huge grin on her face. "We get to be roommates! Sisters! You'll be living here now!"

I gave Rebekah a confused look.

"Honey, you can't go back home. That bloodhound knows your scent, now. It is very good that he didn't touch you or else he would be able to track you very easily. When you and Beth dispatched the car and burned your clothes, you destroyed your scent. The dog only has the lingering scent from where he first saw you to go on and not a physical piece of you or something close to you. Your scent is very strong at your house, especially since you walked to and from school. Your trail is all around there. It is possible he could follow your scent there. We pulled as much out of your house as we could, but I'm afraid you cannot return."

Beth walked around the island so that she was standing across from me. She leaned forward and rested her elbows and forearms on the cold marble. "When we escaped into the ocean the other day, we cut off the bloodhound's ability to track us. You haven't left the house since that day, so you're completely safe here, so far."

I raised my eyebrows. "So far?"

"We'll have to be very careful with you two from now on," Rebekah said.

"How am I ever going to go anywhere again?"

"Jonah goes to UCSD, too," Beth said. "There's a legitimate reason for him to be there. He'll always be close by. We'll be safe with him near. He wouldn't be able to protect you as well if you lived so far away."

I snorted. "That takes care of school, but what about the rest of my life?"

A proud air surrounded Beth as her chin rose. "We have ways of masking our scent. Jonah has taught us what to wear to help keep our scent contained, and how to cleanse ourselves to reduce our trail. It can never fully be contained, but there's a lot we can do to protect ourselves, including having him infuse us.

"Infuse you? Do I want to know what that means?"

"Yeah, he makes this drink and infuses it with, uh, Angel magic that helps to mask our human scent."

I crossed my arms. "Angel magic. Really?" My tone was sarcastic.

Beth rolled her eyes. "Anna, seriously. After all you've seen, *and felt*, don't you think a little Angel magic is possible? Anyway, I think we're almost out. He'll have to make more soon."

"You drink it all the time?"

"We didn't used to, but ever since we met you, he's been making us drink it every day. It's good. You'll like it."

It only took a second for me to figure out what she was talking about. "The tea. Rebekah told me it's Jonah's secret recipe. I've had it before. It's red. It has his blood in it, doesn't it? Angel magic – Angel blood?"

Both Beth and Rebekah stared at me with awed expressions. "How did you know that!" Beth stuttered.

"It smells just like him. Rebekah gave me some last week. I wondered why she said it was tea. I thought it was cranberry juice at first because it's red. You drink his blood?" I was horrified.

"Anna, calm down," Rebekah said, as she crossed the kitchen toward me.

"Why doesn't it taste like blood?"

"Anna, honey, we weren't trying to cover anything up, honestly. We would have told you eventually. All things in time, dear. Just so you know, it really *is* tea. Jonah brews it himself. It contains herbs and spices that help to detox the human body. There are only a few drops of his blood in each batch. His blood is so potent that it turns the entire batch red."

I ground my teeth. "I'm making your lives messy and complicated. Maybe I should just move away. Then Jonah wouldn't have to protect me, infuse me, or struggle between his mission to protect me and living his life with you. You all could get back to your lives."

Just saying those words made my heart ache. "What would have happened if Beth never wanted to become my friend and I never met any of you? Would I be dead now?"

"Possibly," Rebekah said, in a grave tone. "Honey, we can't just let you go. You're too important. Not just to us, but to the world. There are so few Pure Bloods left that we have to do everything in our power to protect you."

"I can ignore him. I can spend more time at school and less time here."

"Although less physical proximity would ease his chances of his interaction with you, it would no doubt cause him pain at this point. He *will* be watching you most of the time now, whether you're aware of it or not. Staying close to him would be the best chance for your successful protection."

"How could being far from me cause him pain?" Protecting me was all that seemed to matter to them now. If it wasn't for me bulldozing my way into this family, they would be living their sweet little lives and no one would be confused, in danger, or torn. I hated the fact that I was causing Jonah pain for whatever the reason may be. Now his hot-one-minute-and-cold-the-next, made sense.

"Anna, he's connected to you now in a way we can't even understand. He's tried to explain it to us before, but there are no words that can describe the connection he has with a Pure Blood. It's what he was sent to Earth to do. He was given special powers to assist him in this task that he has never lost. He will have this connection to you your entire life. Time and distance from you will cause him pain. I know this doesn't make it any easier on you, but just remember that he's experienced this before, with the other Pure Bloods he's protected. He knows how to handle himself."

"Except that now there's confusion added because I'm a female, because I'm living with you, because I feel something different from his touch, need I go on? To use his words, he's 'swimming in uncharted waters'." I crossed my arms in front of my chest. "Can I take a walk on the beach?"

Beth stood up. "Of course. The ocean cleanses the beach every day. It's probably the safest place for you to be."

I stood up, grabbed my plate and headed for the sink. Rebekah stopped me. "You're a guest, Anna. You don't have to do these sorts of chores."

I looked at her with determination. "A guest? I thought I was part of this family now. Doesn't that mean I should pitch in just like everyone else? All you need to do is show me how to open this thing."

I felt around the edges of the fancy dishwasher and gave it a few hard pulls.

Beth walked over, with a superior look on her face and slid her finger down the side. It whistled open.

"Oh," I muttered.

I put my dish in and jabbed my thumb over my shoulder out the window in the direction of the beach. Rebekah nodded and I slipped out the door.

Chapτξr 24

As I headed down the steep wooden stairs, the refreshing sea air swept around my body. The beach was barren. No one seemed to use it except the Gwenaëls.

I made my way to the warm, soft sand, not getting very far when I sat down and lay back. I closed my eyes and remembered the last time I was here. I was so exhausted I was unable to move. Then Jonah lifted my head to give me a drink of water. Remembering the feel of his hand on the back of my neck excited me. Tingles ran over the surface of my skin.

My life was forever connected to him, now. What would this new life be like, I wondered. Would I always live with the Gwenaël's? Would I always live with Jonah? Deep in thought, a presence stirred around me. I was not alone.

I sat up and scanned the beach. But I *was* alone. This was the same feeling I had a few weeks ago, the morning after I met Beth's family for the first time and I awoke from that strange dream. This is the same feeling I had just this morning, when Jonah and I connected from across the kitchen. Like my spirit was being held in a satin embrace and every empty facet of my soul was being filled. A flash of green eyes appeared in my head.

Dang-it! My mind was instantly consumed with thoughts of Jonah – the dimple in his cheek, the tattoo scrawled across his back, his generous, caring nature, the way it feels when he touches me.

"*Anna*," a whisper filled my head.

I bolted up and looked around frantically, spinning in circles. No one was around. I was sure I just heard Jonah call my name. I turned and looked up at the glass wall of the beach house and caught him just as he was turning away.

He couldn't have yelled my name. The voice I heard sounded like he was standing right next to me, whispering in my ear.

I sprinted up the stairs and shook the sand out my clothes as I flew into the house. Through the windows, I caught a glimpse of Jonah outside on the patio.

I ran outside just as he jumped into the pool. The lightning-fast laps he swam sent water thrashing around him in a white frenzy. I could barely see him.

This seemed like an escape tactic. I wasn't going to let him get away with this. I *knew* what I heard.

I unbuttoned my shirt, tossed it onto the deck and then hesitated for a moment. What would happen to the feathers if they got wet?

Jonah's complete lack of acknowledging my presence infuriated me. The feathers would dry. I jumped into the pool in my tank top and shorts. He immediately stopped swimming, and stood up. I waded toward him vigorously, forcing him to step back until his shoulder blades hit the edge.

Standing on my tip toes, I took a giant step toward him, closing the gap between us. Our faces were mere inches apart.

I spoke through my teeth. "What. Was. That!"

He looked me in the eye and shrugged.

"Don't tell me you didn't do that on purpose." I growled at him.

A coy smile broke across his face, and he did this insanely cute thing with his eyebrows. "You're turning red, Anna."

I took a step back and stumbled into the middle of the pool. It was just deep enough that I had to tread water to get back to where I could touch. I found myself face-to-face with him again.

"How am I going to live here if I'm always wondering what the HECK is going on!" I teetered as I spoke, about to fall back into the deep water again.

He put his hands on my hips to steady me. My heart pounded.

"You can get inside my head, can't you?"

The grin on his face widened as he gave my hips a tiny squeeze. He peered deep into my eyes. "Can I?"

"You've been trying?" I shrieked. I felt totally invaded. What had he picked out of my brain?

"Yes," he said, softly. "I didn't know it was working."

I squinted angrily at him. "So you *can't* hear what's in my head?"

He shook his head. "No."

This was so frustrating! I understood everything they'd told me about the Fallen Angels, Nephilim and bloodhounds, but I couldn't grasp what was going on between me and the person that was supposed to be my life-long protector!

"You send electricity through my entire body when we touch and I can hear you in my head. Why!"

The grin left his face. "I'm sorry, Anna. I can't feel what you feel when we touch. I can't hear you in my head. But you can feel these things from me. This is part of the connection that forms between a Watcher and his charge. It will grow in many ways, eventually giving me access to enter your thoughts in order to guide you and protect you. This would have happened eventually, though I'm surprised it has progressed so quickly. It usually takes many years for this particular connection to grow. You must be very in tune with me."

"Great. It's a one-way street and I'm a stalker," I muttered under my breath.

He grabbed my face, resting his full hands on each of my cheeks and held it directly in front of his. My body tensed as he pulled my feet off the pool floor. I grabbed his arms to steady myself. His thick biceps felt like softballs under my grip.

His energy bolted through my face and down my body, but I was determined to hold steadfast through it. I closed my eyes and used my mind to focus the energy into my legs.

"It's *not* a one-way street and *I'm* the one who will be stalking you for the rest of your life," he said to me emphatically.

I opened my eyes and spoke through my teeth. "You know what this does to me."

"You seem to be learning to control it," he said, with an amused look on his face.

"Barely," I spat. My heart raced. I concentrated on my breathing. In. Out. In. Out. It slowed a fraction.

"If you learn to control it, you might be able to use it to protect yourself." He didn't let go.

I wrapped my fingers around his wrists and slid his hands off of my face. My shirt had ridden up in the water, exposing my midriff. I put his hands on the bare skin of my waist. An uncontrollable gasp followed. I hated when that happened.

His eyes widened as he gave my waist a firm grip.

I let go of his wrists and floated my arms out at my sides, letting him steady me in the water.

I could prove to him that I could control his power over me! I closed my eyes and concentrated on his energy humming through my body. I drew the energy from my legs up, into my hands. They burned with his current. I imagined balls of light pooling in my palms. I reached out to the sides of me and thrust the energy out of my hands.

Jonah gasped and let go of me, sending me toppling backward into the deep water.

"What?"

"You sent ripples out of your hands into the water."

"I did?"

"Yes. How did you do that?"

"Uh, I'm not sure. When you touched me I imagined holding your energy in my hands and throwing it away from me."

"Anna, I can't even do that," he said, with awe.

He gazed intensely into my eyes and moved his hands under the water as he reached out for me. A shock webbed its way through my veins as he wrapped his hands around my waist and drew me near to him. "Try again. Try sending it back to me," he asked earnestly.

My hands found his wet, bare chest. I closed my eyes.

I brought the energy that was pulsing through me, into my arms and imagined the balls of light forming in my palms, again. I collected more and more energy as it surged into me. I held the energy at my fingertips. But this time, I waited.

I looked directly into his eyes and thrust the energy into him, sending lightning through his skin, straight to his heart.

His jaw clenched, his eyes shut tight. Goose bumps cascaded down his chest. Veins popped out of his neck and over his biceps as his arms tightened around my ribs. He enveloped me and squeezed me tight. I rested my cheek on his chest and let the energy flow between our wet skin.

We exchanged this power for only minutes before I began feeling dizzy. I knew we had to stop soon, before I passed out.

I envisioned the energy retreating from his legs and then his arms. His embrace around me loosened. I pulled the energy away from his back and then slowly away from his heart.

I pushed it down into my legs.

He let out a sharp exhale as if he'd been holding his breath. His eyes opened. A look of shock befell his face. We were embracing.

I expected him to push me away; his usual reaction to any close proximity to me, but he stood frozen, gazing into my eyes.

The energy he sent to me flowed through my body intensely, but it did not overtake me. I forced it into the muscle tissue of my legs where it swirled and engorged each cell. I could probably run a marathon in half the time with this power!

I peered up at him. He was breathing heavily; his eyes welled up with tears.

He unwound one of his arms from my waist and lifted my chin with his finger. My breath sped even faster. Was he really doing this? Wasn't this the very thing that was forbidden?

I knew I should try to stop him, but I found myself yearning for this more than anything I had ever wanted before.

I moved a sliver of energy from my legs to my mouth. He closed his eyes and gently brushed his lips against mine. Energy left my lips and transferred into his. He gasped unexpectedly, opened his mouth on mine and drank in the power. His embrace tightened. His kiss became urgent and intense.

His biceps bulged, squeezing me tightly as he lifted me partially out of the water. I was now at his height, my arms wound around his neck. Our skin touched along the length of our bodies as my legs dangled in the water.

The exhilaration of kissing him, mixed with his electric touch. I could no longer hold onto, or control this power. It overflowed as I sent back to him what I could not contain. He responded as his lips eagerly assaulted mine with a passion that was completely pure, completely transparent. I touched my tongue to his and let an intense tingle flow between our mouths. I couldn't imagine any two people more utterly enraptured with each other as we were this instant.

The voltage he sent to me did not overtake me, now. Completing the circuit between our skin removed the fire, as the electricity flowed easily between us. Each time we touched, our connection created a new sensation. It adjusted naturally, connecting us on a deeper level with each rendezvous.

Mid-kiss, Jonah grunted. He began to struggle against the bond that held us tightly together. I could feel his spirit pulling away from mine, as he attempted to gain control over the current. His arms rigidly unwound from my waist until his hands gripped my shoulders. In one swift move, he pushed me away.

Chαρτξr 25

As the color drained from Jonah's face, his eyes locked on mine in an empty stare. I reached for his hand, our fingers brushing for an instant before he disappeared from in front of me. He quickly waded toward the steps and I saw his bare back for the first time. The tattoo I had only caught glimpses of before, was fully facing me, now and it was breathtaking. Tattered wings were tattooed across the span of his shoulder blades with a cross-shaped sword strapped to his back. When he moved, the ripples in his muscles shifted the wings in such a manner that it gave the illusion that he was flying.

"Angel wings," I whispered to myself. The meaning of the art inked deep into his skin hit me. He was a warrior, a protector, defected from his army, but still holding onto his heavenly connection by a thread. He still considered himself active duty.

The haunting dream rushed into my mind as I examined a chunk of absent feathers. It looked as if there were three missing; the same number of feathers I had pulled out of my dream. A quick breath caught in my throat.

Jonah was on the pool deck in an instant. Grabbing a towel from the lounge chair, he turned to face me. "Out of the pool, Anna. We need to talk."

I swam over and walked up the steps. He draped the towel around my shoulders.

"We need to discuss this with the family and possibly even the Light Ones. Go change, then meet me in the library as soon as you can." He ran off, disappearing around the corner of the house.

I felt abandoned, standing by myself wrapped in the warm towel. My fingers gently ran over my swollen lips. I had never felt such passion, such pure love.

Love . . . right . . . like he would love me. Attraction to the forbidden was something Fallen Angels obviously had a hard time denying themselves. But that's all it was. I was sure of it. I was just forbidden fruit. The battle inside him wasn't because he was in love with me. He was captivated by the unknown, drawn to the allure of a Pure Blood; a rare female amongst a sea of Nephilim half-breeds.

I shuffled slowly in the kitchen, carefully navigating the slick, marble tile. Rebekah was sitting in an overstuffed chair, reading a book when I walked past the library, dripping wet.

"What on Earth?" she exclaimed. "Are you okay?"

I paused at the door of the library. "Jonah wants to call a family meeting. Are Isaac and Beth around?"

Rebekah scurried over to me. She threw her hands up to my face and pushed my hair back, inspecting for wounds. "Beth is out but Isaac is around somewhere. Are you sure you're okay? You're fully dressed and soaking wet!"

I huffed out a short breath. "Yeah, I jumped in the pool because I was angry with Jonah." I searched my mind for a moment. I didn't know exactly how to explain it, or what it was that I was explaining. "Something happened. Can you get Isaac and Beth here right away? I need to go change. I'll meet you back here in a few minutes."

"Of course, dear," Rebekah said, with obedience, as she hurried off to round them up.

The complete trust and devotion they all had with each other was something I'd never experienced before. It caught me off guard. I was barking orders at her, and she took them and followed them directly.

I bounded up the stairs and into my room. My room. It was surreal. Had it only been this morning that I woke up in this very room unable to move, realizing that my life had completely changed? It felt like someone had pressed the fast forward button and I was speeding through a part of a movie I hadn't seen before, wondering what was happening.

I peeled off my wet clothes, tossed them into the bathtub and dug around in the dresser until I found shorts and a tank top. I threw them on as quickly as I could, wrung out my wet hair and twisted it into a clip.

I opened the bedroom door and dashed out, practically running over Jonah in the hall. Our bare arms touched. He gasped as he grabbed my shoulder to steady himself. The electricity that flowed between us was completely organic this time, like it was a natural part of both of us, connecting us. I didn't even concentrate on sending it to him. It was like a switch had been turned on. The energy flowed between us without a conscious effort.

I seemed to have more control over the energy exchange than he did. I lifted his hand off my shoulder and dropped it to his side.

Behind his eyes, a private war took place: to stay or to go. He shuffled forward as I stepped back. He had me against the wall, leaned in and stared into my eyes. He inched toward my face and stopped only a breath away from my lips. A beautiful glossy, brown curl fell over his forehead and his emerald eyes peered into my soul. He hovered there, breathless.

"I'm home!" Beth yelled, as she walked through the front door. Jonah turned away, breaking our stare and greeted her from atop the stairs.

"Beth, grab the *Angelus Secreta* journal and meet us in the library," he ordered.

Chills ran down my arms as I listened to his deep voice. It held such authority. When he spoke to me, his tone was soft and caressing. This was different. I wasn't used to hearing him use his full voice.

She looked up, eyeing us on the landing and gave Jonah a swift nod.

"How does every member of this family follow orders so easily? Rebekah practically saluted me when I told her you had called a family meeting."

He turned to me and pressed his lips against each other in a way that revealed a dimple in his left cheek.

"The family knows that protecting you is the most important thing we'll ever do. None of us take your safety and well-being lightly. When I make a request, because I am an Angel I have certain powers over my half-breed relatives."

"Isn't that like, most of the world?"

He chuckled. "Yes."

Was I allowed to ask? I desperately wanted to know what he could do. I gulped down an awkward swallow and peered up at him bashfully. "What powers do you have . . . exactly?"

Jonah took a step toward me, which forced me to take a step back until my back pressed against the wall. He leaned toward me.

"Although I have lost many of my celestial powers, there are still many abilities I retained after I turned from grace. My abilities to connect with the one I protect have remained intact. I can also hold authority over any human with Angelic blood in their veins; any Nephilim. They are submissive to my voice for the most part, but it depends on how diluted they are. I have no authority over you, but I have varying degrees of influence over almost everyone else."

"But, I've seen you move so fast and you seem so strong."

"It's true, there are some physical attributes that have been preserved as well. I can move very fast, as you've seen, and I *am* very strong. More importantly," he paused as his gaze meandered down my body. "Has Rebekah told you of how I became a part of this family?"

"Yes, they adopted you as a baby." He's going to explain how he shrank from an adult to a baby? Now, this was something I *had* to hear.

"That's right. I have the ability to change my appearance." He paused uncomfortably.

What could be so bad about being able to change your appearance? I had always dreamed about being taller. I had always wanted curly hair.

"As a Watcher, morphing is something that is vital to the success of the protection of the Pure Bloods we're assigned to. We are able to roam incognito of our preferred appearance, in order to gain access to the ones who are a threat. Unfortunately, this is one of the Angelic attributes that the Dark Ones desire the most. They have bred for centuries to strengthen this aspect in their offspring. Some have become very good at it, but none that

I know of can completely change their appearance, only mask it or throw it."

"You mean you can completely change the way you look? Like turn into a tree or a dog?" Part of me was laughing inside, but part of me was terrified that the gorgeous Jonah I loved was really a dark and horrific beast.

"I guess if you think of it that way, yes, but that's not something I've ever really done. Other than becoming an infant to experience life from the beginning and growing myself up over the years, I have only ever copied existing human appearances, or morphed into shadows."

The thought of his Angelic appearance plagued me. Looks tend to be categorized as a shallow subject, but they're still important. No matter how kind and virtuous someone is, if they looked like the elephant man, it would be hard to love all of them, wouldn't it? "What do you really look like, Jonah?" I felt ashamed for asking. I was in love with him. I should love *all* of him, no matter what he looked like, but I couldn't keep my curiosity at bay.

"What I *really* look like? I don't understand. I'm standing right in front of you."

"No. What I mean is . . . is this your morphed appearance or your natural appearance? Humans imagine Angels as beautiful beings of light. We imagine demons as dark, hideous monsters. I know you were once a beautiful Angel, but did anything happen to you when you fell? What do you *really* look like, Jonah?"

He ran his fingers through his hair as he shuffled back and let out a sigh. "What you see in front of you was the form that was chosen for me when I was created. I am in my original state, only my wings are missing."

With a distant focus, he grabbed a strand of my hair that had fallen out of the clip and tucked it behind my ear.

"We have a lot of work ahead of us, Anna. We will know each other our entire lives. You will have decades of time to discover these things about me. Right now, we need to focus on your training. It must begin right away. I promise to tell you everything I can, so you won't feel like you're left in the dark. I know how that frustrates you. But for now, let's concentrate on you. The next few weeks will be very strange. Please, try to trust me."

I raised my hand to touch the side of his face, consciously keeping the energy of his touch locked inside myself. Electricity jolted through my arm as I rested my hand on his cheek. I pulled his face close to mine.

"I trust you. Completely," I whispered.

He brought his hand up and rested it on top of mine and gave it a few pats. "We have to figure this out. Are you controlling it now, not sending it back to me?"

I nodded.

The corner of his mouth crept up into a half-smile. "Send me just a little," he asked.

My heart pounded at his touch. I closed my eyes and imagined a thread of energy passing between my hand and his cheek. His face smiled under my palm.

"Amazing," he whispered.

"You realize this is all freaking me out, right? I feel like I'm losing control over everything. My life, my body, my mind . . ."

His eyes turned soft. He wrapped his arms around me and pulled me close, pressing his body against mine. A warm flood of energy enveloped me, calming every cell in my body. He was attempting to comfort me, but something felt strangely familiar about our embrace. This was the first time he had held me in this sort of soft, warm hug, but I had felt this before. My heart pounded harder. My eyes flung open. This was the same embrace my spirit had felt three times now.

I pulled back and looked at him, astonished. "Uh," I knew what I wanted to say, but how could I phrase this feeling, this invisible force flowing through me? "Have you . . ."

"What is it, Anna?" he asked fervently.

"I've felt this before."

He twisted his head slightly and gave me an inquisitive look. "Felt what before, exactly?"

I took a step back, breaking our embrace and motioned my hands around his body. "This! You! Except you weren't near me and we weren't touching!"

His lips twisted adorably to the side as one eyebrow lifted. A slow smile spread across his face. "You could feel me?"

My face tensed. "Something else you were doing to me that I didn't know about?"

He chuckled. "I had no idea you could feel me."

I put my hands impatiently on my hips. "Feel you, dream of you, bring your feathers back from my dream! Yes! All of the above!"

"You have my feathers?" He looked anxious. "Anna, where are they? Do you have them here, in the house?"

"I have them right here," I admitted sheepishly. The day I snatched them off of his wing, I gently wrapped a green, satin ribbon around them and held them in the waistband of my pants. I couldn't bear to part with them. Having them so close to me, touching my skin, felt like I carried a piece of home around with me.

I pulled them out and handed them over. "So they *are* yours?"

He took them, gently examined them, then tucked them in his back pocket. "Yes. The night I found you in your dream was the night I established my link to you. You chose a strange place to meet. How long were you alone before I found you?"

"It felt like I was in the cold for days. Wait, the dream was *my* idea?"

"Yes it was, and it took me hours to find you after you began the dream. It appears you've had a lot of contact with the otherworld, to be able to protect yourself for that long."

I nodded.

"I am able to morph my appearance in the unconscious as well as physical worlds, but that night I chose to come to you as my true self. You just asked me what I looked like in my natural state. Do you remember that from your dream?"

"I remember the velvet softness that enveloped me."

"My wings."

"I remember the warmth that filled me."

"My spirit."

"And I remember your green eyes, but I don't remember what you looked like." I hung my head, so sad that I couldn't recall his angelic appearance.

"There will be time for that," he said, as he stroked my hair. "Anna, bringing something back from an unconscious encounter is something I didn't even know was possible. And the experience you say you just felt, that was my spirit connecting with yours. None of the Pure Bloods I've protected before have had the power to give back to me, only to receive. You're indeed a unique creature that has been given many special Gifts, most of which I don't fully understand yet."

"So, we're linked now?"

He shuffled forward and took my hand. "While on Earth, yes, but I'm not human, Anna. Even though I have this human body, I'm still a celestial being and thus have a celestial soul. My being will go on forever, as will yours, but in a different celestial plane. We will know each other in this lifetime, but not the next. Heaven is the final dwelling for humans who have been saved; hell is the final dwelling for those who have not. As for me, I am Fallen. I am here now, but I do not know what will become of my soul; if it will end up in heaven or the Tartarus, or worse, somewhere else entirely."

"You really don't know where you'll end up?"

"Because of my unique situation, no. But I do know that even after I decided to stay on Earth rather than return to heaven I was not stripped of most of my powers, which has puzzled me for centuries. One of the most effective skills is to be able to connect with the Pure soul. It's what I was created for. It's what I was sent to Earth for. The only other human soul I've ever been able to connect with was the human I was originally sent to Earth to protect. My assignment protecting him was successful in most part because of my connection to his soul. My bond with you, however, is different. The extent of our connection is quickly growing past the link that I had with him. This is one of the things we need to work on."

"Goethe," I said.

"Yes, the connection I have so easily made with your soul makes perfect sense. You're his blood relative. These past few days, I've been thinking a lot about that. My turning from heaven has enabled me to guard generations of Pure Bloods. It seems that my protective abilities have come full-circle, now that I am protecting a direct descendant of Goethe."

Voices carried up the stairs and I ducked around him and started down the hall. "Everyone's probably waiting for us. We should go."

Chαρτξr 26

When we entered the library, Isaac, Rebekah and Beth were standing at a round stone pedestal table with a large leather-bound book in the center of it.

Jonah guided me into the room with his hand on the small of my back. I was nervous knowing that the family could see him touching me in this way. Our intimacy, not even an hour old, was only known between us. Would they be upset if they found out we'd kissed? Would Jonah disappear into the Tartarus because he was getting involved with me? These were answers I needed. Quickly.

Isaac spoke first. "Jonah, is everything okay? You know you have our support, no matter what it is."

"Thank you for coming so quickly. Please, sit," Jonah said, with an authoritative tone. The family sat on command as Jonah continued. "Anna and I have discovered some interesting things today. This has also been a whirlwind of change for her. We need to fill her in on everything we can, to get her up to speed. She needs to start training."

"Training, already?" Rebekah said, worriedly.

Jonah nodded and smiled at me. "I've never experienced anyone like her. Our connection is the strongest physical force I've known here on Earth. She appears to be absorbing some of my celestial powers. She's been able to harness some of my energy. This is something I cannot even do."

I raised my hand and peered around the circle meekly.

"Anna, dear, you don't need to raise your hand. Please speak what's on your mind."

"Um. What's training?"

Beth scooted her chair up to the table and spoke with enthusiasm. "Jonah's been working with us for years, discovering

Cris L. P. Olsen

what our Gifts are and helping us develop them. He's taught us everything he knows about the Nephilim, the Dark Ones and the Light Ones." She patted the aged leather book in front of her gently. "All of his research and first-hand experiences with people who have different Gifts or powers are in this journal. He's also trained us how to recognize the ones who mean to harm us and how to escape them when being pursued. When we escaped from the Hunter and the bloodhound at Seaport Village . . . yeah, I didn't always know how to drive like that," she giggled as her cheeks blushed. "You should have seen me the first time I ditched a car. I was a blubbering wreck. If Jonah hadn't trained me, we would have been dog food a few days ago."

Jonah sat tall in his chair. "I think it's most important that we discuss the issue of our Gifts first. It is crucial that Anna understand where these Gifts come from and how they're used. I believe she has many Gifts and I think it will be easier for her to accept what is happening to her if she understands that these Gifts are given for a purpose and not randomly."

Beth reached out and pulled the journal toward her. She thumbed through it and found a page with gold lettering on the top. She pushed the book toward me. "Read this."

I bowed my head to read the page in front of me.

> Now to each soul, a gift is given for the common good. To one there is given a message of wisdom, to another a message of knowledge, to another faith, to another the gift of healing, to another miraculous powers, to another prophecy, to another distinguishing between spirits, to another speaking in different kinds of tongues and to still another the interpretation of tongues. All these are given from the Spirit, and He distributes them as He determines.
>
> —1 Corinthians 12:7-11

I raised my head. "So we're all given some sort of Gift?" They nodded in unison. "Who gives us these Gifts?"

"The Holy Spirit," Jonah said, with esteem. "Most people don't know that they've been given such a powerful bestowal. They don't know what their Gift is, or how to use it, or that they have the ability to strengthen it. Unfortunately, most Gifts lie dormant and untapped in each human. They can only be strengthened when a soul seeks out the Truth."

"So, that's what you meant when you said that you've been *working* with everyone?"

Jonah reached out and slid the journal toward himself. "Yes. I've been close to Isaac, Rebekah and Beth for so many years, that I have been able to determine what their Gifts are. We've worked diligently on enhancing them."

I spoke tentatively. "What are their Gifts, if you don't mind me asking? Is that a silly question?"

Rebekah reached over and rested her hand on mine. "That's exactly the right question, Anna. There's nothing we will hide from you. You need to know everything we know. You will be part of this family for a very long time. We need to have complete trust in each other."

Isaac nodded and spoke. "Rebekah's Gift is that of patience, compassion and generosity. Her job suits her very well. She's able to use her Gifts for the greater good. Being a social worker is difficult and often times saddening, but Rebekah has a way about her that comforts and soothes. She is very successful in bringing families back together after tragedy or abuse.

Beth's Gift is that of intuition. She can sense the true nature of one's soul. That's the reason she was drawn to you, Anna. She has told me that you have the purest soul she's ever come across. Now we know why."

As soon as Isaac was finished, Jonah stood, walked behind him and patted him proudly on his shoulders.

"Isaac has the ingenious Gift of persuasion. He is able to use his position as an attorney to mediate the differences between people and their situations to find the outcome that best suits everyone. He has brought hundreds of people back together who were having legal battles among their families or businesses, and he's negotiated hundreds of lawsuits toward peace instead of destruction. He has saved many lives he doesn't even know about. All the while, working free of charge."

"He saves lives? How could someone talk someone else out of death?"

Jonah gave Isaac's shoulders a firm squeeze. "Because Isaac is so successful in his negotiations, many people's lives have become better. They are living in peace with each other. He has been able to persuade people to help one another. People who once lived in poverty, in abusive relationships, or despair have been assisted by others who discovered their own generosity and compassion by helping their neighbor. Those who would have otherwise perished from these circumstances have found peace and a better way of life because of the generosity and compassion given by others. Isaac has negotiated many of these outcomes."

Jonah looked down at Isaac. "Surely, father, you know how many lives you've saved."

He looked over to Rebekah. "Mother, you have also saved many. You navigate your Gifts well."

Jonah walked over to Beth and ruffled her hair. "Beth, here, has given us the greatest Gift of all." He looked straight at me. "You, Anna."

Pride was tangible in the room as they were all receiving compliments on their hard work for the greater good. I felt small and insignificant, sitting next to these people who had done so much for others. What had I ever done for anyone?

I dipped my chin down and stared at the table, ashamed at my own self-pity. I had been so consumed in my own thoughts of *why me*, I hadn't thought of the millions of others in the world who have far less than I do, who are desperate, hungry, hopeless. Compared to them, I lived like a queen.

Jonah crouched next to me. "Anna, you have the ability to give the world what it needs most – more Pure Bloods."

My head shot up and I looked sternly at him. "That's not a Gift! That's reproduction! I'm just supposed to have tons of babies! With who? Beth told me you've only met seven Pure Bloods in your entire life!"

Rebekah rose from her chair. She stood at my other side and put her hand on my shoulder. "Anna, darling, you're not here to breed. Jonah was simply stating that you have the ability to give pure life and what a fantastic Gift that is."

I felt deflated. That wasn't a spiritual Gift, it was a physical one. That had nothing to do with character; it had to do with bloodline.

The day was almost gone and I hadn't done any homework. I was completely unprepared for class tomorrow. I scooted back from the table and silently climbed the stairs to my room.

I'd acted childish, just leaving without saying anything. I felt so cheated and upset, that my purpose was to procreate.

I spent the rest of the evening in my room, studying.

After a few hours, I couldn't concentrate on calculus anymore. No one had bothered me, except when Rebekah brought me a sandwich for dinner. I took my time soaking in a hot bath and was having a hard time finding my pajamas, so I organized the clothes in my new dresser drawers.

I'd ignored my Giants research completely. Too much of it reminded me of what was happening in my own life. How was I going to write this paper objectively, if my own future was tied to everything I uncovered?

I slumped down on the floor next to the bed.

My future. There was a big question mark looming over it. The thought of birthing a new line of Pure Bloods turned my stomach. I'd always wanted children, but with a husband that I loved, not as the matriarch of a new bloodline of Pure humans. And why was that the only Gift Jonah had mentioned? I had other Gifts! I could feel his energy! I could send it back to him!

Tears ran down my cheeks as I started sobbing, utterly overwhelmed. Jonah tapped on the door.

"Yeah," I squeeked.

"Oh, Anna," he said, as sat next to me on the floor and kissed the top of my head. "This has been so much in such little time."

He pulled his sleeves down so they covered his hands and nudged his finger under my chin to lift my face up. "You need some time to digest these changes and live a few normal days before beginning your training. Beth or I will accompany you to each of your classes this week. Just try to concentrate on school, and we'll revisit this again when you're ready."

When I'm ready? Try never!

Jonah used his shirt to dab the tears streaming down my face. He reached down, picked me up off the floor and set me gently on the bed.

It unsettled me each time he touched me. Not because of the electricity that lay behind the thin layer of his clothes, but because of how completely safe I felt in his arms. By his own admission he was struggling, trying to deny the attraction he had to me, while I was completely consumed with him. It was so clear. Whatever this connection was that we had, it had permeated every facet of my soul.

He lay me down on the bed and pulled his arms out from under me.

I grasped his shirt. "Please stay," I whispered.

Without a second thought, he reached over to the nightstand and turned out the light as he pulled the covers over me, then he lay on top of the covers next to me.

"Is this okay?" I whispered into the darkness. "I mean, having you near makes me feel safe."

He rolled onto his side and rested his arm over me. He stroked my hair, carefully avoiding the skin on my face.

"I'll always be here for you, Anna. I'll always give you what you need. You've had a very full day. Just sleep now."

Mentally exhausted, I closed my eyes. With him near, sleep found me within minutes.

Chapτξr 27

A bright moon shone in through sheer curtains, casting a blue glow across Jonah's sleeping face. His beauty stunned me. His square jaw seemed powerful, even in sleep. His lush, black eyelashes twitched. He was not only sleeping, but dreaming as well. How could he be so human and so divine at the same time?

A single, shiny lock of his wavy, brown hair rested on his forehead. I rolled onto my side to face him. Carefully, I raised my hand and swept the curl from his face. My finger brushed across his cheek, surging a white-hot, electric trail down my arm. I pulled my hand away quickly.

Inhaling a deep breath, his eyes opened slowly. He'd caught me. I was awake and staring at his beautiful face.

He rolled onto his side and propped his head up with his arm. Pulling his sleeve down to cover his hand, he rubbed the back of his finger down my cheek.

His touch was so tender. My heart swelled with an overwhelming urge to be even closer to him. I grasped his strong forearm gingerly and pulled the shirt up to his wrist, exposing his hand.

He shook his head.

I nodded.

An anxious expression befell his face, as he slowly ran the back of his bare finger down my cheek again. His fingertip traced my jaw line before he rested his hand on my collarbone.

I controlled a gasp as my heart raced at his touch. His energy hummed through me, flowing through every muscle and vein.

Allowing only a fraction of what was pulsing into me to remain throughout my body, I isolated the excess and pushed it down into my legs. The farther I could get it from my lungs, the easier it was to breathe. My breath slowed as I fought to gain control of this new power.

We lay motionless, staring at each other. I concentrated on his eyes, quickly losing myself in his gaze, remembering in silence his commanding, yet compassionate voice the night before. I hadn't had time to piece together all of the details from the conversation at the stone table, or attempt to figure it out. I stormed out, perturbed at my lack of Gifts, my obvious "purpose" infuriating me. I'd cut off any explanation before it had a chance to be heard.

Blunt statements stabbed at my memory. I was their greatest Gift. I had the power to create more Pure Bloods. Frustration welled up within me as I lay, thinking of the future breeding I would be urged to take part in.

Then something Jonah had said pierced through the frustration. He said he thought I had more than one Gift. How could I have more than one Gift if my Gift wasn't really a Gift at all, but a biological rarity? Did he think . . . could it be possible that maybe I wasn't just created to breed?

He had the confidence in me that I lacked. He thought I had something more. Was feeling his power a Gift or a fluke? How was I able to send the ripples into the water? Why could I send the jolt back to him so that he could feel it, too? By his own admission, no other Pure Blood had been able to feel what I feel – his touch amplified by a thousand. What could possibly lie ahead of me, where I would need that sort of power?

We were locked in a wondrous gaze. A hint of a smile caressed Jonah's lips.

Positive that my tortured thoughts showed on my face, I nuzzled into his shoulder to hide. His sweet, fresh scent enveloped me as my forehead rested on his shoulder. I longed to press my lips against the warmth of his flesh.

The springs in the mattress wavered beneath us as he brought his hand to my face and brushed aside a few stray hairs that had wound themselves around my throat. He slipped his fingers around to the back of my neck. I became breathless.

"This energy you feel, it is a good and unprecedented Gift, Anna. You should be proud that it has been given to you. I am."

I looked at his angelic face and touched my hand to his cheek. "How can something so evil come from something so good?" I whispered. The thought of Angel and human DNA mixing to create such monsters frightened me.

"Not all Nephilim are evil, Anna. The Light Ones are very virtuous and honorable."

"Light Ones?"

"There are just as many good Nephilim as there are evil ones. They're called "Light Ones." Most people live in between these vast opposites. They struggle between balancing the good and evil inside them. The Light Ones and Dark Ones are the exceptions . . . the anomalies."

"How can such evil and such good exist in the same world?"

Jonah curled his arm under his head. He gazed down on me affectionately. "Good comes from above," he said, as he caressed my cheek. A tingle shot down my neck. "In the beginning, there was no sin in the world; until the fall of man. You know the story of Adam and Eve, right?"

"Of course, doesn't everyone?"

Jonah chuckled. "Unfortunately, not. After Adam and Eve let sin into the world, it penetrated everything, including the earth. Earthquakes, hurricanes, disease, these are all a result of sin. The root of all of this comes from below. Lucifer fell before the Earth was created. He has been here from Day One. His goal is to cause chaos and win souls, by keeping people disillusioned from the only way to heaven: redemption. And the only way to redemption is by using our free will to choose God. Each soul must make the choice to let Him in.

Lucifer studies us. His cunning is subtle. His evil can invade our minds in the simplest of ways. Most are unaware of his presence. When he gets desperate, he sends his demons after us to keep us separated from God. This is the epic battle of good versus evil. It's this very battle that will damn souls to hell or ascend them to heaven on Judgment day.

As the Nephilim grew in numbers and spread over the face of the earth, they found that they had the ability to strengthen certain powers through careful breeding. This breeding began the Dark and Light societies."

Bits and pieces of stories I had heard over the years came rushing together. Even though this was new information, somehow, it all made sense.

I looked down at Jonah's chest, averting my gaze from his. "I'm sorry I ran out on the family meeting you gathered yesterday. I was so upset at my . . . purpose that I didn't stick around to hear you out. It sounded like you were about to explain all of this. I'm sorry."

Reaching out, he wound a strand of my hair around his finger. His lips parted, caressing my face with his sweet scent. His stare was focused on my mouth as he slowly inched closer.

No. I couldn't let him do this. I put my fingers gently over his lips. "Won't you end up in the Tartarus? None of this is worth *that.*"

He leaned back and sighed. "I'm not really sure. I'm the only Fallen Angel I know of who hasn't ended up there, but I don't think falling in love warrants a life sentence. All of the Fallen ones who are there, have fathered Nephilim children. That's something I will never do."

"What do you mean by . . ." he had just said something that I was intensely curious about, but I just couldn't ask.

"Anna, please don't ever hesitate to ask me anything. Your life is changing so drastically. I want to do everything in my power to help you through it."

I looked back up at him. "I can ask you anything?"

He ran his hand from my temple to my chin. "Of course."

I took a deep breath. If I didn't ask now I would regret it forever. "What did you mean when you just said, 'falling in love won't warrant a sentence there'?"

His eyebrows pulled together. His face turned businesslike. "That's a good question, one that deserves an answer." He sighed and exhaled loudly, as if pondering the question in his head, searching for just the right words. "I've spent centuries living next to humans. I've grown to love them very much. I've had many friends I've cared about so deeply that I would have given my life for them. Now I have a family that I would do the same for. I'm still here."

My face dropped without my consent. My deepest hope was that he was talking about loving me, but the love he spoke of was a generalized love for humanity. His answer was virtuous and compassionate. I was proud to know someone as kind as him. It was selfish of me for wanting him for myself.

I was sure my embarrassment was apparent.

The corner of Jonah's mouth turned up and he did that insanely cute thing with his eyebrows. "Anna, you're unlike any human I've ever known. You're pure, and good, and broken, and all I want to do is put you back together. I want to strengthen you. Build you up. Teach you to protect yourself and to seek the right path to walk. Protect you so you can live the life that's meant for you."

"Oh," I whispered. I tried to hide it, but I knew disappointment filled my voice. I fiddled with the edge of the blanket.

His face gently contorted into a million different expressions as we lay there, facing each other in silence. What could possibly be warring inside him at this moment for him to look so conflicted?

He let out a large sigh. His voice was soft and tentative as he spoke to me. "I want to do all of that at your side, Anna – as your partner – as your love."

My heart raced as his words sunk in. Did he just throw centuries of denying himself the one thing he wants the most, out the window – for me? I stared into his clear, emerald eyes in awe.

"I'm in love with you, Anna. The past few months have been some of the hardest of my life, trying to deny it. In almost two hundred and fifty years here on Earth, I've never felt this way before. I've never allowed myself to be open to romantic love because of the potential consequences, but I'm so incredibly drawn to you, I can't hide the love I feel for you."

"Past few months? I've only known you three weeks!"

He reached out and caressed my face, his energy pulsing into my cheek so pure and so vital, that I flinched. "Beth noticed your pure soul the very first day at orientation, before classes even started. She was drawn to you from across campus and followed her intuition. It led her straight to you. We suspected you might be a Pure Blood from that very day, but we needed to let things happen naturally. We didn't want to invade your life, just keep you safe.

Your friendship with Beth has blossomed into something beautiful and for that I will be eternally grateful. I've been watching you since the very first day Beth told us about you."

"You've been watching me for two months?" My voice cracked on the last word. How many times was I going to feel invaded by this family – by Jonah himself?

The web of electricity spinning its way into my face ceased. Softly, he took my hand and placed it over his heart. "The day we met in the library, I smelled the blood from the cut on your finger, confirming to me that you were Pure. The scent of blood from a Pure human is the sweetest smelling thing on Earth to an Angel. I knew at that moment, you would be in my life forever."

Warm waves of heat radiated out from his chest. Under my hand, his heart leapt into a full gallop. I had never seen him nervous before.

He breathed in a large gulp of air before continuing. "It took all of my willpower to contain myself and not kiss you right there in the stacks. The reaction I had to you confused me so much that I almost left, fearing I might have finally succumbed to the fate of the rest of the Fallen Angels."

His eyes closed, as a pained expression crinkled his brow. "It had been explained to me that the draw to the women who eventually became the Fallen Angels mates was so powerful, that any punishment would be worth it to them, for just one moment with their love. The Angels who were sent as Watchers that fell, fell out of pure love. They loved their mate so intensely that they could not restrain themselves. Each time I'm near you, I feel the same way. Maintaining control around you is next to impossible."

When Jonah's eyes opened, clear, luminous flecks sparkled in them, like diamonds gleaming in the moonlight.

"It took a few weeks of intense soul searching to reach the decision to stay. I decided to protect you forever, no matter what my feelings for you might be. I decided that protecting you was more important than anything else."

He caressed my face again, tracing the lines of my nose and lips. "I can understand now, how the other Angels fell so easily. Being near you brings out feelings I never dared to believe I could have. The intensity of the love I feel for you consumes me. It also brings with it feelings of jealousy, selfishness and fierce protection. I have never wanted anything for myself as much as I want you. If I end up in the Tartarus, it will be worth it to be near you, to protect you, to love you."

He cupped my chin in his hand and tilted it up. His exhilarating power wound through my jaw and down my throat. He exhaled, filling the air around my face with his sweet scent, then his lips were on mine. This kiss was unlike the one before. Our first kiss in the pool was unexpected, tense and filled with anxiety. This kiss was soft, tender. I moved my hand from his chest and slid it to the back of his neck. I let a thread of energy escape my fingers and flow down his spine. His body shivered. I brought a thin layer of energy to my mouth and let it flow through my lips into his. His lips curled into a smile as he let out a small chuckle. His arm wrapped around my shoulders as he pressed me against him tighter.

I imagined a million points of light filling my breath and I breathed into his open mouth. He inhaled deeply and moaned. His kiss deepened as he twisted his fingers in my hair and held my face in both of his hands. My cheeks surged with the heat and power of his touch.

He gently pulled away, then pecked his lips on my skin, each time giving me a tingle of power. He worked his way down my jaw, and rested his cheek in the cove of my neck. His current thrummed directly into my carotid artery and pulsed into my bloodstream.

In only a few minutes, I was breathless. I either needed to send the energy back to him or ask him to move, but I couldn't imagine asking him to move, even an inch away from me. I put my hand on his cheek and slowly began to release the energy I had trapped in my muscles. He gasped. The flow began small, then grew, as I shared with him the power he sent to me with his mere touch. His muscles tensed. Now, it was his turn to try to control this power.

"Slow, deep, breaths," I whispered into his ear. His eyes closed as he forced slow breaths. At last the circuit was complete, and I released the last of the current. As it flowed through us, our souls bonded together. He was my other half and I, his.

Chαpτξr 28

We lay like that until the sun peeked through the curtains, neither of us wanting to break our embrace. Beth stirred in her room next door. It was time to start the day.

"You have myth and calculus class today?" Jonah asked, his voice muffled as it nuzzled in my neck.

"M-hm," I sighed.

He sat back. "I will go with you to your classes today. I want to scope out the campus for any possible dangers before letting you and Beth attend by yourselves."

I nodded lightly.

He kissed my forehead. In a flash, he was gone, leaving behind a trail of his sweet scent.

Seconds later Beth skipped through the door in her pj's. "Ready for Prof. D's myth class? The giant better not call us down again. He needs to pick on someone his own size!"

"Jonah's going with us today," I said, stretching.

Beth leapt on the bed and bounced up and down. "Oh, goody! My best friend and my brother make a good Bethie sandwich!"

I glowered at her. "How much sleep did you get last night? You've got far too much spunk for seven a.m.!"

"IIIIII'm a morning person," she snickered. "Breakfast will be in thirty," she said, as she bounded out of the room.

I ran my hand over the blanket where Jonah had just been lying. It was still warm. I rolled over onto his pillow, feeling his lingering warmth against my face and inhaled the mixture of jasmine, herbs and Angel – a scent that was uniquely him.

"Jonah loves me," I whispered to myself into the pillow. "An *Angel* loves me."

I felt the same, but I hadn't been able to bring myself to say it back to him. It seemed too soon. Society scoffs at lovers that divulge the "three little words" prematurely. What was premature, though? A week, a month, a year? Jumping in with both feet is what fools do. Smart people wait, right? Wait for what, though? For the lover to cheat? To find out some deep, dark secret or lie that would change everything?

I couldn't help but make comparisons to Seth. He was the only other person who I had been close with in a romantic way. I had always doubted him. He said words, but never backed them with actions. He told me he loved me, but always flirted with other girls. He helped me when my parents died, but wanted payment in return. The more I thought about it, the more my memories of Seth turned dark. He was a Nephilim; considering his height, maybe even a second or third generation Nephilim. The darkness of his words and actions began to make sense. Was he assigned to infiltrate . . . *me*?

Jonah's stark contrast to Seth's evil stood out like a white light in my mind. He was good. I knew his secret. I knew I loved him. I was angry with myself for letting society control my actions. I would tell him I loved him. Soon.

A quick shower, followed by a frenzy of hair and makeup, and I would just make it to breakfast on time. I tugged on my favorite tattered men's button-fly jeans and paired them with a snug white T-shirt that said "Angel" across the bust in silver glitter. I looked at myself in the mirror and giggled.

"How ironic," I said, to my reflection.

Feeling good about my appearance for the first time in days, I bounded down the stairs and found Rebekah spooning fresh blueberries into gorgeous, fluffy crepes. A breakfast casserole sat on the island, bubbling and sizzling as the eggs, sausage and cheese continued to cook in the pan.

"It smells wonderful in here! Are you *sure* you're not a gourmet chef?"

Rebekah scooped a crepe onto a plate and pushed it toward me as she chuckled in response. "Beth told me you're lactose intolerant, so I've stocked the fridge with organic soymilk and all sorts of dairy-free products for you. The casserole is made with soy cheese. I tasted it and it's really not that bad."

"Not that bad. That's a nice way of saying it's totally disgusting, isn't it?" I laughed.

She smirked, and shook her head as a dainty snort slipped out of her nose. Her thoughtfulness was astounding. She cared for me enough to take the time to find out about lactose intolerance and went shopping just for me. I gave her a morning hug just as Jonah floated into the kitchen.

Our embrace loosened as my eyes followed after him. He was stunning. The first time I saw him, he was wearing khakis, a Polo shirt and a name tag; normal library volunteer wear. Every time after that, I'd only seen him in a tank top and board shorts. He looked totally different, dressed in regular clothes. His dark, snug jeans were worn and frayed and the black T-shirt he wore stretched tight across his chest and biceps.

Rebekah strode toward the stove to tend to the crepes, leaving me motionless, staring after Jonah. As he passed the window, the sun coming in caught his clear, emerald eyes. A flash of green sparkle filled the room for an instant. He peered at me from under his lush eyelashes. His mouth crept up into a sly smile, only meant for me to see. He ran his fingers through his damp hair and walked by me, discreetly brushing his free hand over my wrist as he passed.

Isaac's voice entered the room before I saw him. "Class today, kids?"

Jonah turned coolly to face him. His smile turned innocent. "Myth 101 and calculus today, right, Anna?"

I had just shoved a huge bite of crepe into my mouth. My hand flew up to cover my lips. I tried to say "yep" but it came out as "blup."

Isaac chuckled.

I nodded.

"I'll be accompanying Anna to her classes this week. I need to check things out before I feel comfortable letting her and Beth roam campus without a chaperone."

Beth pranced into the kitchen and squealed. "Oooh, crepes! Yummy!"

I lowered my head and shook it back and forth. "Beth, I'm gonna start calling you bubbles."

She shot me a confused look. "Bubbles?"

"Yeah, you're always so bubbly! You know, it's the perfect disguise too. No one would ever guess you're the intuitive soul reader that you are. Your façade is much too sunny for such a deep Gift!"

"I've never thought of that before," Jonah said, with surprise. "All this time we've been working on Beth's Gift and I never thought of trying to cloak her talent under a façade to throw people off. You might be onto something there, Anna!"

Beth gushed. "You know, Anna might have an intuition Gift, too! She can put pieces together we never even knew were there."

Jonah and Beth went back and forth, naming some of the talents they thought might be hidden within me, as if I weren't there.

But Beth was wrong. I might be able to put things together, but when it came to myself, I felt completely lost as to what my role would be in this new life.

Beth looked at her watch. "Ooh, we better get going, or we'll be late for class!"

I looked at her straight on. "Uh, Beth, how are we getting to school? You killed your car, remember? By the way, where's mine?"

They all looked at each other in silence.

Isaac spoke first. "Your car is in a locked container in a shipyard in Long Beach. We couldn't take the chance of the bloodhound finding it, and gaining access to a physical piece with your scent on it. Long Beach is far enough away that they shouldn't be able to track it there."

"Wait. If my scent is in my car, wouldn't it be in my house, too? What if they figure out where I lived? Rebekah said that's a real possibility since they were most likely already watching me."

Isaac looked apologetically at me. "Movers came and packed your household belongings the first night you were here. We have already had the carpet switched out and the entire house repainted. The paint is water based, so it covers up the scent well. We had a water truck clean the roads and sidewalk between your house and the school, so the path of your scent should be cleansed from there, as well. If the Hunter did trace you to your previous address, he would find nothing that would help him track you. It would be a dead end. As for a car, we will go this weekend to purchase a new one for you and Beth to share. Until then, you can use my car."

Jonah's deep voice startled me. "Actually, I will take them in my car this week. I'm tailing them, remember?"

Beth let out a peal of giggles. "Yay! We get to ride in the Morgan!"

"The Morgan? You mean that vintage thing sitting in the garage? It actually runs?"

Beth nodded vigorously and urged me to finish breakfast quickly. My plate not yet cleared, she yanked me outside just as Jonah was pulling the Morgan out of the garage. Beth got in first and slid into the backseat, quickly pulling the seat back in place, forcing me to sit in the front. We rolled down the steep driveway as the car growled under Jonah's control. He slipped his sunglasses on, flashed me a brilliant white smile and we were off.

I felt a world away as I breathed in the smell of the old leather and hint of grease from the car's mechanical upkeep. I gazed around, wondering how long Jonah had owned it. I imagined an entire other lifetime that he might have lived in this car.

I closed my eyes. Images of women in ornate vintage gowns complete with elbow-length gloves and heeled boots that buttoned up beyond the ankle played out in my head. I envisioned Jonah in a three-piece suit with cufflinks and a tophat. I sighed, longing to be part of his past that I had never known.

With the top snapped off, there was no barrier between us and the beautiful morning sky and gentle breeze ran it's fingers through my hair. My worries melted away as we drove. Jonah's scent found its way to me. I breathed it in deeply, letting it comfort and excite me. His scent meant he was near; having him near felt like I was home.

He reached over the gearshift and unexpectedly rested his hand on mine. I jumped as his spark entered my hand and made its way through my body. I let the feeling pulse through me for a moment before pushing it down into my legs, which would give us a few minutes of contact before I would have to pull away.

A giggle came from the back seat. I turned and shot Beth a self-conscious glance. No one knew about Jonah's professed love for me. No one knew we had kissed. Wasn't it supposed to be a secret? Wasn't romance between us forbidden?

Beth bit her lip to hide a huge smile as she gave me an enthusiastic nod. Is this what she had been hoping for? Was this the reason for her little speech on the beach stairs the first day I had visited their home? She wanted what was best for Jonah, but disagreed with her parents about what that was. I could understand now, why she thought Jonah had been denying what was "good for him," when "good for him" could have so many consequences. Her encouragement made my worries about keeping a distance from Jonah, for the sake of my friendship with her, vanish.

At that moment, thoughts of Cain flashed through my head. I remembered how talking to him made me feel as though I was betraying my feelings for Jonah . . . feelings I knew were there, but had been denying. All those speed bumps were gone now. Jonah loved me. What our future would hold was uncertain. Did this mean he was my boyfriend? The thought sent my heart into a frenzied gallop, intensified by Jonah's energy pulsing into my hand. Boyfriend didn't seem to accurately describe our bond. I couldn't find the right word to connect us. My mind wandered as I searched for a phrase that felt right. The energy of Jonah's hand on mine threaded its way through my veins and was about to overtake me. I couldn't send it back to him, or certainly, we'd end up in an accident. I pulled my hand away and disguised the move as brushing hair out of my face.

The cold emptiness rushed in and my throat let out an uncontrollable sob.

"Anna, are you okay?" He whispered from the driver's seat.

I nodded. A lie. If I let Jonah's touch consume my entire body, emptiness filled me when it ceased. I would have to figure out a way to be close to him and not be devoured by the frigid sadness when he left my side. I resolved to make that my next project.

Chαρτξr 29

We pulled into a private, underground parking lot. "Wow."

Jonah looked at me and flashed a million-dollar smile. "You can get a nice spot, but you have to donate a lot of cash to the school for it. The car *is* a bit obvious. This helps to preserve my anonymity. No one even knows it's here."

As I opened the door and gently pulled the seat forward to let Beth out, I took in the immaculate interior and glossy paint. A car this old should have been in the junk yard decades ago. A lot of time had been put into keeping it so pristine.

"What's with you and this car, anyway?" I asked Jonah.

His eyes lit up. "This is one of the original Morgan four-seater 4/4's ever produced. About seventy years after my first assignment with Goethe, I found another Pure Blood and protected him and his family for two generations. His name was Harry Frederick Stanley Morgan. He founded the British Morgan car company. He gave me this car in nineteen thirty-six, fresh out of the factory where it was made by hand. It has great sentimental value to me."

"Don't get him started on the car," Beth whispered. "He'll have you here all day, looking at engine pieces he's had to recreate to keep the thing running."

I stifled a giggle as I turned to Jonah. "My dad hot-rodded old cars as a hobby. My mom and I were always grateful for the neighbors who would stop by to gawk at them. He would monopolize them for hours in the garage talking about axle this and crank shaft that. His last project was a fire engine red nineteen thirty-five Ford Slantback."

"A thirty-five, really? Those were . . ."

Beth interrupted Jonah mid-sentence. "Okay you two. No car talk in my presence, *capiche*? It's like a foreign language that I don't speak," she said, as she walked ahead of us.

"The girl has a point," I said to Jonah.

He nodded, reluctantly.

Car talk was as boring to girls as flat-iron talk was to boys. I was grateful for Beth stifling the conversation. Car talk also made me long to be back in my old world with my parents.

My life had two parts . . . the one before I met the Gwenaël family and the one after. The two worlds were black and white.

I couldn't imagine my parents being a part of this new life. They were never ones to believe in the supernatural, the real existence of heaven and hell, or even fantasies. They never would have believed any of this.

And here, I believe without question or hesitation. The thought made me wonder what was so different between me and them.

Jonah led the way out of the underground parking garage. As we ascended a staircase, we exited through a side door of a building and found ourselves right in the middle of campus.

"I had no idea UCSD had a secret underground parking lot!"

Jonah leaned down and brushed his lips against my ear. "That's why it's a secret, love." Heat sizzled down my neck into my spine. I shivered.

His gaze meandered down my body to my hand, where he laced his fingers through mine. My body tensed. I reacted by giving my hand a small jerk away from his.

The expression on his face made it clear that it had just dawned on him that I may not be ready to manage appropriate control in such a public situation. As he began to pull away, I squeezed his fingers tightly, not letting him loosen his grip. Our eyes met. I nodded and passed him a look of encouragement. His head dipped down, and his mouth pulled to the side, as he tried to conceal a smile while he pulled me along. My hand tingled from his current. I pushed his energy into my legs and fought to maintain a steady heartbeat, but the sight of his beauty made it palpitate uncontrollably. When he ran his fingers through his windblown hair, the sleeve of his T-shirt crept up his arm and revealed his toned bicep. My knees wobbled and I had to pull my fingers from his grip.

Beth caught our exchange and rolled her eyes. "A-hem," she announced loudly to gain our attention. "I guess now is as good a time as any to let you in on something that's becoming *glaringly* obvious to me," she said, sarcastically.

She stepped toward me and wrapped her arm around my neck until her mouth was right next to my ear. "Anna . . ." she whispered, " . . . the longer I know you and the more I'm around you, the more I perceive about you. You have power that I've never sensed in anyone before . . . and it's growing. Your soul is changing with it."

She reached up and grabbed Jonah's shirt, pulling his head close to ours. "You tell me your angelic soul is not like a human soul, brother, but since you met Anna, your soul is changing, too. I can sense a link between you and Anna. The two of you are becoming one."

Jonah stood up straight, concern filling his face.

This seemed an inopportune time for Beth to drop such a heavy load on our minds, with class just about to start, but knowing her, she had probably been dying to say this for days. I can't imagine her being able to hold something like that in for very long. Now that she had seen us "together," she was able to disclose the information freely.

Judging from Jonah's reaction, this was something that he hadn't expected.

He shook his head as if purging the idea from his mind and forced a smile. "Let's go, ladies, you don't want to be late for class."

"That's for sure!" Beth blurted.

She threaded her arm through mine as we hurried along. Jonah lagged behind. A quick look back over my shoulder revealed that he was deep in thought. His reaction worried me.

"C'mon slow poke!" Beth hollered. Within a few amazing strides Jonah caught up to us just as we entered the back doors to the theater-style lecture hall of myth class.

The back of the class always filled up first with the guys who were intimidated by Professor Dhampir. The front was filled with all the girls who thought he was hot. The only seats left were in the middle.

As we fought our way across the isle, Beth coaxed a student to scoot over so we could all sit together. As soon as I sat down between them, a hush rolled over the class. Professor Dhampir had walked in. He was wearing a long-sleeved charcoal, gray button-down shirt that barely fit around his chest. His black slacks almost brushed the floor in the back when he walked. They must be custom made, just for him. Where else do you get pants that tall?

His back was to the class as he shuffled papers over his desk, searching for something. Mumbling to himself, he finally turned around. Without looking up, he brought his papers to the podium and started to speak.

He spoke in a loud tone to himself as if no one was even there. After a long while, he looked up and scanned the class, exuding an annoyed obligation-to-be-there attitude. His eyes passed over his audience not looking at any particular person before he stopped at the three of us. He froze. His voice wavered and the papers he was holding dropped unexpectedly to the floor.

Jonah took my hand and gave it a nervous squeeze. My body tensed and I gave him a curious look. What was going on?

Beth nudged my knee and gestured her chin at Professor Dhampir. I turned my head to find his eyes blazing into Jonah.

A ringing cell phone broke the tension.

"You! Out!" Professor Dhampir growled as he pointed to a boy with curly red hair and freckles. The boy was shaking as he picked up his books and tiptoed over his classmates to escape.

As Professor Dhampir turned back to face the rest of the class, his gaze scanned over us. A look of deep satisfaction filled his face. He turned abruptly to hide his reaction. It took him an uncharacteristically long amount of time to gather himself. When he did, he put a concerted effort into focusing on his podium the rest of class. He lectured intensely, not asking one question, not looking up again. He didn't even notice two girls passing notes and whispering to each other incessantly the entire time. Either that, or he was ignoring them.

When class was dismissed, Beth and I lingered putting things in our bags.

Cris L. P. Olsen

Jonah grabbed my arm. "Let's go. Now. Get Beth." I'd never seen him agitated before. The urgency in his voice frightened me. Jonah practically pulled my arm off as he dragged me out of class. I towed Beth behind me.

"Ouch!" Beth complained as we trained out of class and into the quad.

"What was that all about?" Beth asked in an annoyed tone.

Jonah gave Beth a flabbergasted look. "Haven't you noticed something strange about Professor Dhampir, Beth?"

"Yeah, he's huge and gorgeous and intimidating . . . does that mean something?"

Jonah shoved the back of his hand up to Beth's forehead. "With all the work we've done developing your intuition, you can't tell your myth professor is an NG?"

"What? He is? How can I not see that?"

Jonah tucked his arm into the strap of her backpack and pulled her over to the edge of the grass under the shade of a grove of trees, where students weren't likely to overhear.

I was lost. "Wait, how could you tell that, Jonah?"

"His reaction to you makes sense to me now," Beth stated plainly.

"His reaction, as in, he could tell Jonah was a Fallen Angel just by looking at him?"

Jonah's voice was distressed. "I personally know a New Generation Nephil who can see celestial energy emanations. Luckily, he's a Light One, but this ability is one of the powers the Dark Ones covet. They breed specifically to strengthen this Gift. Until we know more about your professor, I don't want you going anywhere near that class, understood?"

I nodded. Beth squeaked out a tiny "okay." She looked close to tears. "I'm so sorry Jonah, I had no idea. I've never gotten anything from him except a draw to his hotness. How can I not see he's an NG?"

Jonah paused, as if figuring something out in his head. He stared at the grass. "Glamour," he whispered to himself.

The word instantly brought to mind a movie I had watched as a kid, about four girls who were witches. One of their "crafts" was to change their appearance.

"A Glamour? As in covering up who you really are?" I whispered to Jonah.

He nodded. "That's got to be why Beth hasn't been able to sense him. To sustain a Glamour, you must be very powerful . . . and very good at it. It appears he can use his charisma to project an image of himself as well. Beth thinks he's hot . . ." Jonah said, as he rolled his eyes, " . . . for lack of a better word, which is the opposite of what his soul really is. Evil."

A pained look crossed Beth's face. She rubbed at her forehead.

"We should really head home. It's not safe here until I figure out what's going on," Jonah said, formally.

"I missed an entire week of school last week, Jonah. I'm going to fail chemistry if I miss much more. I really have to go to class." Beth rubbed at the back of her neck and stretched it from side to side, as if it were stiff.

"Beth, are you okay?" I asked.

"Yeah, just getting a headache, that's all." She looked pale.

The concern in my heart for my friend overpowered the logic in my head that it was *just* a headache.

"Don't you think you should go home and lie down? Your last headache turned into a nasty flu. Maybe you're sick."

Beth stood motionless and stared at the ground.

A stale breeze tentacled its way around me, bringing with it an icky feeling. I felt queasy. I shifted my shoulders and stretched my back, bending the air around me, as if making sure nothing was touching me. I glanced behind me at the invisible fingers of nothingness that brushed against the back of my neck.

"Something's not right." I looked up at Jonah. He was at my side in an instant, with his hand on the small of my back.

"What is it, Anna?"

"I'm not sure how to explain it, but something's wrong with Beth." I squeezed my eyes closed, hard. The explanation was just within grasping distance, but it eluded me. All I knew was that we needed to get Beth home. "Beth, how do you feel?"

"I'd feel better if everyone would stop asking me how I feel and just let me go to class!"

She was usually so positive, so resilient. I had never seen her act so ugly. Her intuition should be telling her something dark was looming around, but she seemed oblivious to it. Even I could feel it.

"Can you feel that?" I whispered to Jonah.

"Anna?" He peered down at me.

"There's something dark moving around us."

Beth's face turned pale white. Suddenly she was short of breath. "Oh, crap!" Beth whispered. "The Hunter!"

"What? Where!" Jonah's voice was filled with anger as he hissed through his teeth.

Beth outstretched her arm and pointed to the Hunter that found us at Seaport Village. He walked briskly, straight toward Professor Dhampir's office door, his eyes locked on his goal. His dirty blonde dreadlocks burst out under a black motorcycle helmet that he was hastily unbuckling.

"I can feel it too," Beth whispered. "I can feel the darkness. It's coming from him. I've felt it before, but didn't recognize it until you said you felt it too. I can feel Professor Dhampir now. He's teeming with power. It's as if a floodgate just opened. I can feel everyone around me, now."

Beth's knees gave out from under her. Jonah caught her by her backpack. He held her in one arm and wrapped me in the other, enclosing both of us in a firm grasp. The Hunter stopped in his tracks and looked up, turning his head slowly as he scanned the quad. As his gaze moved in our direction, Jonah dragged us into the cover of the nearby shadows of the trees and started chanting words I'd never heard before.

"*Hidam et protegat o Deum. Hidam et protegat o Deum.*"

Jonah picked both of us up off the ground and ran like hell to the underground parking garage. He ran so fast it sucked the air out of my lungs. A defeating whooshing sound filled my ears. I gasped for air but my lungs were locked.

Seconds later, Jonah dropped me to the ground, landing me right in the middle of a greasy smudge on the parking garage floor. Jonah had Beth in his arms and gently put her in the car.

Choking and gasping for air, I watched him lay Beth in the front seat. He immediately started blowing air into her lungs. After only a few rescue breaths, she was breathing on her own. Jonah checked her pulse and felt her forehead. Her face was pale white, but she was breathing normally.

I coughed and choked into a few breaths before my lungs fully opened again to accept life-saving air into them.

"Anna, are you strong enough to get in the car?" Jonah said, with heavy anxiety in his voice.

I nodded and crawled to the car and pulled myself up and over the side, landing in the back seat.

"Can you sit up? I want to lay Beth's head in your lap. Make sure she keeps breathing. I'll get us home as fast as I can."

I took several deep breaths, forcing the black spots before my eyes to fade away.

"What was that?" I whispered through coughs.

"I can run fast enough not to be seen, but it's painful for those who travel with me. I'm sorry, Anna. I didn't have time to warn you. Are you breathing all right, now?"

"Yes."

Sitting under the open sky of the conspicuous convertible car, exposed us in a way that made me want to slump down to hide. The wind whirled across my face, stinging my eyes and I wished the Morgan had its top on. Jonah raced home, on the phone with Isaac the entire time.

Chaptξr 30

As we pulled into the driveway, Isaac and Rebekah were waiting for us at the garage door.

"I summoned Doctor Salutari. He'll be here in about ten minutes," Rebekah said, frantically.

Jonah nodded.

Isaac and Rebekah worked as a team, unloading Beth from the car.

Something still felt wrong. "I'm not sure it's a doctor that Beth needs," I said, hesitantly, not knowing exactly what I meant as I said it.

Isaac disappeared into the house, carrying Beth in his arms. Rebekah nodded at Jonah and quickly disappeared into the house. Standing in the middle of the garage next to the Morgan, Jonah looked at me as he put his hands on my shoulders.

"Beth is not exactly sick, Anna. We believe Beth is having physical issues with her Gift. Doctor Salutari is a Light One. He has an incredible Gift of inner intuition that is similar to Beth's. His Gift is not unlike fortune tellers who use their vision to see one's inner struggles and unresolved issues; but unlike those who misguidedly use their Gifts, Doctor Salutari knows how to use his properly. He will be able to assess what's going on with her."

Everything was happening so fast, I couldn't keep up with it all. So many strange things spun around in my head. I looked up at him, my cheeks hot with frustration.

"What happened at school, Jonah?"

He paused long enough that I didn't think he was going to answer.

"Do I need to spell it out?" I spat at him.

I held my hands out and started to count on my fingers as I spoke. "Beth was fine this morning, now she's unconscious. The

Hunter was on campus. I could feel him before I saw him. Professor Dhampir freaked out when he saw you; then we disappeared from the quad, getting practically suffocated on the way and ended up in the parking garage! What the . . . *bleep*, Jonah!" Swearing right now wasn't going to help anything.

His hands fell from my shoulders as he hung his head. "I'm so sorry. I can't imagine how confusing this is for you, not to mention scary."

Just then the door leading from the garage into the house flung open. "Jonah!" Isaac shouted through the open door. "We need you, now! Bring Anna!"

Jonah grabbed my hand and pulled me along behind him as we flew up the stairs into Beth's room.

She was still unconscious as she lay silently on her bed. Rebekah patted her hand and pressed a cool cloth to her forehead in an attempt to revive her.

I squeezed Jonah's hand in despair, hoping for some reassurance that Beth was going to be all right. He squeezed back, then let go gently. My empty hand hung at my side. The sweet scent of him whirled around me as he breezed out of the room. In the same instant, I heard a loud knock on the front door.

"Welcome, Doctor Salutari. Thank you so much for coming. What is *he* doing here?"

A low mumbling came from the foyer at the bottom of the stairs.

"Beth? Beth!" Zech shouted from the front door.

He clomped loudly up the stairs and flew into the room, dropping to his knees at Beth's side.

Jonah entered the room directly behind him. "You shouldn't be here, Zech," Jonah said, sincerely, as he placed his hand on Zech's shoulder.

"What's wrong with her?" Zech asked, with tears in his eyes.

"Zech, why don't you come with me, dear," Rebekah cooed as she tried to coax him out of the room.

"Why is he here?" Isaac whispered to Jonah.

"He came with Doctor Salutari."

We all traded perplexed glances. What could we say to him? How could we possibly tell him that Beth wasn't sick, but that it was her Gift – her intuition that was going haywire and that we had no idea how to heal her?

The tension in the room broke, as Doctor Salutari entered. A small gasp caught in my throat. His appearance shocked me. He was at least six foot eight and there was a glow about him. His pale skin had a healthy luster and the sheen of his silver hair gleamed as it shone in the light of the window. But that wasn't where the glow emanated from; his glow came from within. He had an inner calm and radiance that filled the room.

He strode to Beth's bedside, knelt and immediately began assessing her condition.

Jonah relieved Zech of his position at Beth's other side and began rambling off his observations.

"Her pulse and respiration are steady. Her temperature and blood pressure are normal, although she is not usually this pale."

Doctor Salutari nodded in agreement and glanced around the room, stopping at me. His eyes widened.

"I was unaware you had found a Pure Blood." His eyes immediately shot over to Jonah as he squinted a burning stare at him. "Isaac, you have been out of touch for some time, old friend. How long has she been under your care?" He spoke as he continued to glare at Jonah.

I was taken aback. How did this man know I was a Pure Blood by merely looking at me? Why was he scowling at Jonah? And how come he was talking about this in front of Zech?

The doctor looked back at me, and then down to my stomach. Did he suspect that Jonah was trying to father a New Generation Nephil with me? I surprised myself at how this new language and accompanying understanding came so easily.

Jonah followed Doctor Salutari's gaze as he stared at my midsection. "Doctor Salutari, I think it is best that we discuss these matters in the privacy of the family," he said, as he shot a look at Zech.

"Zechariah is with me," Doctor Salutari stated. "He is a young Light One and very brilliant. I discovered him only a few years ago while I was studying a Dark One not too far from here. It was Zechariah who discovered that one of the professors on your college campus is a Clan leader. Zech and I have been working closely on this issue for some time."

Doctor Salutari scowled at Zech. "He failed to mention, however, that he had become involved with a young lady . . . who turns out to be the sister of the only known Fallen Angel in history who is still pure. You know how to pick 'em, son. This one here is quite a catch, and quite over stimulated it seems," he said, as he placed his hand on Beth's forehead.

As Doctor Salutari pulled his hands from Beth's face, his eyes wandered back to me. "I don't believe I've met Miss Pure Blood," he stated as he addressed me.

Rebekah floated to my side and wrapped her arm gently around my shoulders. "It is my great pleasure, Doctor Salutari, to introduce you to Miss Ananiah Immaculada. We have had the honor of knowing her about a month now. She began living with us just recently, after a bloodhound and Hunter picked up her scent a few days ago. Anna and Beth narrowly escaped." Rebekah's voice was full of reverence and pride as she spoke of me like I were some sort of royalty. It made me uncomfortable.

"It's an honor to meet you, Miss Immaculada."

Jonah was at my side in an instant, not bothering to reserve his lightning movement in front of me, the good doctor or even Zech. He kept his distance from me, though. We stood side by side, but he was careful not to touch me in any way. I couldn't blame him. I didn't want the doctor to know about our feelings for each other, either, which we both knew could get us into a great deal of trouble.

"Anna, do you remember when I told you that I knew a Light One who could see celestial energy emanations?" Jonah spoke in a soft, low voice.

"Yes."

"Doctor Salutari is the Light One I spoke of. He and I have known each other for many decades. When he initially found me, he attempted to take my life, thinking I was a Fallen one, destined to infiltrate a Pure bloodline as most of the Fallen Angels do. He can see the great celestial aura I produce in contrast to the lack of aura you emit."

"It's usually very clear, Miss Immaculada, like seeing the world in black and white. Jonah emits a powerful black emanation that spirals around him, practically engulfing him, making it difficult for me to even see him. The darkest of his celestial tentacles twist out into almost wing-shaped sails behind him. It's beautiful, but also very disconcerting to see such a powerful Fallen Angel standing next to a Pure Blood. Most Nephilim produce varying degrees of emanations. Isaac and Rebekah produce very light auras and Beth, here, is one of the most diluted Nephilim I've ever met."

Doctor Salutari's eyes were shut tight, now. His hands were on either side of Beth's head at her temples as he focused on evaluating her condition. "We need to let her rest. I believe her Gift is increasing rapidly. While the training Jonah has given her has been beneficial in understanding and recognizing this Gift, it is not sufficient to deal with such power. She has obviously been surrounded by quite a few very strong auras lately. She can feel them, just as I can see them.

Although the intuition of feeling such powerful beings far exceeds my visual abilities, seeing them is easier to deal with. The interpretation is clear for me. I can assess what I see instantly. She will need to learn how to recognize and interpret what she's feeling with much more diligence. She needs time to rest. When she awakens, she will need to be trained by the Council to fine-tune her Gift, and use it effectively."

He looked at Jonah. "You've done a superb job of guiding her in her Gift."

I spoke for the first time since Doctor Salutari entered the room. "Doctor Salutari . . ." I trailed off.

"Please, call me Doctor Sal, Miss Immaculada."

I nodded in his direction. "Then please, call me Anna," I said softly as I patted my chest.

"Of course." He placed his hand over his heart and bowed his head at me in admiration.

I sighed and scratched at my forehead, although it wasn't itching. I felt undeserving of this level of respect.

"Um, I felt the Dark One before Beth did. It was only after I mentioned the icky feeling that she pointed out the Hunter at school."

He looked at me with wide eyes. "Tell me, Anna. What Gifts has the Spirit given you?"

I shot Jonah another wary glance, unsure of how to answer.

He put his hand on my shoulder. "It's okay, Anna. Just tell Doctor Sal anything you feel is out of the ordinary. This is something I would also like to hear. We haven't really gotten a chance to talk about these things yet."

Jonah looked at each person standing in the room. "If you don't mind, I would like to continue this discussion downstairs so as not to disturb Beth. I can log Anna's responses in the *Angelus Secreta* journal as well."

Now I felt like a science project.

With the imminent worry of Beth's well-being diffused, we all descended the stairs quietly. The men took seats in the comfortable tan and red family room as they caught up with each other, talking of their latest dealings with the supernatural. The Gwenaëls seemed to have complete trust in Doctor Sal. Since Zech was Doctor Sal's pupil, he was silently welcomed into the circle of trust seamlessly and without hesitation.

Rebekah raced ahead of us. I could hear her in the kitchen frantically getting some refreshments together for our guests. I followed behind. She seemed flustered, no doubt worried about her daughter and the challenge that lay ahead of her.

I felt guilty. If it weren't for me, none of this would be happening to sweet little Bethie. I placed my hand on Rebekah's, while I grasped the pitcher of iced tea from her and took over pouring detail. A look of gratitude filled her face. She began placing an assortment of cookies on a silver tray.

I carried a tray filled with crystal goblets of Jonah's red tea as I followed Rebekah into the cozy family room and placed it gently on the coffee table. I took a glass and sat in the only empty spot left, directly next to Jonah.

I had picked up on Doctor Sal's concern for Jonah's close proximity of a Pure Blood. No doubt Doctor Sal had his reservations about the situation. If he learned of our love, would it ignite his worries further? My guess was yes.

I rose and grabbed a fluffy pillow on my way to the end of the coffee table. I tossed the pillow on the ground and sat on it quickly, before anyone could protest.

"Now I can see everyone better," I commented innocently.

"Anna, would you mind telling us of anything out of the ordinary that you've experienced?" Doctor Sal began.

My eyebrows raised as a gush of air escaped through my lips, puffing out my cheeks.

"Well, I guess . . ." I couldn't imagine where to start.

"Can I start with the most recent things and work my way back?" I asked.

Every head in the room bobbed up and down in response.

"Well, like I said, I felt the darkness before Beth did this morning. She didn't understand what she felt until I said *I* felt it, then she was able to zone right in on the Hunter. The darkness he brought with him felt cold and suffocating. *I* felt nauseous just before *she* passed out. I made ripples in the pool water by imagining throwing balls of light out of my hands, I feel an electric shock when Jonah touches me . . ."

I was on a roll. It felt as if I was rambling off a laundry list of supernatural powers for a sci-fi movie.

"I can hear Jonah in my head, I can feel his spirit, I can send his power back to him . . . oh, and I've had hallucinations and have been haunted by ghosts and stuff my entire life."

I tried to ramble off the last part as lightly as I could by flashing a smile at the end of the sentence. If I was going to confess my insanity to any group of people, this would most likely be the only group that would understand.

Jonah wrote furiously in his book, but stopped as soon as the last part flew out of my mouth. Everyone held blank stares as they processed my words. Crap, they *did* think I was crazy.

"You can see them, Anna?" Jonah seemed thrown that I was aware of the supernatural things going on around me.

"Y-eah . . ." I answered reluctantly. "I can see them, feel them, smell them . . . ugh, they smell disgusting."

"Only ones with a spiritual disposition can actually see those from the otherworld. That's why there are so many skeptics and non-believers; most cannot see them. Possessing the ability to see spirits is a Gift, Anna." Jonah jotted down another Gift to my mounting list of abnormalities. At least, that's how *I* thought of them. *He* thought they were special; tools to be used for the greater good. Great, more pressure.

"My therapist, Ms. Seraph, said I was 'spiritually sensitive'," I said, as I made finger quotes in the air. "She tried for years to get me to go to some "LO" therapy, but my parents refused."

I paused for a long moment. Wait . . . no way. "You don't think she meant Light Ones therapy, do you?"

Doctor Sal spoke up. "Does Ms. Seraph have an office in Mission Valley, Anna?"

I nodded slowly. This couldn't be happening. My life with the Gwenaëls hadn't crossed over into my life before them, until now.

I stared intently at the carpet and began to hyperventilate. Rebekah knelt beside me and wrapped her arm around my shoulders. "This is too much for her, Doctor Sal," she pleaded.

"Rebekah," he replied in a commanding, yet gentle tone. "Your compassion and empathy for her is commendable, but we have to get a full understanding of her life until now." He shifted his focus to me. "Can you elaborate on any of your encounters, Anna?"

I pushed rewind on my mental list of supernatural occurrences. There were gaps between happenings. "I don't remember having any encounters while I was with Seth, but since his death, I've had a lot the last few months."

"Excuse me please, Anna, who was Seth?" Doctor Sal spoke earnestly.

I wasn't sure I wanted to relive this part of my life with him in the room. My repeated abandonment hurt too much.

"Seth was my boyfriend," I said, as tears welled up in my eyes. I hadn't cried even once over his death, but the pain of everything combined, began to crash down on me.

"Was?" Doctor Sal asked.

I felt ashamed for some reason. I nodded. "Seth and I knew each other from a young age. We were together as a couple for about two years. He was in a car accident only a few months ago. He died in the hospital."

Doctor Sal's eyes filled with concern. "Was Seth's last name Malum?" he asked sharply.

Now I was freaking out. "Yes."

Doctor Sal's words turned dark. "We found Seth the night his accident happened. He was evading us when he ran his car into a tree. When we learned that he was in the hospital recovering rapidly, we had to end him. He had been assigned by his Dark Clan to infiltrate you, Anna."

I could feel them. The tears were coming. "I knew him from the time I was twelve years old. We practically grew up together." My voice grew louder. "I knew his parents! You must be mistaken! You killed him?" I screeched.

Even though I knew deep down that Doctor Sal was right, the reality of what happened hit me hard. I had already guessed Seth might be a Dark One, but having my suspicions confirmed made it feel entirely different.

Doctor Sal seemed agitated. "Anna, we've been looking for you for months. It was Seth's Clan-mates, the Nephils that posed as his parents that killed your mother and father. The Archangel cleansed them from the Earth within days, squelching the leads we had on the Clan. Seth was the only one of his Clan left. When he died, his Clan died with him. Without Seth near, the demons that constantly search for Pure blood have had no barrier between you and them. There was no Dark infiltration to respect. They have, no doubt, been seeking you out since Seth's death. They have to make full contact to confirm that you are Pure. Has that happened?"

I scratched at my neck nervously. "The second week after classes began I woke up in the early morning to the sound of someone climbing the stairs in my house. The cold crept into my bedroom, then there was a loud bang on the wall, but nothing materialized. That same day, I felt something following me at school and I felt the cold again, but I didn't see anything.

"Actually, Doctor Salutari," Jonah began, "I chased away the very spirits Anna is speaking of. I've been watching over her for some time, now."

"What!" I screamed at him.

"We haven't had time to discuss this yet, Anna. Things have been happening so quickly," Jonah defended.

He turned to me with apologetic eyes. "The morning the spirit entered your home, I cloaked myself as a shadow and followed it. As soon as I knew it was trying to make contact with you, I revealed myself. The demon tried to run, but I bound him and took him far away from here. The very next day another spirit followed you around the quad. He suffered the same fate as the first. Unfortunately, I was only able to remove them from the immediate vicinity. My power to send them to hell was stripped when I lost my wings."

I kept forgetting that Jonah used to have wings. It was so difficult to imagine him alight, soaring up into the heavens.

"Jonah is correct, Anna," Doctor Sal confirmed. "The ability to see spirits is a Gift of sight. This has been given to you for a reason. Your very protection could lie in your ability to see your predator coming. There are spirits who live to cause mischief and chaos and who answer to a dark power. They are the deceased Nephilim."

"But if the Nephilim die and become evil spirits, does that mean that anyone who dies who's not a Pure Blood is wandering the earth as a spirit, looking for trouble? Are there billions of spirits roaming the earth, then? Pure Blood or not, that seems like too large an army for anyone to take on."

"Not all who die doomed to walk the earth, hungry and thirsty. The breeding that has gone on for centuries has diluted the blood in so many, that they are able to make the journey to heaven or hell. Only the first generation Nephilim who are conceived directly by a Fallen Angel, become spirits that roam until Judgment day.

Pure human blood is a powerful thing, Anna. It only takes one generation of dilution to save a Nephilim from this ghostly fate.

There is, however, another race to be more worried about. Demons. They are the Angels who fell with Lucifer."

My heart raced. It was evident that there had been an evil plan designed for me for quite some time; a plan that had been following me my entire life. "Like the devil?"

"Yes. Lucifer and the Angels that fell with him have created a web of power and deceit on Earth. Many Clan leaders have sold their souls to Lucifer in exchange for earthly power. They can directly control the demons here on Earth. It is part of Satan's plan to have ones on Earth who can carry out his wishes."

Hyperventilating again! "So, there *are* things stalking me?" I squeaked. "I mean, I do have an active imagination. I hallucinate sometimes. But you're telling me that I'm not crazy? I haven't been imagining this stuff my whole life?"

"Yes, there are evil forces after you, I'm sure of it. No, you're not crazy, and no, you haven't been hallucinating these things," Doctor Sal stated confidently. "Hallucinations would be easier to expunge. These things you've experienced throughout your life have been one-hundred percent real."

I always knew deep down that these strange happenings were real. Not being able to blame these things on my imagination anymore terrified me.

"I hallucinated Professor Dhampir the other day and felt his icy hand on my shoulder. Was *that* real?"

Jonah interjected in an informative, formal tone as he addressed Doctor Sal. "We believe the professor is a Dark One with the capability of producing a Glamour. I had an encounter with him just this morning. Based on the little history I know of the professor, he has all the tell-tale signs of a Dark One. A powerful Dark One. Maybe even a first or second generation. Beth had no idea. He has been cloaking his true self under a very strong Glamour."

"Professor Dhampir is the Dark Clan leader that Zech discovered, and the one we have been studying." Doctor Sal was lost in thought for a moment. "Jonah, your situation is very unique. What was the professor's reaction to you?"

I could answer that one, easy. I couldn't get the look on Professor Dhampir's face out of my mind. "He was shocked, then smug. He seemed really satisfied when he saw an Angel in his classroom."

Doctor Sal rose and paced around the room. "There is much evil surrounding you, Anna," he said. "Jonah, do you believe these are all of Anna's Gifts?"

"I don't think we've even scratched the surface, Doctor Sal. Anna is very unique. She possesses many qualities I've never come across. Her Gifts keep revealing themselves."

"Has anyone thought that she may possess the greatest Gift of all . . . the one that could very well save her mortal life and certainly save her spiritual life?" Doctor Sal directed the question to the entire room. He sounded upset that no one had thought of something very important. He turned to me. "Are you a believer, Anna?" he asked, inquisitively.

"A believer . . . of what?" I wondered back at him.

"To believe in God the Creator and His death and resurrection is the greatest choice we can make with the free will He has given us. We can choose to believe . . . or not."

"Yeah, I remember all the Sunday school lessons about that stuff. I guess I've always believed that was the Truth."

Doctor Sal's smile lit up the room. "The first step is believing, next step is accepting the invitation He extends to us to ask for His Holy Spirit to dwell inside of us."

I searched my memory of any such thing happening. "Yeah, I remember doing that when I was a kid. That was so long ago, though."

He leaned forward and held my gaze intently. "Once you've accepted the invitation, it lasts forever. It can offer you some very powerful protection and control over the supernatural beings around you. The innocent little question you asked as a child may be the very reason that your interludes with the supernatural have been fairly benign until now. They can't hear your thoughts or possess your body because the Holy Spirit that dwells within you protects you from this sort of evil. You can develop this protection and even use this power against these occurrences. You just need to be taught how."

He relaxed back into his chair. "This is a good development," he boasted.

The look of astonishment on my face must have been apparent. There was no invisible force protecting me, was there? I'd never given the idea much thought. I'd always thought I was on my own with all of this . . . until I met an Angel. If he was possible, wasn't anything?

"Anna, dear, are you okay to continue?"

I shook my head, as the corners of my mouth unwillingly turned down on their own. The tears I had been holding back were finally rising to the surface. There was no way to keep them in this time. There was just too much crap rumbling around in my head to process. Everything seemed a blur. My life felt as if it were crumbling. I couldn't keep my emotions in as the tears poured out of my eyes, and sobs made my entire body shudder with their sheer force.

Rebekah rose again from her chair to comfort me. I put my hand up in front of my face, stopping her where she stood. I didn't want a pat on the back and her voice telling me it would be okay, when I knew it would do nothing to make me feel better. In fact, right now her touch would surely make me long for the touch of my own mother so intensely, I wouldn't be able to bear it.

I looked into Jonah's brilliant, emerald eyes. Sadness and pity filled them as he gazed back at me. I wanted desperately for him to hold me in his arms and consume me with his spirit. Everything was okay when I was near him. His spirit could melt the world away.

I didn't care if Doctor Sal saw us, or if Isaac or Rebekah saw us. I didn't care if our love was forbidden. I had to get into Jonah's arms. It was the only relief I could think of that could ease the pain of my unraveling life.

I stood on wobbly legs and tripped my way over three steps to where Jonah was sitting. I threw myself into his lap and wrapped my arms around his neck tightly. If it were anyone else, I might have choked them to death. The sizzle of his skin on mine bolted through me, causing me to inhale a loud jagged breath that I knew everyone heard. I squeezed my eyes together as tight as I could, hoping it would make the truth of my life disappear.

It wasn't Seth's death that was so difficult to swallow. No, it was the fact that my bloodline had been hunted down for years and no one had told me. My own parents may have known, but never spoke a word, leaving me to discover it myself. Maybe they hoped I never would.

"Please, Jonah, send me your spirit, make this pain go away," I whispered into his ear through heavy sobs. I pulled my head back enough to rest my cheek on his and let the scorch of his electricity radiate through my entire face and body. I let the sharp stabs of his electric touch impale me, sending an attack of power under my skin and through my veins.

Jonah wrapped his arms around me and whispered in my ear, "Anna, it will be okay. I will never leave you. I will protect you all the days of your life."

Chαpτξr 31

A tremendous calm enveloped me. It wasn't just Jonah's velvet spirit wrapping around me like wings concealing me in their satin feathers. This was more. This was a brilliant calm mixed with a soothing, motherly love. I opened my eyes. Both Rebekah and Doctor Sal had their hands on my shoulders.

How they were doing this, I didn't know and I didn't care, as long as they didn't stop. It was working. My sobs faded and only the calm of their combined effort was left. The lightning pulsing into my cheek from Jonah's soft skin began to engulf me and the dizziness crept in. I knew I had to end the embrace soon, but I wanted more of him before I let him go.

I sent back the full force of his energy to him, knowing his arms would tighten around me and not let go until I pulled the power back.

Instantly, his arms tensed around me, giving me exactly what I wanted. At the same time, I heard Doctor Sal and Rebekah gasp as they were pushed to the floor by the force of the energy that had just bolted through them.

I hurled myself off of Jonah's lap and crawled anxiously over the back of the couch to them. They were stunned, but conscious.

"What was that?" Rebekah asked innocently, as she shook her head, dazed.

"I'm so, so sorry! I had no idea you would be able to feel that. I thought only Jonah could."

"Anna, is that what you feel when Jonah touches you?" Rebekah asked. "I feel magnificent."

I nodded. I had accidently zapped both of them. Now they knew what it felt like when a Pure Blood touched a Fallen Angel. Scary and amazing.

Doctor Sal sat up. "Anna, you will go with Beth to the Light Ones Council. We must uncover this ability you possess. You must be trained in how to use it." His tone was stern. His words were an order.

Just then, I had a flash of genius.

"If *you* could feel the energy I channeled from Jonah, do you think it could help Beth?" I directed the question to both Doctor Sal and Rebekah as they sat before me. Doctor Sal seemed confused.

"Anna has used Jonah's power to heal herself in the past." Rebekah explained to Doctor Sal. "If I am hearing her correctly, she thinks that sending some of the, uh, *feeling* she just gave us into Beth might help to heal her."

"Or at least clear her head enough to function until she can get the training she needs to be able to do it by herself?" I added enthusiastically.

The thought of helping my best friend, who was sick and unconscious upstairs, made my worries seem petty. It wasn't even lunchtime yet and the emotional roller coaster I was on had peaked this morning when I saw Jonah in all his gorgeous glory in his black T-shirt and tight jeans. Then it had plunged into dark depths upon learning of my past, and was now being ratcheted up an incline again as the idea of being able to help my friend was coming to light. I hoped this was the end of the ride for the day and another plunge wouldn't follow.

I felt a hand on my shoulder. Jonah had turned around on the couch and was facing Doctor Sal and Rebekah. "I think Anna has a very valid suggestion. If she thinks it will help, I say we try. What is your opinion, Doctor Salutari?"

"If you're really considering this, I think we should test it first. We do not want to harm Beth. Her condition right now is very delicate."

Doctor Sal rose and stood in the middle of the room. Jonah and I followed.

"Jonah, Anna, give me your hands."

I was extremely nervous, knowing that this "test" was all about me being able to control Jonah's energy. If this didn't work, I was sure Doctor Sal wouldn't let me try it with Beth.

"Anna, are you sure about this?" Jonah whispered to me. His lips were so close, they brushed the side of my cheek. A tingle rushed down my jaw. I wanted to grab him and kiss him hard and never let go.

"I can do this," I whispered back, letting my lips touch his ear lobe. He shivered, then laced his fingers through mine.

"Doctor Sal?" Jonah said, formally as he reached out for the doctor's hand.

Doctor Sal, Jonah and I stood in the middle of the room, hand in hand.

"Anna, are you feeling Jonah's energy now?" Doctor Sal asked.

"Yes, I'm just keeping it to myself at the moment." I glanced around the circle, then closed my eyes. I released a filament of energy.

Doctor Sal gasped. "This is nothing like the bolt of electricity I felt a moment ago, Anna."

I opened my eyes. Jonah was standing with closed eyes, reveling in the euphoria. Doctor Sal waited for an answer. "I'm only sending you a tiny amount. I can crank it up if you want more."

Doctor Sal nodded.

I sent out four more threads of the energy. Both Doctor Sal and Jonah's grips grew tighter. "This is about ten percent," I said.

Doctor Sal dropped my hand and rubbed his palms together swiftly. "Normally, I would insist on studying the effects of this power exchange, but it doesn't seem to do harm, in fact, as Rebekah said, I, too, feel wonderful. It's invigorating." The doctor shook his head and shrugged, not quite knowing the correct answer to give us. "If you think it would benefit Beth, I don't think it would do any harm. I give my consent to try."

I looked to Rebekah. I couldn't in good conscience do this without her permission. "If you think it would help, I trust you,

Anna. You're really the only one who knows how it works," she said, frankly.

I nodded her way, then tightened my grip on Jonah's hand and pulled him behind me up the stairs to her room.

We ascended the stairway quickly, both anxious to get to Beth. "They know now. About us," I said. "I'm sorry I outed us like that. Will they be terribly upset?"

Jonah squeezed my hand. "Anna, don't ever apologize for what we feel. We'll be together in one way or another, your entire life. Things will change between us over the years, but no one can change the way we feel about each other except us. As much as I love my family and value their support, *you* are the most important thing in my life now and you always will be. I imagine they are concerned, but they love us. They've never been ones to exile themselves or their feelings because of a decision they don't agree with. It will be okay, please trust that."

His little speech warmed my heart, but somehow I wasn't convinced that everything was *truly* going to be okay; with his family, maybe, but what about Doctor Sal? He had known Jonah for decades. He knows that Jonah loves humans and would never do anything to harm them, especially infiltrate a Pure bloodline. But Doctor Sal seemed very concerned when he learned I was a Pure Blood. There must be holes in his trust. That scared me.

We entered Beth's room. She hadn't moved an inch. Jonah knelt at her bedside.

Now that we were alone, I was dying to kiss him. Each time he sent his spirit to me it gave me an overwhelming sensation to passionately ravage him from head to toe. I couldn't act on any of those feelings downstairs. I just *had* to taste his lips before attempting to find the sort of control I would need to help Beth.

I knelt down beside him. "Kiss me. Please," I whispered.

Without hesitation, he turned to me and held my face in his hands. I closed my eyes, eagerly waiting to feel his lips on mine. Nothing. My eyes fluttered open to see him staring at me.

"Anna. We need to control our desire. We will have our entire lives together, this is not the time to lose control."

I hadn't planned on losing control. I just wanted to feel his soft lips to satisfy my excruciating urge to drink him in.

"I have complete control," I pleaded. "Please, just a little kiss. You don't understand how I long for you every second of the day. It's all I can do to concentrate on anything else anymore. Just one kiss and it will satisfy me enough to be able to focus on Beth." I was begging now.

He leaned over and brushed his lips against my cheek, leaving a wet line where his mouth met my skin.

I wanted more. So much more, but if I begged any further, I would humiliate myself.

"It's difficult for me as well, Anna. I've never felt anything like this before in my life. This desire I have for you assaults me every moment I'm with you and devastates me every moment I'm not. I have to fight to maintain control of it every second of the day."

"That's exactly how I feel. The draw to you is magnetic."

"Yes."

He felt the same. I don't know why I constantly worried that he would somehow get over it and leave me. He had professed his love for me. He had repeated numerous times that he would be my protector for the rest of my life, which should have reassured me, but it didn't. At some point or another everyone I ever loved had left me, or worse, died. That's a hard thing to get over.

I sighed disappointedly, and walked around to the other side of Beth's bed. "Okay," I said, as I rubbed my hands together. Jonah and I reached over Beth and I placed my hand in his. His power pulsed through me.

I sent a filament of energy back to him. "Can you feel that?" I whispered.

"Yes."

I placed my hand on Beth's forehead and closed my eyes. I let out a thread of Jonah's electric power from my palm and across her forehead.

She stirred.

I placed Jonah's hand on my arm so I could touch Beth with both hands, then I turned up the intensity a fragment. With my fingers on her temples, I sent tentacles of healing power over her skull and into the gray matter of her incredible brain.

Her eyes opened slowly. Her gaze met mine. In divine Bethie fashion, she blurted, "what's your hand doing on my forehead, girlie?"

Jonah chuckled.

Chαpτ§r 32

"Are you sure that's all you're going to bring, Anna? We might be there for quite a while, you know," Beth remarked as she peered over my shoulder at the measly bag I had packed.

My suitcase was full, but it was small. I had no idea what we would be doing. I had no idea what to pack.

What *would* we be doing? What did *training* actually mean? I had asked Doctor Sal, but he declined to elaborate, just saying that there were standard exercises and the rest would be tailored specifically to develop my Gifts. I was afraid of what that meant.

"I'm sure if I need anything else, I can buy it there," I answered quietly.

I knew I had enough money at my disposal to buy whatever I might need. Packing a bunch of clothes I had no idea if I would even wear, seemed daunting.

The closest Light Ones Council was up the coast in a city named Avalon on the island of Catalina. Even though the island was a tourist attraction, being surrounded by water, it offered unique protection from the Dark Ones. They also had a base off of Dana Point, which was on the mainland. I hoped it would be a short stay.

Doctor Sal went ahead of us to make arrangements for our extended stay and to prepare the Council for our arrival and all that it would involve. He conveyed to us that the Council was buzzing with excitement at the idea of a Pure Blood training with them. I was the first Pure Blood to train there in over forty years.

All the fuss that was being made over us was completely embarrassing. A month ago I was a loner with no one who cared about me. Now I was in the center of an ever-expanding circle of the supernatural, surrounded by a new family.

Beth bounced around my room, picking pieces of jewelry off of my dresser, and examining them carefully as she voiced her concern, yet again, about missing her classes for an undisclosed period of time. I had to remind her that as long as we finished Prof. D's Giants paper, we would at least complete the quarter. The syllabus didn't contain any work we couldn't read on our own and since Zech was the professor's TA, he had reassured us he would send us any work Prof. D surprised the class with. As for her other classes, I left the task of squelching her worries about those to Jonah.

"Zech said he would visit," Beth announced excitedly. "Doctor Sal said that they welcome all Light Ones there and has extended an invitation to him to visit anytime. Zech can't wait to be in the presence of other Light Ones."

Beth boasting about her interludes with Zech, filled me with mixed emotions. I was jealous at her excitement to experience this with the boy she loved. Jonah wasn't coming with us and I had no idea when I would see him next. My heart ached.

Rebekah strode gracefully into the room. "I've packed each of you a thermos full of Jonah's tea. Make sure you keep sipping it on the way and keep the windows closed as you drive. We wouldn't want anyone to pick up Anna's scent."

I nodded and took the thermos from her, flashed her an affectionate smile, then turned to finish packing. Rebekah and Beth chattered in the background.

In our absence, Doctor Sal suggested that now would be a good time to give the house a good once-over cleansing. He hoped that when we returned, we would have been on Jonah's infused tea for long enough, that our essence would be practically untraceable by then. When he said *we*, I knew he meant *me*. Jonah made a large batch of his tea just this morning, which had been loaded into the car.

Before Doctor Sal left, he had called Leah, the Gwenaël's maid, to stop by the house. He revealed to us that she was an apprentice of the Light Ones, assigned to keep an eye on Jonah and report back on a regular basis. Doctor Sal announced her station after consulting with the Council. They determined it was time to tell us they had a sleeper watching over Jonah the whole time.

She was fully trained in the cleansing techniques to remove my Pure human scent and would be staying at the house to watch over things.

Even though Jonah had explained that the scent and taste of Pure blood is the sweetest, most alluring scent and taste on Earth to the Angels and Nephilim, the whole cleansing issue was beginning to bother me. I felt like a stinky dog that left the couch smelly from napping on it. At any moment I expected for my owner to toss me in the tub and scrub me down.

The Light Council kept their existence and whereabouts a secret, even from Jonah, sending only sleepers to watch the Gwenaëls and not interfere. I wondered what made them finally reveal themselves and become involved? Then I remembered; Jonah was the only anomaly until now and he had been behaving himself. When I came into the picture, everything changed. My arrival had uprooted their very existence, never to be the same.

Rebekah gave me a pat on the back and turned to leave. "Girls, would you like to come to the market with me to pick up some last minute items to take with you? Beth, we can stock up on your favorite granola bars and get some of that beef jerky that Isaac likes so much."

She turned to me. "Anna, would you like anything, dear? You're welcome to come with us, although I did notify the Council of your dietary restrictions. I'm sure they'll take into consideration your limitations accordingly. You needn't worry."

"I'm fine," I sighed. "I need to finish packing."

"All right, honey. Isaac just left to gas up the car. We will be back shortly."

I stood beside the bed of my new room and stared off into space. A melancholy sigh escaped from my throat.

Doctor Sal and Isaac had decided it was best for Jonah to stay behind so he could check into Professor Dhampir and the Viking Hunter we saw on campus. Jonah's chest rose when he proudly claimed it would be a "reconnaissance mission," but I could see the agony behind his eyes. Any length of separation would cause him physical pain, now. We had barely figured out how to be together, only to be forced apart.

I couldn't hide my disappointment that Jonah wouldn't be the one to train me and guide me into this new life. None of this seemed worth it without him.

I sat on the bed with a half folded shirt in my lap. Nothing seemed in my control. Nothing made sense without Jonah near. He was home to me now, and he was going to be far away for so long.

Uncontrollable sobs shook my body and tears flowed freely down my cheeks. With no one home, I could have a good cry without anyone seeing. I sat sobbing, until the folded shirt in my lap became damp with tears.

A strong hand stroked my hair, followed by a flurry of Jonah's sweet, clean scent. I thought he had gone with Isaac to get the car ready, but he was here.

"Anna, please don't cry. This is all for the best, I promise. Beth will get the guidance she requires and the Council will uncover the answers we need and learn how to best protect you, now."

His comment filled me with anger and frustration. My mere existence was making everyone's life so messy.

I stood up and walked briskly to the dresser, determined to find some nondescript piece of clothing that was vitally important to pack, requiring me to start digging around in the top drawer frantically.

Jonah saw through my attempt to cover the anguish festering inside of me. He walked up behind me and slid his hands from my shoulders down to my waist. He wrapped his arms around me and turned me to face him.

When I looked up, he had tears in his eyes. "I'll miss you like crazy, too."

All my frustration melted away as I saw Jonah truly vulnerable for the first time. Breath escaped from my lungs, deflating all my anger and my heart went out to him.

As if a magnetic force I couldn't control pulled us together with all its might, I stood on my tiptoes and flung my arms around his neck and kissed him hard. His hands found my hips. He tried to push away from me but I didn't let up. I sent him back the full force of electricity he gave me as I crushed my lips against his.

His mouth opened and he let out a grunt of surprise. I found his tongue and sent a thousand threads of energy into it. He inhaled a ragged gasp. His hands ran down my back, over my hips and grabbed the back of my thighs. He lifted me up and wrapped my legs around his waist as he sat me on the dresser.

His hands searched my body until his fingers made contact with the skin around waist. Heat from his touch scorched my skin, electrifying it like never before, sending bolts of fever flaming up my spine. The intensity of his energy was more than I'd ever felt, so much that my body couldn't contain it. I sent it back to him as soon as he gave it to me. The current passed through our bodies, forming a continuous circuit of electricity. We were bound together by our touch, by our souls, by our love.

As his hands caressed my skin, the feathers tucked into the waistband of my pants poked out. He pulled on them gently.

"I didn't know you carried them with you."

My face flushed with embarrassment, "I haven't let them out of my sight since the day I pulled them off of your wing. Even before I knew what they really were, the feel of them on my skin comforted me."

The look in his eyes was one of adoration and torture. He stroked the feathers lightly and held them against my skin as his hands found my face. He held it firmly, moving it in time with his, as his lips vigorously attacked mine. I gasped for air between the movements of our lips.

"God help me, I love you, Anna," he whispered through hungry breaths.

My heart pounded at his words. I knew now, what Beth saw in us. We were one. Our hearts bound by an unseeable force that pulled us together, never to be torn apart. His power was mine and mine was his. This bond between us, created by our love for each other, was a power that I never knew existed in the universe. We would be able to create anything together with this bond.

His fingers laced through my hair and up the back of my head, as he kissed my neck and collarbone. His other hand found the small of my back and pulled me closer to him until our bodies pressed against each other so tightly, they molded together.

The amount of blazing power that flowed between us was nearly impossible to control. It was on the brink of overcoming me completely. With all my might, I shoved the power into my legs, then one by one, I slowly pulled back threads of energy from Jonah's core until I felt his muscles relax. A long, soft, satisfying moan came from deep inside him and I knew the current had left his body. His embrace loosened.

He inhaled deep breaths to recover as I sat with my legs still wrapped around him doing the same. Our clothes were the only barrier between sweet serenity and overwhelming power. He peered down at me, his clear green eyes bright and luminous, but tainted with a single tear.

"What is it?" I asked.

He closed his eyes and sent his spirit to me, wrapping me in a luxurious warm embrace as his arms followed, squeezing me gently. In his presence I was completely at peace and at home. I could have lived in his invisible velvet wings forever, but the embrace lasted only moments, before he spoke.

"It breaks my heart to know we can't ever end up together. It's what I want more than anything in this world. I've never wanted anything more. Now I understand how the Angels of the past fell, knowing they would have to endure darkness and chains until Judgment. This feeling I have for you is overpowering. Resisting you, knowing none of that can happen for us, breaks my heart every day.

I know you notice it. One minute I'm at your side and the next I'm distant. I'm so torn between my own selfish desire for you and what I know I must ultimately do . . . give you up, so you can live your life with another."

My heart broke as he spoke, knowing his words were true. My head, however, refused to think that this connection between us was useless.

He moved closer until his lips were at my ear. "Do you hate me?" he whispered.

"No," I whispered back, my voice wavering. I barely held back a sob at the mere thought of hating him.

"The best part of you is at arms length. It's so hard to bear," he said.

"The best part?"

"Your heart. You're capable of such great and honest love. I've seen it as you've embraced and fallen in love with my family. I don't have a piece of it . . . but I don't want just a piece of it, I want all of it. My selfishness and desire for you overwhelms me. It makes me feel guilty every second of the day. I don't deserve you."

A lump rose in my throat as I listened to him speak of his tortured feelings for me. I was causing him such intense torment. Couldn't he see that he already *had* my heart? Or had he held romantic love at arm's length for so long that he didn't recognize it when it was right in front of him? Maybe he just couldn't imagine a human, me, loving a creature that had purposefully fallen from grace.

I whispered into his perfect ear. "I know that what we have between us . . . what you've allowed yourself to feel, is *not* all for nothing."

He began to pull away. I squeezed him tight with my legs and gripped the back of his neck forcing his eyes to again meet mine. I concentrated on the touch of my hand on the back of his neck and sent tingling energy down his spine. I wanted him to remember this moment. I knew what I wanted to say, but I also knew I had to choose my words carefully so that he didn't think he had provoked them from me. He had to truly believe every word I was about to speak.

"You can't deny what we have is pure and real. I can feel it. We're connected on a deeper level than I can explain. I know you feel it, too. I'm in love with you, Jonah. I love you more than I've ever loved anyone in my entire life. The love I have for you is the strongest bond I've ever felt. We may not be able to be together in the way we want, but until we figure that out, I'm not giving you up. Please don't give up on me, either."

The tear that was welled up in his eye floated down his beautiful cheek.

"You *love* me? I'm not even human," he muttered.

His pure transparency was endearing. It made me love him even more. He was so strong, yet so exposed as he doubted his deserving of my love.

"Completely. With all of my heart and soul. *What* you are, a Fallen Angel, is part of *who* you are. The man that I love."

He took my face in his hands and ran his thumb over my lips before wrapping me in his velvet spirit again.

"I'll love you for the rest of my life, Ananiah Immaculada. You have my whole heart and my whole spirit," he whispered into my head.

"And I'll love you for the rest of my life," I replied.

He kissed me softly.

For more information about this story, visit
www.thepurebloodchronicles.com.

COMING SOON . . .

Reδεεμεδ Blooδ

The Pure Blooδ Chronicles

Booк 2

Νεω Blooδ

The Pure Blooδ Chronicles

Booк 3

Resources

1. Bob Curran, *An Encyclopedia of Celtic Mythology* (McGraw-Hill; 1 edition, January 11, 2000)

2. Gustav Davidson, *A Dictionary of Angels: Including the Fallen Angels* (Free Press, October 1, 1994)

3. David Noel Freedman, *The Anchor Bible Dictionary* (Bantam Doubleday Dell Publishing Group, Inc., June 1, 1992)

4. Craig Hines, *Gateway of the Gods: An Investigation of Fallen Angels, the Nephilim, Alchemy, Climate Change, and the Secret Destiny of the Human Race* (Numina Media Arts, January 9, 2007)

5. John Lindow, *Handbook of Norse Mythology (World Mythology)* (ABC-CLIO, June 1, 2001)

6. Dr. A. Nyland, *Complete Books of Enoch: 1 Enoch (First Book of Enoch), 2 Enoch (Secrets of Enoch), 3 Enoch (Hebrew Book of Enoch)* (CreateSpace, October 16, 2010)

7. Charles Russell Coulter and Patricia Turner, *Encyclopedia of Ancient Dieties* (McFarland & Company, October 2000)

8. http://www.ancienttexts.org/library/ethiopian/enoch/1watchers/wcenter.htm